In Dreams Begin Responsibilities

Delmore Schwartz

•

IN DREAMS
BEGIN RESPONSIBILITIES
and other stories

Preface by Lou Reed

*Edited with an introduction
by James Atlas*

Afterword by Irving Howe

A NEW DIRECTIONS BOOK

Grateful acknowledgment is made to the editors and publishers of *The Kenyon Review*, *New
Directions in Prose and Poetry*, *The New Yorker*, and *Partisan Review*, in which the stories in
this book first appeared. "Screeno" was originally published in 1977 in *Partisan Review*.

The story "The Track Meet" appears by arrangement with Corinth Books, Inc., publishers of
Successful Love, a collection of stories by Delmore Schwartz.

Special thanks are made to the Collection of American Literature, Beinecke Library, Yale
University, for use of the holograph manuscript of "Screeno" in its possession.

Thanks are also due for permission to quote from the following copyrighted sources: for a
selection from "Gerontion" in *Collected Poems* by T. S. Eliot (copyright © 1936 by Harcourt
Brace Jovanovich, Inc.; copyright © 1963, 1964 by T. S. Eliot), reprinted by permission of
Harcourt Brace Jovanovich, Inc., and Faber and Faber, Ltd.; for a passage from *Axel's Castle*
by Edmund Wilson (copyright © 1931 by Charles Scribner's Sons; renewal copyright © 1959
Edmund Wilson), reprinted by permission of Charles Scribner's Sons and Farrar, Straus &
Giroux, Inc.

Manufactured in the United States of America
First published clothbound and as New Directions Paperbook 454 in 1978.
Reissued with a new preface by Lou Reed as NDP1233 in 2012.

Library of Congress Cataloging-in-Publication Data
Schwartz, Delmore, 1913–1966.
In dreams begin responsibilities and other stories / Delmore Schwartz ; preface by Lou Reed ;
edited with an introduction by James Atlas ; afterword by Irving Howe.
p. cm.
ISBN 978-0-8112-2003-3 (acid-free paper) — ISBN 978-0-8112-2021-7 (acid-free paper)
I. Atlas, James. II. Title.
PS3537.C7915 2012
813'.52—dc23   2012002923

10 9 8 7 6 5

New Directions Books are published for James Laughlin
by New Directions Publishing Corporation
80 Eighth Avenue, New York 10011

CONTENTS

PREFACE

O Delmore how I miss you. You inspired me to write. You were the greatest man I ever met. You could capture the deepest emotions in the simplest language. Your titles were more than enough to raise the muse of fire on my neck. You were a genius. Doomed.

The mad stories. O Delmore I was so young. I believed so much. We gathered around you as you read *Finnegans Wake*. So hilarious but impenetrable without you. You said there were few things better than to devote one's life to Joyce. You'd annotated every word in the novels you kept from the library. Every word.

And you said you were writing "The Pig's Valise." O Delmore no such thing. They looked, after your final delusion led you to a heart attack in the Hotel Dixie. Unclaimed for three days. You— one of the greatest writers of our era. No Valise.

You wore the letter from T. S. Eliot next to your heart. His praise of IN DREAMS. Would that you could have stopped that wedding. No good will come of this!!! You were right. You begged us—Please don't let them bury me next to my mother. Have a party to celebrate moving from this world to a hopefully better one. And you Lou—I swear—and you know if anyone could I could—you Lou must never write for money or I will haunt you.

I'd given him a short story. He gave me a B. I was so hurt and ashamed. Why haunt talentless me? I was the walker for THE HEAVY BEAR WHO GOES WITH ME. To literary cocktails. He hated them. And I was put in charge. Some drinks later—his shirt undone—one tail front right hanging—tie askew—fly unzipped. O Delmore. You were so beautiful. Named for a silent movie star dancer Frank Delmore.

O Delmore—the scar from dueling with Nietzsche.

Reading Yeats and the bell had rung but the poem was not over you hadn't finished reading—liquid rivulets sprang from your nose but still you would not stop reading. I was transfixed. I cried—the love of the word—THE HEAVY BEAR.

You told us to break into ——'s estate where your wife was being held prisoner. Your wrists broken by those who were your enemies. The pills jumbling your fine mind.

I met you in the bar where you had just ordered five drinks. You said they were so slow that by the time you had the fifth you should have ordered again. Our scotch classes. Vermouth. The jukebox you hated—the lyrics so pathetic.

You called the White House one night to protest their actions against you. A scholarship to your wife to get her away from you and into the arms of whomever in Europe.

I heard the newsboy crying EUROPE EUROPE.

Give me enough hope and I'll hang myself.

Hamlet came from an old upper class family.

Some thought him drunk but—really—he was a manic-depressive—which is like having brown hair.

You have to take your own shower—an existential act. You could slip in the shower and die alone.

Hamlet starting saying strange things. A woman is like a cantaloupe Horatio—once she's open she goes rotten.

O Delmore where was the *Vaudeville for a Princess*. A gift to the Princess from the stage star in the dressing room.

The Duchess stuck her finger up the Duke's ass and the Kingdom vanished.

No good will come of this. Stop this courtship!

Sir you must be quiet or I must eject you.

Delmore understood it all and could write it down impeccably.

Shenandoah Fish. You were too good to survive. The insights got you. The fame expectations. So you taught.

And I saw you in the last round.

I loved your wit and massive knowledge.

You were and have always been the one.

You can lead a horse to water but you can't make him think.

I wanted to write. One line as good as yours. My mountain. My inspiration.

You wrote the greatest short story ever written.
IN DREAMS.

—LOU REED

INTRODUCTION

When Delmore Schwartz's first book, *In Dreams Begin Responsibilities*, was published in 1938, the critics were virtually unanimous in their acclaim. His poetic style marked "the first real innovation that we've had since Eliot and Pound," Allen Tate declared, and George Marion O'Donnell heralded the book as "the one genuinely important modification to come out of the 1930s in America." From then on, Schwartz's reputation as a poet was secure. He was the first of the new generation to establish his own voice, and at a remarkably young age; he had just turned twenty-four the week of publication. Before Robert Lowell, John Berryman, or Randall Jarrell had published a line, Schwartz had become, in Irving Howe's later estimate, "the poet of the historical moment quite as Auden was in England." The pathos and controlled intensity of his style fused the language of the Jewish immigrants among whom Schwartz had grown up with a Modernist weariness that echoed Baudelaire.

Schwartz's most famous poems were to be found in *In Dreams Begin Responsibilities*: "In the Naked Bed, in Plato's Cave," his insomniac elegy to the remorseless forces of history and the passage of time; "The Heavy Bear Who Goes With Me," a majestic reflection on the conflict between the body's gross, importunate demands and its ultimate dissolution; and many others that were to achieve the status of contemporary classics. But there was also a work of prose in this collection, a story that in seven pages managed to express the poignant experience of pride, anxiety, and disappointed hope that characterized his parents' generation. In spare, evocative prose, Schwartz portrayed the doomed courtship of his mother and her temperamental suitor, the vanity and tenacious ambition that had wrecked their marriage from the start. Seated in a darkened movie theatre, the narrator dwells on the features of that distant era: the tree-lined Brooklyn avenue on which "a streetcar skates and gnaws"; the courtly manner of Rose's father when Harry Schwartz comes to call; the restaurant on the Coney Island boardwalk where he blurts out his marriage proposal, "lifted up by the waltz that is being played." And when the narrator stands up and cries, "Don't do it.... Nothing good will come of it, only remorse, hatred, scandal, and two children whose characters are monstrous," Schwartz dramatized in that impassioned outburst the traumatic history of his own childhood, the conflict between his parents' wills that he used to liken to O'Neill's *Strange Interlude*.*

Schwartz wrote "In Dreams Begin Responsibilities" over a July weekend in 1935, when he was only twenty-one. A day later, his friend William Barrett appeared at the boarding house off Washington Square where Schwartz was living that summer and found the author ecstatic; he knew he had written a masterpiece, a verdict later confirmed by Vladimir Nabokov, who singled it out as one of his "half a dozen favorites" in contemporary American literature, and by the editors of *Partisan Review*, who published it two years later as the lead piece in their first number, before contributions from Edmund Wilson, Lionel Trilling, and James T. Farrell, among other eminences.

---

* The story's veracity was attested by his mother, who scrawled on the back of the original typescript: "If there is another word besides wonderful I dont know I dont remember telling you all these so accurate."

Schwartz's reputation as a poet has perhaps obscured his achievement as a writer of prose fiction. For a time in the mid-thirties he concentrated more on his stories than on his verse, and there survive among his papers several prose drafts and fragments that showed considerable promise—autobiographical fiction in the vein of "In Dreams Begin Responsibilities." One story Schwartz did complete but never published (or even typed up; it existed only in a holograph copy until *PR* published it more than a decade after his death), was "SCREENO," a charming tale that features the youthful, vaguely alienated persona who appeared under so many variations in his work: as Hershey Green in the two-hundred-page poem *Genesis* (1943); as Shenandoah Fish, who figures in the verse play *Shenandoah* and in three of the stories collected in *The World Is a Wedding* (1948); and in several unpublished novels about Delmore Schwartz-like characters.

Written during three days in November 1937, "SCREENO" introduced the Washington Heights milieu Schwartz could evoke with such laconic ease. In this story, Cornelius Schmidt escapes from a dreary existence to the movies, which promise to dissipate the "tasteless, colorless mood" that descends on him at home. Once there, however, he finds himself embroiled in a fantastic series of events very different from the realistic situations Schwartz was to write about later on; the strange atmosphere in which Cornelius wins the lottery, recites a passage from Eliot's "Gerontion" to the bewildered audience, and impulsively hands over his prize money to a pathetic old man who protests that he, too, has won, recalls the comic, implausible world of Kafka's *Amerika*.

"The Commencement Day Address," written during the same period and published in *New Directions in Prose and Poetry* in 1937, was just as implausible—and just as precocious. Still in his early twenties, Schwartz had fashioned a vivid, inventive prose resonant with images of the city's life. After the curious speech given by Dr. Isaac Duspenser, a kibitzer out of Schwartz's gallery of wise, garrulous, bitter old men—the ghosts in *Genesis* and in his verse plays—the audience disperses into "the metropolitan city, narrow and tall on all sides, full of traffic, accident, commerce, and adultery, of a thousand drugstores, apartment houses and theatres, its belly veined with black subways, its towers and bridges grand, numb, and without meaning." Such impressive rhetorical flights enlivened these stories, and one can only wonder why he chose not to include them in *The World Is a Wedding*.

Schwartz's letters during the early forties, when he was writing *Genesis*, are filled with accounts of novels—plotted, proposed, and in the works. *Genesis* itself was first composed in prose, and the title story in *The World Is a Wedding* was originally intended to be a sort of sustained *Bildungsroman*. Many chapters survive that deal with his years at the University of Wisconsin and New York University, his courtship with his first wife Gertrude Buckman, and episodes from his adolescence; but the only trace of the novel in print is "The World Is a Wedding," about Paul Goodman and his circle. The two writers met in 1934, when Goodman was living with his sister in Washington Heights and struggling—with far less success than Schwartz—to establish himself as a writer. But Goodman had the advantage over Schwartz of an admiring group that gathered around him to proclaim his genius. Moreover, he had acquired a certain worldliness that intimidated his rival, a knowing manner encouraged by his friends. "That he seemed ill at ease in Paul's home is understandable," one member of the circle noted, "the atmosphere was satirical and many of the jokes were almost impolitely private." That he was beginning to publish meant little there, since the world outside Goodman's living room was irrelevant to the hermetic coterie that thrived on its own wit. Schwartz's aspirations to literary fame indicated to them only that he was "living beyond his intellectual and artistic means." "The World Is a Wedding" was, in part, an act of revenge for their ill-treatment of him on the few occasions when he attended the Saturday evenings at which Goodman's work was read aloud.

It was in 1946, Schwartz noted in his journal, that he "formulated fiction as reality-testing," a principle suggested to him by Turgenev's stories. But he had been "testing" reality for over a decade by then, producing character sketches of his friends—whom he conveniently initialled in the margins of his manuscripts to obviate any doubt as to their identities. It is a pity that he never finished a story labelled "Philip & Mary"—about Philip Rahv and Mary McCarthy—but at least we have the portrait of Goodman and his circle; and in "New Year's Eve," published in 1945, a brilliant depiction of the *Partisan Review* crowd. Inspired by a *PR* party at the close of 1937, when Schwartz was just becoming known, "New Year's Eve" was written with a fine sardonic eye toward the frailty of his intellectual friends, all of whom are readily recognizable. F. W. Dupee, at the time an editor of *PR*, he depicted as "an interesting and unfortunate human being" goaded by his failure as a novelist into cynical pronouncements on literary history; Dwight Macdonald, caricatured in the person of Grant Landis as having a "pathological excess of energy," was shown making endless phone calls to raise money for some jailed labor leaders; the hapless Leon Berg, universally resented "because his chief activity was to explain to all authors that they were without talent," was a malicious version of the critic Lionel Abel; Schwartz's close friend William Barrett, the Nicholas O'Neil of the story, "who was unhappy and suffered from a cold," spent the evening soaking his chilled feet in a pail of hot water; Gertrude Buckman, as Wilhelmina Gold, was said to have the "sensibility ... of an only child who for twenty-four years has been adored, tended, and nagged by her parents"; and Schwartz himself was again represented by Shenandoah Fish, the promising author of "a satirical dialogue between Freud and Marx," who "had for long cherished the belief that if he were an interesting and gifted author, everyone would like him and want to be with him and enjoy conversation with him." Caught up in academic disputes, afflicted by excessive self-consciousness, the guests wore one another down until everyone shared the same condition, "what was soon to be a post-Munich sensibility: complete hopelessness of perception and feeling."

Schwartz had by this time perfected a unique style that enabled him to depict his characters with a sort of childlike verisimilitude, a deliberate naivete; wry, satirical, subdued, his stories had a nostalgic flavor that made them seem like parables. "The evening of the profound holiday drew much strength and unhappiness from such depths as the afternoon, the week, the year of unhappiness, and the lives that had long been lived," "New Year's Eve" began; and he prefaced "The World Is a Wedding" with the observation that "In this our life there are no beginnings but only departures entitled beginnings, wreathed in the formal emotions thought to be appropriate and often forced." Alert to the universal character of his experience, the sadness and vulnerability that oppressed his friends and family, Schwartz rendered their predicament in a language at once limpid and rhetorical. And in keeping with this tactic of amplifying the lives of his characters to yield some larger significance, he would invariably conclude with a Joycean epiphany, as in "America! America!" where Shenandoah stares in a mirror and muses: "No one truly exists in the real world because no one knows all that he is to other human beings, all that they say behind his back, and all the foolishness which the future will bring him." It was a style that had more in common with Isaac Babel or Sholom Aleichem than with Hemingway.

"America! America!," a charming story about the fortunes of a typical Jewish family early in the century, was Schwartz's testament to what he liked to call "the Atlantic migration, that made America." Based on his mother's involved tales of the Salomon family, who had lived next door to the Schwartzes in Washington Heights, his chronicle of the Baumanns reproduced with a precise fidelity the attitudes and habits of language that defined them. In a symposium "On American Literature and the Younger Generation of American Jews," Schwartz gave an account of how he had acquired such a sensitive ear for their speech:

To be the child of immigrants from East Europe is in itself a special kind of experience; and an important one to an author. He has heard two languages through childhood, the one spoken with ease in the streets and at school, but spoken poorly at home. Students of speech have explained certain kinds of mispronunciation in terms of this double experience of language. To an author, and especially to a poet, it may give a heightened sensitivity to language, a sense of idiom, and a sense of how much expresses itself through colloquialism. But it also produces in some a fear of mispronunciation; a hesitation in speech; and a sharpened focus upon the characters of the parents.

For the Baumanns, as for Schwartz's parents, America was a source of wonder, "a subject much loved by all the foreign-born." As their own fortunes declined, and their children failed to become "millionaires ... rabbis, or philosophers like Bergson," they were left to their dreams of a future prosperity announced in the newspapers read aloud at the dining-room table. Drinking tea from a tall glass, Mr. Baumann was the very type of the Jewish immigrant businessman, talkative, enthusiastic, at once provincial and shrewd. Schwartz brought the particular idiom of his parents' generation to life by italicizing the vocabulary that defined their characters. Mr. Baumann was said to be *doing business* when he paid a social visit; he was *well-informed*, involved in *deals*, and the owner of a *going concern*; he was sensitive to *the finer things in life*. Anyone whose parents or grandparents came over on the boat will hear in these phrases and inflections the familiar tonalities expressive of the Jewish immigrant experience; and Schwartz was the great commentator on this experience. His family's claustrophobic milieu, constricted by a longing for assimilation in conflict with an ineradicable sense of estrangement from the dominant values of American life, has never been written about with such imaginative force. And when he turned to their immediate history, in "The Child Is the Meaning of This Life," Schwartz produced a vivid, if unsparing portrait of his own childhood.

The story of the Hart family's faded expectations—the promising uncle who died young; his brother's compulsive gambling; the clashes between Sarah Hart and her husband (Schwartz's parents); her sister's marriage late in life—was entirely autobiographical. Schwartz's portrait of his mother as "suspicious, rejected, ambitious to win more than most human beings desired," and of his father as a handsome, philandering businessman rehearsed what had by now become an obsession: to discover and define "the Furies of the Family Life." "What was the freedom to which the adult human being rose in the morning, if each act was held back or inspired by the overpowering ghost of a little child?" Jasper speculates on leaving the hospital where his beloved grandmother lies ill. "This freedom seemed to Jasper like the freedom, dangerous, dark, and far-off, to become the father of new children without knowing at all what would become of them, what kind of human beings they would be." This was Schwartz's theme, acquired from his absorption in the past and from an assiduous reading of Freud; and he made of it a history of the aspirations bequeathed those whom Irving Howe once labelled, in a famous essay, "the New York Jewish intellectuals." Gossip, the rudiments of philosophy, and a study of manners mingled in his stories with a narrative art of homiletic simplicity; the result was, in one critic's estimate, "the definitive portrait of the Jewish middle class in New York during the Depression."*

Schwartz had expected *Genesis* to establish his reputation as a great American poet; it was to have taken its place beside Pound's *Cantos* and "The Waste Land" among the major poems of his time, and when the critics proved indifferent to its virtues, he was inconsolable. During the mid-1940s, he began one story after another about a failed author whose hopes had come to nothing. It was in this period that signs of Schwartz's eventual tragic decline became apparent, and his prose grew impossibly diffuse. Only one significant story, "The Track Meet," a bizarre hallucination in the Kafkaesque manner of his earliest work, dates from

* R. W. Flint, "The Stories of Delmore Schwartz," *Commentary*, (April 1962).

after *The World Is a Wedding*. He continued to labor on several novels—*The Brothers Kennedy*, so accented to echo *The Brothers Karamazov*; *A History of the Boys and the Girls*; and a group of stories about one Richmond Rose—but all of them were abandoned. When he died alone in a midtown Manhattan hotel in 1966, Schwartz left behind no undiscovered masterpieces. But the stories collected here constitute one of the durable achievements of that culture and era now known as "the world of our fathers."

—JAMES ATLAS

In Dreams Begin Responsibilities

IN DREAMS BEGIN
RESPONSIBILITIES

I

I think it is the year 1909. I feel as if I were in a motion picture theatre, the long arm of light crossing the darkness and spinning, my eyes fixed on the screen. This is a silent picture as if an old Biograph one, in which the actors are dressed in ridiculously old-fashioned clothes, and one flash succeeds another with sudden jumps. The actors too seem to jump about and walk too fast. The shots themselves are full of dots and rays, as if it were raining when the picture was photographed. The light is bad.

It is Sunday afternoon, June 12th, 1909, and my father is walking down the quiet streets of Brooklyn on his way to visit my mother. His clothes are newly pressed and his tie is too tight in his high collar. He jingles the coins in his pockets, thinking of the witty things he will say. I feel as if I had by now relaxed entirely in the soft darkness of the theatre; the organist peals out the obvious and approximate emotions on which the audience rocks unknowingly. I am anonymous, and I have forgotten myself. It is always so when one goes to the movies, it is, as they say, a drug.

My father walks from street to street of trees, lawns and houses, once in a while coming to an avenue on which a streetcar skates and gnaws, slowly progressing. The conductor, who has a handle-bar mustache, helps a young lady wearing a hat like a bowl with feathers on to the car. She lifts her long skirts slightly as she mounts the steps. He leisurely makes change and rings his bell. It is obviously Sunday, for everyone is wearing Sunday clothes, and the street-car's noises emphasize the quiet of the holiday. Is not Brooklyn the City of Churches? The shops are closed and their shades drawn, but for an occasional stationery store or drug-store with great green balls in the window.

My father has chosen to take this long walk because he likes to walk and think. He thinks about himself in the future and so arrives at the place he is to visit in a state of mild exaltation. He pays no attention to the houses he is passing, in which the Sunday dinner is being eaten, nor to the many trees which patrol each street, now coming to their full leafage and the time when they will room the whole street in cool shadow. An occasional carriage passes, the horse's hooves falling like stones in the quiet afternoon, and once in a while an automobile, looking like an enormous uphol-stered sofa, puffs and passes.

My father thinks of my mother, of how nice it will be to in-troduce her to his family. But he is not yet sure that he wants to marry her, and once in a while he becomes panicky about the bond already established. He reassures himself by thinking of the big men he admires who are married: William Randolph Hearst, and William Howard Taft, who has just become President of the United States.

My father arrives at my mother's house. He has come too early and so is suddenly embarrassed. My aunt, my mother's sister, an-swers the loud bell with her napkin in her hand, for the family is still at dinner. As my father enters, my grandfather rises from the table and shakes hands with him. My mother has run upstairs to tidy herself. My grandmother asks my father if he has had dinner, and tells him that Rose will be downstairs soon. My grandfather opens the conversation by remarking on the mild June weather. My father sits uncomfortably near the table, holding his hat in his hand. My grandmother tells my aunt to take my father's hat. My uncle, twelve years old, runs into the house, his hair tousled. He shouts a greeting to my father, who has often given him a nickel, and then runs upstairs. It is evident that the respect in which my father is held in this household is tempered by a good deal of mirth. He is impressive, yet he is very awkward.

II

Finally my mother comes downstairs, all dressed up, and my father being engaged in conversation with my grandfather becomes uneasy, not knowing whether to greet my mother or continue the conversation. He gets up from the chair clumsily and says "hello" gruffly. My grandfather watches, examining their congruence, such as it is, with a critical eye, and meanwhile rubbing his bearded cheek roughly, as he always does when he reflects. He is worried; he is afraid that my father will not make a good husband for his oldest daughter. At this point something happens to the film, just as my father is saying something funny to my mother; I am awakened to myself and my unhappiness just as my interest was rising. The audience begins to clap impatiently. Then the trouble is cared for but the film has been returned to a portion just shown, and once more I see my grandfather rubbing his bearded cheek and pondering my father's character. It is difficult to get back into the picture once more and forget myself, but as my mother giggles at my father's words, the darkness drowns me.

My father and mother depart from the house, my father shaking hands with my mother once more, out of some unknown uneasiness. I stir uneasily also, slouched in the hard chair of the theatre. Where is the older uncle, my mother's older brother? He is studying in his bedroom upstairs, studying for his final examination at

5

the College of the City of New York, having been dead of rapid pneumonia for the last twenty-one years. My mother and father walk down the same quiet streets once more. My mother is holding my father's arm and telling him of the novel which she has been reading; and my father utters judgments of the characters as the plot is made clear to him. This is a habit which he very much enjoys, for he feels the utmost superiority and confidence when he approves and condemns the behavior of other people. At times he feels moved to utter a brief "Ugh"—whenever the story becomes what he would call sugary. This tribute is paid to his manliness. My mother feels satisfied by the interest which she has awakened; she is showing my father how intelligent she is, and how interesting.

They reach the avenue, and the street-car leisurely arrives. They are going to Coney Island this afternoon, although my mother considers that such pleasures are inferior. She has made up her mind to indulge only in a walk on the boardwalk and a pleasant dinner, avoiding the riotous amusements as being beneath the dignity of so dignified a couple.

My father tells my mother how much money he has made in the past week, exaggerating an amount which need not have been exaggerated. But my father has always felt that actualities somehow fall short. Suddenly I begin to weep. The determined old lady who sits next to me in the theatre is annoyed and looks at me with an angry face, and being intimidated, I stop. I drag out my handkerchief and dry my face, licking the drop which has fallen near my lips. Meanwhile I have missed something, for here are my mother and father alighting at the last stop, Coney Island.

III

They walk toward the boardwalk, and my father commands my mother to inhale the pungent air from the sea. They both breathe in deeply, both of them laughing as they do so. They have in common a great interest in health, although my father is strong and husky, my mother frail. Their minds are full of theories of what is good to eat and not good to eat, and sometimes they engage in heated discussions of the subject, the whole matter ending in my father's announcement, made with a scornful bluster, that you have to die sooner or later anyway. On the boardwalk's flagpole, the American flag is pulsing in an intermittent wind from the sea.

My father and mother go to the rail of the boardwalk and look down on the beach where a good many bathers are casually walking about. A few are in the surf. A peanut whistle pierces the air with its pleasant and active whine, and my father goes to buy peanuts. My mother remains at the rail and stares at the ocean. The ocean seems merry to her; it pointedly sparkles and again and again the pony waves are released. She notices the children digging in the wet sand, and the bathing costumes of the girls who are her own age. My father returns with the peanuts. Overhead the sun's lightning strikes and strikes, but neither of them are at all aware of it. The boardwalk is full of people dressed in their Sunday clothes and idly strolling. The tide does not reach as far as the boardwalk, and the strollers would feel no danger if it did. My mother and father lean on the rail of the boardwalk and absently stare at the ocean. The ocean is becoming rough; the waves come in slowly, tugging strength from far back. The moment before they somersault, the moment when they arch their backs so beautifully, showing green and white veins amid the black, that moment is intolerable. They finally crack, dashing fiercely upon the sand, actually driving, full force downward, against the sand, bouncing upward and forward, and at last petering out into a small stream which races up the beach and then is recalled. My parents gaze absentmindedly at the ocean, scarcely interested in its harshness. The sun overhead does not disturb them. But I stare at the terrible sun which breaks up sight, and the fatal, merciless, passionate ocean, I forget my parents. I stare fascinated and finally, shocked by the indifference of my father and mother, I burst out weeping once more. The old lady next to me pats me on the shoulder and says "There, there, all of this is only a movie, young man, only a movie," but I look up once more at the terrifying sun and the terrifying ocean, and being unable to control my tears, I get up and go to the men's room, stumbling over the feet of the other people seated in my row.

IV

When I return, feeling as if I had awakened in the morning sick for lack of sleep, several hours have apparently passed and my parents are riding on the merry-go-round. My father is on a black horse, my mother on a white one, and they seem to be making an eternal circuit for the single purpose of snatching the nickel rings which are attached to the arm of one of the posts. A hand-organ is playing; it is one with the ceaseless circling of the merry-go-round.

For a moment it seems that they will never get off the merry-go-round because it will never stop. I feel like one who looks down on the avenue from the 50th story of a building. But at length they do get off; even the music of the hand-organ has ceased for a moment. My father has acquired ten rings, my mother only two, although it was my mother who really wanted them.

They walk on along the boardwalk as the afternoon descends by imperceptible degrees into the incredible violet of dusk. Everything fades into a relaxed glow, even the ceaseless murmuring from the beach, and the revolutions of the merry-go-round. They look for a place to have dinner. My father suggests the best one on the boardwalk and my mother demurs, in accordance with her principles.

However they do go to the best place, asking for a table near the window, so that they can look out on the boardwalk and the mobile ocean. My father feels omnipotent as he places a quarter in the waiter's hand as he asks for a table. The place is crowded and here too there is music, this time from a kind of string trio. My father orders dinner with a fine confidence.

As the dinner is eaten, my father tells of his plans for the future, and my mother shows with expressive face how interested she is, and how impressed. My father becomes exultant. He is lifted up by the waltz that is being played, and his own future begins to intoxicate him. My father tells my mother that he is going to expand his business, for there is a great deal of money to be made. He wants to settle down. After all, he is twenty-nine, he has lived by himself since he was thirteen, he is making more and more money, and he is envious of his married friends when he visits them in the cozy security of their homes, surrounded, it seems, by the calm domestic pleasures, and by delightful children, and then, as the waltz reaches the moment when all the dancers swing madly, then, then with awful daring, then he asks my mother to marry him, although awkwardly enough and puzzled, even in his excitement, at how he had arrived at the proposal, and she, to make the whole business worse, begins to cry, and my father looks nervously about, not knowing at all what to do now, and my mother says: "It's all I've wanted from the moment I saw you," sobbing, and he finds all of this very difficult, scarcely to his taste, scarcely as he had thought it would be, on his long walks over Brooklyn Bridge in the revery of a fine cigar, and it was then that I stood up in the theatre and shouted: "Don't do it. It's not too late to change your minds, both of you. Nothing good will come of it, only remorse, hatred, scandal, and two children whose characters are monstrous." The whole audience turned to look at me, annoyed, the usher came hurrying down the aisle flashing his searchlight, and the old lady next to me tugged me down into my seat, saying: "Be quiet. You'll be put out, and you paid thirty-five cents to come in." And so I shut my eyes because I could not bear to see what was happening. I sat there quietly.

V

But after awhile I begin to take brief glimpses, and at length I watch again with thirsty interest, like a child who wants to maintain his sulk although offered the bribe of candy. My parents are now having their picture taken in a photographer's booth along the boardwalk. The place is shadowed in the mauve light which is apparently necessary. The camera is set to the side on its tripod and looks like a Martian man. The photographer is instructing my parents in how to pose. My father has his arm over my mother's shoulder, and both of them smile emphatically. The photographer brings my mother a bouquet of flowers to hold in her hand but she holds it at the wrong angle. Then the photographer covers himself with the black cloth which drapes the camera and all that one sees of him is one protruding arm and his hand which clutches the rubber ball which he will squeeze when the picture is finally taken. But he is not satisfied with their appearance. He feels with certainty that somehow there is something wrong in their pose. Again and again he issues from his hidden place with new directions. Each suggestion merely makes matters worse. My father is becoming impatient. They try a seated pose. The photographer explains that he has pride, he is not interested in all of this for the money, he wants to make beautiful pictures. My father says: "Hurry up, will you? We haven't got all night." But the photographer only scurries about apologetically, and issues new directions. The photographer charms me. I approve of him with all my heart, for I know just how he feels, and as he criticizes each revised pose according to some unknown idea of Tightness, I become quite hopeful. But then my father says angrily: "Come on, you've had enough time, we're not going to wait any longer." And the photographer, sighing unhappily, goes back under his black covering, holds out his hand, says: "One, two, three, Now!", and the picture is taken, with my father's smile turned to a grimace and my mother's bright and false. It takes a few minutes for the picture to be developed and as my parents sit in the curious light they become quite depressed.

They have passed a fortune-teller's booth, and my mother wishes to go in, but my father does not. They begin to argue about it. My mother becomes stubborn, my father once more impatient, and then they begin to quarrel, and what my father would like to do is walk off and leave my mother there, but he knows that that would never do. My mother refuses to budge. She is near to tears, but she feels an uncontrollable desire to hear what the palm-reader will say. My father consents angrily, and they both go into a booth which is in a way like the photographer's, since it is draped in black cloth and its light is shadowed. The place is too warm, and my father keeps saying this is all nonsense, pointing to the crystal ball on the table. The fortune-teller, a fat, short woman, garbed in what is supposed to be Oriental robes, comes into the room from the back and greets them, speaking with an accent. But suddenly my father feels that the whole thing is intolerable; he tugs at my mother's arm, but my mother refuses to budge. And then, in terrible anger, my father lets go of my mother's arm and strides out, leaving my mother stunned. She moves to go after my father, but the fortune-teller holds her arm tightly and begs her not to do so, and I in my seat am shocked more than can ever be said, for I feel as if I were walking a tight-rope a hundred feet over a circus-audience and suddenly the rope is showing signs of breaking, and I get up from my seat and begin to shout once more the first words I can think of to communicate my terrible fear and once more the usher comes hurrying down the aisle flashing his searchlight, and the old lady pleads with me, and the shocked audience has turned to stare at me, and I keep shouting: "What are they doing? Don't they know what they are doing? Why doesn't my mother go after my father? If she does not do that, what will she do? Doesn't my father know what he is doing?"—But the usher has seized my arm and is dragging me away, and as he does so, he says: "What are *you* doing? Don't you know that you can't do whatever you want to do? Why should a young man like you, with your whole life before you, get hysterical like this? Why don't you *think* of what you're doing? You can't act like this even if other people aren't around! You will be sorry if you do not do what you should do, you can't carry on like this, it is not right, you will find that out soon enough, everything you do matters too much," and he said that dragging me through the lobby of the theatre into the cold light, and I woke up into the bleak winter morning of my 21st birthday, the windowsill shining with its lip of snow, and the morning already begun.

AMERICA! AMERICA!

When Shenandoah Fish returned from Paris in 1936, he was unable to do very much with himself, he was unable to write with the great fluency and excitement of previous years. Some great change had occurred in the human beings he knew in his native city, whom he had sought out before his stay in Europe. The depression had occurred to these human beings. It had reached the marrow at last; after years, the full sense of the meaning of the depression had modified their hopes and their desires very much. The boys with whom Shenandoah had gone to school no longer lived in the same neighborhood, they no longer saw much of each other, they were somewhat embarrassed when they met, some of them were married now, and many of them were ashamed of what they had made or what had been made of their lives. After visits which concluded in perplexity, Shenandoah ceased to try to renew his old friendships. They no longer existed and they were not going to rise from the grave of the dead years.

Yet Shenandoah was not troubled by his idleness. He would have liked to be in Paris again, and he expected to go back next year. He did not know then that it would be impossible for him to go back. Meanwhile, as his mother said, he was taking it easy, and enjoying an indolence and a relaxation which, though peculiar in him, seemed unavoidable after the prolonged and intense activity of the year before.

He slept late each morning, and then he sat for a long time at the breakfast-table, listening to his mother's talk as she went about her household tasks. It was simple and pleasant to shift attention back and forth between what his mother said and the morning newspaper, for in the morning sunlight, the kitchen's whiteness was pleasant, the newspaper was always interesting in the strength of attention possible in the morning, and Shenandoah found his mother's monologue pleasant too. She spoke always of her own life or of the lives of her friends; of what had been; what might have been; of fate, character and accident; and especially of the mystery of the family life, as she had known it and reflected upon it.

After two months of idleness, Shenandoah began to feel uneasy about these breakfast pleasures. The emotion which often succeeded extended idleness returned again, the emotion of a loss or lapse of identity. "Who am I? what am I?" Shenandoah began once more to say to himself, and although he knew very well that this was only the projection of some other anxiety, although he knew that to work too was merely to deceive himself about this anxiety, nonetheless the intellectual criticism of his own emotions was as ever of no avail whatever.

On the morning when this uneasiness of the whole being overtook Shenandoah seriously, his mother's monologue began to interest him more and more, much more than ever before, although she spoke of human beings who, being of her own generation, did not really interest Shenandoah in themselves. She began to speak of the Baumanns, whom she had known well for thirty years.

The Baumanns, said Mrs. Fish, had given Shenandoah a silver spoon when he was born. Mrs. Fish brought forth the silver and showed Shenandoah his initials engraved in twining letters upon the top of the spoon. Shenandoah took the spoon and toyed with it nervously, looking at the initials as he listened to his mother.

The friendship of the Fish family with the Baumann family had begun in the period just before the turn of the century. Shenandoah's father, who was now dead, had gone into what was then entitled the insurance *game*. The word rang in Shenandoah's mind, and he noted again his mother's fine memory for the speech other people used. Mr. Baumann who was twenty years older than Shenandoah's father, had already established himself in the business of insurance; he had been successful from the start because it was just the kind of business for a man of his temperament.

Shenandoah's mother proceeded to explain in detail how insurance was a genial medium for a man like Mr. Baumann. The important thing in insurance was to win one's way into the homes and into the confidences of other people. Insurance could not be sold as a grocer or a druggist sells his *goods* (here Shenandoah was moved again by his mother's choice of words); you could not wait for the customer to come to you; nor could you like the book salesman go from house to house, plant your foot in the doorway, and start talking quickly before the housewife shut the door in your face. On the contrary, it was necessary to become friendly with a great many people, who, when they came to know you, and like you, and trust you, take your advice about the value of insurance.

It was necessary to join the lodges, societies, and associations of your own class and people. This had been no hardship to Mr. Baumann who enjoyed groups, gatherings, and meetings of all kinds. He had in his youth belonged to the association of the people who came from the old country, and when he married, he joined his wife's association. Then he joined the masonic lodge, and in addition he participated in the social life of the neighborhood synagogue, although he was in fact an admirer of Ingersoll. Thus he came to know a great many people, and visited them with unfailing devotion and regularity, moved by his love of being with other human beings. A visit was a complicated act for him. It required that he enter the house with much amiability, and tell his host that he had been thinking of him and speaking of him just the other day, mentioning of necessity that he had just *dropped* in for a moment. Only after protestations of a predictable formality, was Mr. Baumann persuaded to sit down for a cup of tea. Once seated, said Mrs. Fish (imposing from time to time her own kind of irony upon the irony which sang in Shenandoah's mind at every phase of her story), once seated it was hours before Mr. Baumann arose from the dining room table on which a fresh table-cloth had been laid and from which the lace cover and the cut glass had been withdrawn.

Mr. Baumann drank tea in the Russian style, as he often explained; he drank it from a glass, not from a cup: a cup was utterly out of the question. And while he drank and ate, he discoursed inimitably and authoritatively upon *every topic of the day*, but especially upon his favorite subjects, the private life of the kings and queens of Europe, Zionism, and the new discoveries of science. A silent amazement often mounted in his listeners at the length of time that he was capable of eating, drinking, and talking; until at last, since little was left upon the table, he absentmindedly took up the crumbs and poppyseeds from the tablecloth.

Mrs. Fish had not known Mr. Baumann until he was near middle age. But she had heard that even in his youth, he had looked like a banker. As he grew older and became quite plump, this impression was strengthened, for he took to pince-nez glasses, and handsome vests with white piping. Shenandoah remembered that Mr. Baumann resembled some photographs of the first J. P. Morgan. His friends were delighted with all the aspects of his being, but they took especial satisfaction in his appearance. They were shamed often enough into allowing him to *write* a new insurance policy for them, for it was a time of general prosperity for these people: most of them were rising in the world, after having come to America as grown or half-grown children. Their first insecurity was passed and hardly borne in mind, except in the depths of consciousness; and now they were able to *afford* an insurance policy, just as they were able to look down on newcomers to America, and their own early lives in America, a state of being which was expressed by the word, *greenhorn*. Mr. Baumann's friendship was a token of their progress; they liked him very much, they were flattered by his company, and when he paid them a visit, he conferred upon the household a sense of the great world, even of intellectuality. This pleased the husband often because of what it implied to his wife; it implied that although he, the husband, was too busy a man in the dress business to know much of these worldly matters, yet he was capable of having the friendship and *bringing into the house* this amiable and cultivated man who spoke English with a Russian accent which was extremely refined.

Shenandoah's mother explained then that in the insurance business a good man like Mr. Baumann soon arrives at the point where there is no urgent need to acquire new customers and to write new policies. One can live in comfortable style off the commissions due you as the premiums continue to be paid from year to year. You must maintain your friendship with the policy-holders, so that the stress of hard times as it recurs does not make them give up their policies or stop paying the premiums. But this need of reassuring and cajoling policyholders did not for Mr. Baumann interfere with a way of life in which one slept late in the morning and made breakfast the occasion for the most painstaking scrutiny of the morning newspaper. One can go for vacations whenever one pleases, and Mr. Baumann went often with his family, on religious holidays and on national holidays. In fact, Mr. Baumann had frequently written some of his best policies during the general high spirits which are the rule on vacations and at resorts. He was at his best at such times and amid such well-being.

Here Shenandoah recognized in his mother's tone the resentment she had always felt toward those who lived well and permitted nothing to stop their enjoyment of life. It was the resentment of one who had herself never felt the inclination to live well, and regarded it as unjustified, except on the part of the very rich, or during holidays.

Mrs. Fish continued, saying that an insurance man is faced with one unavoidable duty, that of putting in an appearance at the funerals of human beings with whom he has been acquainted, even though he has not known them very well. This is a way of paying tribute to one of the irreducible facts upon which the insurance business is founded. And it provides the starting-point for useful and leading conversation.

"Yes," Mr. Baumann often said, "I was at L——'s funeral today." His tone implied the authoritative character of his presence.

"Yes," he reiterated with emphasis, squeezing the lemon into his tea, "we all have to go, sooner or later!"

Then he dwelt on the interesting incidents at the funeral, the children's lack of understanding, the widow's hysterical weeping, the life-like appearance of the corpse.

"He looked," said Mr. Baumann, "just like he was taking a nap."

And indeed, apart from *doing business*, Mr. Baumann enjoyed funerals for their own sake, for they were comprehensive gatherings of human beings with whom he had everything in common and to whom he was a very interesting and very *well-informed* man, even a man, as he seemed to some and to himself, who was a sage although without rabbinical trappings.

Here, having said this with unconscious disdain, Mrs. Fish finished ironing a tablecloth, folded it carefully, placed it with other ironed linens, took a new piece, and permitted herself no pause in her monologue.

She said that Mrs. Baumann was the one person who was unable to take Mr. Baumann with the seriousness he expected and received in all quarters. She preferred the neighborhood rabbi as a sage. She and her husband shared so many interests that there was a natural and extensive antagonism between them. Whatever gentleman occupied the rabbinical position in the neighborhood synagogue surpassed her husband at his own game, so far as she was concerned: surpassed him in unction, suavity, and fecundity of opinion.

Next to her husband, Mrs. Baumann seemed small and almost tiny. She was nervous and anxious, while he was always assured; and he merely smiled when she attacked him or criticized him before other people, or told him that he was talking too much, or said that he did not know what he was talking about. However, they loved the same things, and some of her resentment of her husband had as its source his freedom to have a full social life while she had to take care of the children. For her children, her friends, and all things Jewish, she had an inexhaustible charity, indulgence, and attentiveness, and consequently she sometimes neglected her household in order to make many visits and tell many stories, stories of patient detail and analysis which had to do with her friends. In the time before the World War, Freud and Bergson were celebrated in Jewish newspapers as Jews who had made a great fame for themselves in the Gentile world. Mrs. Baumann relished their fame to the point of making out a misleading and mistaken version of their doctrines; and in this way, Shenandoah's father, who visited the Baumann household very often before his marriage, learned of the teachings of Freud and passed them on to the salesmen who worked for him in the real estate business.

Only one thing excited Mrs. Baumann more than the success of a musician or an inventor who was Jewish; and that one thing was a new fad, especially fads about food. She often spoke of herself as having a new *fad*, and she often said that everyone should have fads. For the word pleased her, and some of its connotations had never occurred to her. She said often that she wished that she were a vegetarian.

As Shenandoah listened to his mother, he became nervous. He was not sure at any given moment whether the cruelty of the story was in his own mind or in his mother's tongue. And his own thoughts, which had to do with his own life, and seemed to have nothing to do with these human beings, began to trouble him.

What is it, he said to himself, that I do not see in myself, because it is of the present, as they did not see themselves? How can one look at oneself? No one sees himself.

As the Baumann children grew up, they seemed to gain vitality from the intensive social life of the household. For their small apartment near a great park came to be a kind of community center on Sunday nights. All whom Mr. Baumann met on his leisurely rounds were invited to come at any time. Both husband and wife knew very well how glad lonely human beings are to have a house to visit, a true household; and especially the human beings who have gone from the community life of the old country and foundered amid the immense alienation of metropolitan life. And the Baumanns also knew, although they were too wise to express the belief, that it was very important to have something to eat amid the talk, for people do not continue very long without the desire to eat; and in addition, the conversations, the jokes and the comments are improved, heightened, or excited by food and drink, by sandwiches, cake, and coffee; and the food one gets in another's household seems *exceptionally appetizing*.

Shenandoah as he listened tried to go back by imagination or imaginative sympathy to the lives of these people. Certainly in the old country there had been periods when food was scarce, so that one of the most wonderful things about America was the abundance of food. But it was impossible for Shenandoah, who had always been well fed, to convince himself that he knew what their feelings about food had been. He returned to his mother who had begun genre studies of Sunday nights in the Baumann household.

Each of the Baumann children as they grew up amid these scenes of much sociability acquired social talents which gained them gratifying applause from the visitors, who were expected, in any case, in a profound, unspoken understanding, to make much of the children of any household. Dick, the oldest of the three children, learned to play the piano very cleverly, and he recited limericks and parodies. Sidney, the youngest one, was enchanted by the Sunday nights to the extent that he brought his neighborhood cronies to the house, which was a revelation most children avoided and dreaded because they were ashamed that their parents spoke broken English or a foreign tongue.

Sidney was less gifted than his brother; yet he was liked a good deal because he was small and *cute*. Martha, the girl, suffered from the intense aversions, shames, and frustrations of girlhood; and, as her father remarked, she *took it out* upon the piano, playing romantic music from morning to night. She was very smart and clever; and her remarks were often so biting that she was scolded helplessly, vainly, and tirelessly by her mother. Visitors, however, were charmed and not annoyed, when she was *fresh*. And as she became older, she defended herself by saying that she had learned her wit and irony at the Sunday night school of gossip, when all who were present analyzed the failings of their absent friends. Nonetheless, despite her bitter remarks about the household, she loved its regime very much, though annoyed to see how she depended upon it to nourish the depths of her being.

It was when Dick and Martha were old enough to need jobs that Shenandoah's father and Mr. Baumann went into partnership in the real estate business. Shenandoah's father had been in business *for himself* for some time and he had prospered greatly. It was his need of capital, which however he might have secured elsewhere, and his fondness for the Baumann's household which had made him suggest the partnership. The suggestion was made in a moment of weakness and well-being, when Mr. Fish had just enjoyed a fine dinner at the Baumann's. Whenever Shenandoah's father was pleased and had enjoyed himself very much, he suffered from these generous and unexpected impulses; but this did not prevent him from repairing the evil consequences of his magnanimity with an equally characteristic ruthlessness as soon as it was obvious that it not only had been costly (for then, he might forget about it), but that the cost would continue.

The difficulty soon showed itself, for Mr. Baumann and Dick made it clear that their habits of life were not going to be changed merely because they were now part of a *going concern*. Father and son arrived at work an hour before noon, which permitted them just enough time to look at the mail before departing for an unhurried lunch. They *drew* handsome salaries, and this was what troubled Shenandoah's father most of all. When it was a question of making a sale, Mr. Baumann often allowed his interests of the moment, which were often international in scope, to make him oblivious of *the deal*. He ingratiated himself with the customer very well, but this process ingratiated the customer with Mr. Baumann, and thus the mutual bloom of friendship, made business matters unimportant or a matter for tact and delicacy. Dick followed in his father's footsteps. He took customers to the ball game, which was well enough except that he too forgot the true and ulterior purpose of this spending of the firm's money. In three months, Shenandoah's father appreciated his error to the full; and for a week of half-sleepless nights, he strove to think of a way to free himself of his pleasure-loving partner. In the end, and as often before, he found only a brutal method; he sent Mr. Baumann a letter stating his grievances and dissolving the partnership. For a time, this summary dismissal ended the friendship of the two families. But Mr. Baumann was utterly unable to sustain a grudge, although his wife was unable to forget one, and *pestered* him about his weakness in forgiving those who had injured him.

Dick Baumann seemed to be unable to keep a job and he showed few signs of being able to make his way in the world. But he was popular, he had an *immense* number of friends, he was in request all over because he was always truly and literally the life of every party. At one such party, he met his future wife, an extremely beautiful girl who was also successful and had her own business. She was the only child of a mother deserted by her husband, and never had she been so charmed as by Dick, by Dick's parodies, imitations, out-goingness, and his fine air of well-being and happiness. Although somewhat perplexed by the girl's intense and fond looks, since he had not paid much attention to her, Dick had invited her to the Baumann menage, where Mrs. Baumann immediately fell in love with her. Dick was pliant and suggestible, Mrs. Baumann was the only strong-willed one in the family, and soon she had arranged matters in such a way that after a certain amount of urging on her part, everyone recognized the inevitability of the marriage.

First, however, Dick had to make a living. His intended had her handsome business, which she *ran* with a cousin. But this did not seem right to Mrs. Baumann; it offended her sense of propriety. She expected that it would end very soon, and she spoke of its ending all the time. She insisted that it must end before the marriage took place, since it was not only intolerable that a wife should make her own living, should go to work each day, but it was wrong that the wife should earn more money than the husband. As it happened, Dick was in no hurry to get married. He wished to please his mother, as he wished to please all. But from morning until night, he enjoyed being *single*; yet he did not conceive of his marriage as bringing about any great change in his habits, or any new goodness.

Shenandoah listened with an interest which increased continuously; and yet his own thoughts intervened many times. He reflected upon his separation from these people, and he felt that in every sense he was removed from them by thousands of miles, or by a generation, or by the Atlantic Ocean. What he cared about, only a few other human beings, separated from each other too, also cared about; and whatever he wrote as an author did not enter into the lives of these people, who should have been his genuine relatives and friends, for he had been surrounded by their lives since the day of his birth, and in an important sense, even before then. But since he was an author of a certain kind, he was a monster to them. They would be pleased to see his name in print and to hear that he was praised at times, but they would never be interested in what he wrote. They might open one book, and turn the pages; but then perplexity and boredom would take hold of them, and they would say, perhaps from politeness and certainly with humility, that this was too *deep* for them, or too *dry*. The lower middle-class of the generation of Shenandoah's parents had engendered perversions of its own nature, children full of contempt for every thing important to their parents. Shenandoah had thought of this gulf and perversion before, and he had shrugged away his unease by assuring himself that this separation had nothing to do with the important thing, which was the work itself. But now as he listened, as he felt uneasy and sought to dismiss his emotion, he began to feel that he was wrong to suppose that the separation, the contempt, and the gulf had nothing to do with his work; perhaps, on the contrary, it was the center; or perhaps it was the starting-point and compelled the innermost motion of the work to be flight, or criticism, or denial, or rejection.

Mrs. Fish had gone to the roof for more wash. She told Shenandoah as she returned that it was time for him to dress (for he had been in dressing-gown and pajamas all the while), and in her imperative tone, he recognized the strain and the resistance which was part of the relationship of mother and son; which had its cause in the true assumption that mother and son would disagree about what was the right thing to do, no matter what the problem might be.

The *engagement* of Dick and Susan was a protracted one; and after two years, the youthful couple had begun to take their intermediate state for granted. Mrs. Baumann in pride told her friends that Susan *practically* lived with them. It was by no means unusual for Susan to be at the Baumann household on every weekday evening, and on such evenings, as Dick read the sport pages with care, his mother interrupted him persistently to demand that he admire Susan's profile as she sat near the window, sewing. Susan was very beautiful indeed; and her business grew more and more prosperous as Dick went from job to job, unperturbed that a girl waited for him, a fact to which Mrs. Baumann often summoned his attention.

At last, being impatient, Mrs. Baumann arranged that the marriage should occur at the beginning of one of Dick's business ventures, the capital for which had been provided by Mr. Baumann and Susan. It was as if, remarked Shenandoah's mother, Mrs. Baumann was afraid to await the outcome of the new venture. And she had been right, for within eight months the business had to be given up to avoid bankruptcy, and Susan had to return to work as an assistant where before she had been *her own boss*, a humiliation which left Susan without any further illusions about her mother-in-law. The two never again managed to get along very well, although Mrs. Baumann's admiration of her daughter-in-law remained undisturbed. Mrs. Baumann was unable to understand Dick's failure to get rich, for no one failed to be delighted by his charm and his intelligence; and he always seemed to have a great deal of information about each new business. But somehow he was unable to make a success of it, or even to make it *pay*.

After his marriage, Dick frequented his parents' household as often as before marriage, a simple enough matter since he and his bride had taken an apartment near the parents to please Mrs. Baumann. And when Susan had to go back to work, it became convenient for the young married couple to have dinner every night with the whole Baumann family, a procedure Susan resented very much, although she was of a divided heart, since she too often enjoyed the conviviality of the family circle as much as before marriage.

One subject prevailed above others in the Baumann circle, the wonders of America, a subject much loved by all the foreign-born, but discussed in the Baumann household with a scope, intensity, subtlety, and gusto which was matchless, so far as Mrs. Fish knew. One reason for this subject's triumph was Mr. Baumann's interest in science, and one reason was that he was very much pleased with America.

When the first plane flew, when elevators became common, when the new subway was built, some newspaper reader in the Baumann household would raise his head, announce the wonder, and exclaim:

"You see: America!"

When the toilet-bowl flushed like Niagara, when a suburban homeowner killed his wife and children, and when a Jew was made a member of President Theodore Roosevelt's cabinet, the excited exclamation was:

"America! America!"

The expectations of these human beings who had come in their youth to the new world had not been fulfilled in the least. They had above all expected to be rich, and they had come with a very different image of what their new life was to be. But a thing more marvellous than fulfillment had transformed their expectations. They had been amazed to the pitch where they knew that their imaginations were inadequate to conceive the future of this incredible society. They expected and did not doubt that all the wonders would continue and increase; and Mr. Baumann maintained, against rising and rocking laughter, that his grand-children would return from business by a means of transit which resembled the cash carriers which fly through tubes in department stores. Mrs. Baumann's conception of the future was less mechanical and scientific. She hoped and expected her grandchildren would be millionaires and grandsons, rabbis, or philosophers like Bergson.

Sidney, the youngest child, had arrived at the age when it was expected that he too should earn a living for himself. But the disappointments Dick had caused were nothing to the difficulties Sidney made. Dick had been an indifferent student, but Sidney flatly refused to continue school at all after a certain time, and he displayed unexampled finickiness about the job Mr. Baumann's friends gave him, or helped him to get. He left his job as a shipping clerk because he did not like *the class of people* with whom he had to work, and he refused to take a job during July and August on the ground that he suffered greatly from summer heat, a defense natural to him after the many family discussions of health, food, and exercise. His mother always defended and *humored him*, saying that his health was delicate. But Mr. Baumann was often made furious and at times of an insane anger by his youngest son's indolence. Mrs. Baumann pointed out that Sidney was to be admired, after all, since in being unable to work he showed a sensitivity to *the finer things in life*. But Mr. Baumann knew too much of the world not to be concerned about the fact that both of his sons appeared to be unable to make out well in the world. In anger, he blamed his wife and his wife's family; but on other occasions, he discussed the problem with his friends, once with Shenandoah's father after the two were reconciled.

"I'll tell you what to do," said Mrs. Fish, "but you won't do it."

"Tell me," said Mr. Baumann, although he knew well enough

he was not likely to take his friend's advice.

"Ship Sidney out into the world," said Shenandoah's father, "make him stand on his own two feet. As long as he has a place to come home to and someone else to give him money for cigarettes, and plenty of company in the house, he's not going to worry about losing a job."

"But if a boy does not have ambition," Mr. Baumann replied, "is that enough? I always say, it all depends on the individual. His home has nothing to do with it. It is always the character of the person that counts."

"Sure it depends on character," said Mr. Fish, "but a fellow only finds out about his own character when he's all by himself, with no one to help him. Why if I had been your son," said Shenandoah's father, flattered that his advice was asked and wishing to please his friend, "I would have quit work myself and taken it easy and enjoyed the pleasant evenings."

A year after, Sidney was sent to Chicago to be *on his own*, although not before he had been given the addresses of many friends and relatives of the family. In three months, he was back; he had quarreled with his boss about working hours and he had exhausted his funds. He was welcomed into the bosom of the family with unconcealed joy. Although Mr. Baumann grumbled, and Martha addressed habitual ironic remarks to her brother as a *captain of industry*, no one had failed to feel his absence keenly and to be pleased deeply by his return.

"Well: you can try in New York as well as Chicago," said Mr. Baumann, "a smart boy like you is bound to get started sooner or later."

Mrs. Baumann believed that Sidney would fall in love one day, and this would prove the turning point. Either he would meet a rich girl who would be infatuated with *his personality*, or he would meet some poor girl and his desire to marry her would inspire him. In America, everyone or almost everyone was successful. Mrs. Baumann had seen too many fools make out very well to be able to believe otherwise.

And now all he had heard moved Shenandoah to remember all he himself knew of the Baumann family. The chief formal occasions of the Fish family had always been marked by the presence of the Baumanns. Each incident cited by his mother suggested another one to Shenandoah, and he began to interrupt his mother's story and tell her what he himself remembered. She would seize whatever he mentioned and augment it with her own richness of knowledge and experience.

As a girl, Martha had suffered an attack of polio, which left her with a curvature of the spine, which in turn made it unlikely that she would be able to have children, Martha had then decided that this defect and her plainness of appearance, a plainness which, although she did not know this truth, disappeared in her natural vivacity and wit—would prevent her from getting a husband. She would be an old maid, the worst of shames from the point of view of a Jewish mother. The belief that she would never marry heightened Martha's daring wit and *nerve*. She was the one who continued her father's intellectual interests. As he would cite the authors he had read in Russia as a young man, Pushkin, Lermontov, and Tolstoy, so she was much taken with Bernard Shaw and H. G. Wells, and spoke with bitter passion about women's suffrage.

And then, to the amazement of all, a young doctor who had frequented the household, a very shy young man who was already very successful, asked Martha to marry him, pale with fear that she would laugh at him and attack him with her famous sharpness and scorn. When she told him that he would have to go through life without children, he replied with a fine simplicity that he loved her and expected her to make a home for him which would be like her mother's household.

This marriage became the greatest satisfaction of the Baumanns' life, although it did not *compensate* for the shortcomings of the sons in business. Mrs. Baumann tirelessly praised her son-in-law, and marvelled infinitely at his magnanimity in marrying a girl who was unable to have children. She took especial pride in his being a very good doctor, a fact which impressed the women of her acquaintance because they wished most of all for sons or sons-in-law who were doctors. But it was for Mrs. Baumann a triumph chiefly because of her passionate interest in health.

Martha's harshness and sharpness rose to new heights with her marriage, and she became more relentless than ever with her brother, while often Maurice, her husband, found it necessary to protest gently, from a profound gentleness of heart, because she had once again called both brothers *failures*. Maurice had an admiration for the arts which gave him the conventional independence of conventional business values. He tried to argue with Martha that she was being *very conventional* and accepting conventional views of what *success* was. Martha, inspired by an enjoyment of her own brutality of speech, replied that there was one thing the Baumanns were wonderfully successful at, and that was marriage: they made first-class marriages. She was referring then not only to her own husband's prosperity and generosity, but also to Susan, who had started her own business again, and for years now had supported her husband and herself, and provided Dick with the capital for each new enterprise he attempted, spurred by his mother's anguish at the way things were.

Martha became more impatient with her family year by year, and after a time she did not wish to see them at all. But Maurice gently insisted that she pay her parents a weekly visit, and he sought to soothe the parents' hurt feelings when Martha saw to it that they lived in a suburb distant from the Baumann household.

America! America! The expression began to recur in Shenandoah's mind, like a phrase of music heard too often the day before. He was moved, and in a way shocked, as his mother was too, that Martha the family rebel, the one who had repudiated the family circle many times, should be the one who made out well in life. Shenandoah's mother amazed him by remarking that the two sons were unsuccessful because they were like their father, who had been successful, however, because of what he was. The sons had followed the father and yet for some unclear cause or causes, the way of life which had helped him to prosper prevented them from prospering.

And now Shenandoah remembered his last meeting with Mrs. Baumann, two years before. Late in the afternoon in October, as Shenandoah rewrote a poem, Mrs. Baumann's voice had come through the closed bedroom door. And he had been annoyed because he now had to come from his room, pale and abstracted, his mind elsewhere, to greet his mother's friends. It turned out that Mrs. Baumann had come with a friend, a woman of her own age, and when Shenandoah entered the living room, Mrs. Baumann, as voluble as Mrs. Fish, told Shenandoah in a rush the story of her friendship with this woman.

They had come to America on the same boat in the year 1888, and this made them *ship sisters*. And then, although their friendship had continued for some years, one day at a picnic of the old country's society, a sudden storm had disturbed the summer afternoon, everyone had run for cover, and they had not seen each other for the next nineteen years. And Mrs. Baumann seemed to feel that the summer thunderstorm had somehow been the reason for their long and unmotivated separation. The two old women drank tea and continued to tell the youthful author about their lives and how they felt about their lives; Shenandoah was suddenly relaxed and empty, now that he had stopped writing; he listened to them and drank tea too. Mrs. Baumann told Shenandoah that in her sixty-five years of life she had known perhaps as many as a thousand human beings fairly well, and when she tried to sleep at night, their faces came back to her so clearly that she believed she could draw their faces, if she were a painter. She was sickened and horrified by this plenitude of memory, although it was wholly clear why she found the past appalling. Yet these faces kept her from falling asleep very often, and consequently she was pleased and relieved to hear the milkman's wagon, which meant that soon the darkness would end and she would get up, make breakfast for her family and return to the world of daylight. Mrs. Baumann felt that perhaps she ought to see a psychoanalyst, like Freud, to find out what was wrong with her.

Her companion offered advice at this point; she said that everyone should have *a hobby*. Her own hobby was knitting and she felt that without her knitting in the morning, she would *go crazy*. This woman's daughter had married a *Gentile*, and she was permitted to visit her only child on monthly occasions when the husband had absented himself. Her one longing, one which she knew would never be satisfied, was to return and visit the old country.

"You would like it there," she said to Shenandoah, speaking of the country of her young girlhood. Shenandoah was flattered.

And as he listened to the two old women, Shenandoah tried to imagine their arrival in the new world and their first impression of the city of New York. But he knew that his imagination failed him, for nothing in his own experience was comparable to the great displacement of body and mind which their coming to America must have been.

Although almost finished with her ironing, Mrs. Fish was far from finished with her story. She was able to illustrate all that she said with fresh or renewed memories. And what she said bloomed in Shenandoah's mind in forms which would have astonished and angered her. Her words descended into the marine world of his mind and were transformed there, even as swimmers and deep-sea divers seen in a film, moving underwater through new pressures and compulsions, and raising heavy arms to free themselves from the dim and dusky green weight of underseas.

Shenandoah's mother now had progressed to the period of great prosperity in America. The worst animosity had come to exist between Mr. Baumann and his son Sidney, for whenever Sidney was criticized by his father for not earning his own living, he replied by citing the success of his father's friends, many of whom were becoming rich. Few of them had the charm or presence of Mr. Baumann, but they were able to give their sons a start in life. Sidney, an avid reader of newspapers like his mother, had acquired a host of examples of immigrants who had made a million dollars. The movie industry was for Sidney a standing example of his father's ineptitude, his failure to make the most of opportunity in the land of promise. It seemed unfair to go outside the family circle of friends, but Sidney was merciless when criticized, and *stopped at nothing*. And Mr. Baumann was left helpless by Sidney's attack, for he felt there was something wrong not only with the comparisons his son made, but the repeated and absolute judgment that his life had not been successful. He himself was satisfied and felt successful. He had always provided for his wife and his children, and kept them in comfort. It was true that he did not work very hard, but then there was no need to work very hard, he made out well enough, since he had an income from the insurance policies he had written for the last thirty years, when the premiums were paid or when the policy was renewed. Yet Sidney used these professions as obvious admissions of weakness. He observed that the sons of other men had a *ten-dollar bill* to spend on a girl on Saturday nights, but he did not. The more unsuccessful he was, the more outrageous became his verbal assault upon his father for not having made a million dollars. He was provoked to these attacks by renewed efforts to get him to work, and by the citation of young men of his age who would soon be wealthy men in their own right, although they came from the households of parents who were really *common*.

During the period of great prosperity the Baumanns and Shenandoah's mother became intimate friends, since Shenandoah's father had left her. And often Mrs. Baumann and Mrs. Fish discussed the fate of the Baumann children. Mrs. Fish had once given Mrs. Baumann what she still regarded as very good advice, she had told her friend that the salvation of the family would have been the summer hotel business, which they had once considered seriously as an enterprise. No one would have been better suited for that business than the Baumanns, and this was indeed *a high compliment*.

When his mother said such things, Shenandoah suffered for the moment, at any rate, from the illusion that his mother had a far greater understanding of the difficulties of life than he had. It seemed to him at such times that the ignorance he saw in her was a sign of his own arrogant ignorance. Her understanding was less theoretical, less verbal and less abstract than his, and such privations were in fact virtues. She was never deceived about any actual thing by words or ideas, as he often was. And she had just perceived perfectly a profound necessity which he himself knew very well in literature, the necessity that the artist find the adequate subject and the adequate medium for his own powers. No one could deny that the proper medium for the gifted Baumanns was the summer hotel.

What Mrs. Baumann did not understand and sought to explain to herself and Mrs. Fish was the paradox that her sons, who had a good bringing-up unlike many successful young men, had made out so poorly in comparison with most of them. She wished to know whose fault it was, if it were her fault, if she ought to blame herself, as her husband blamed her, for *humoring* and *indulging* the boys. The head start, and the fine home which the boys had, seemed to be a handicap, but this was an impossible thing to think. Mr. Baumann had remembered the advice given him by Mr. Fish, that the boys would be more ambitious if they had no home to come to, and he had distorted this counsel into an explanation which declared that Mrs. Baumann had pampered her sons. Mrs. Baumann returned with this problem many times, eager to be reassured and anxious to be told that on the contrary she was a wonderful mother. Shenandoah's mother was already prepared to blame someone for everything that happened, but she had a general and theoretical interest in the problem which left her free of her natural prepossessions. She observed that one defect of the Baumann sons was their unwillingness to go from door to door for the sake of getting some business. They had not been reared to expect *hard knocks* and rebuffs, and here precisely was where boys of meaner families had the advantage. It was a strange and sad thing, both women agreed, that a certain refinement—nothing like the Four Hundred, *you understand*—but merely a simple taste for the normal good things of life should be a severe and conclusive handicap. The greatest handicap, said

Mrs. Fish, was the fine family circle; this was what had weakened the boys for a world where you had to fight for everything you wanted, and you had to fight all the time just to keep what you had. Mrs. Fish observed again that this was *a cut-rate cut-throat world*, an expression which was her version of the maxim, *dog eat dog*. The best preparation for such a world, as Mrs. Fish's experience had proved many times, was to be born into a family of thirteen children where there was never enough for everyone to eat.

After 1929, when those who had been successful lost so much, Sidney mounted to new summits of scorn. Before 1929, he had been contemptuous of *the system*; now that no one made out well Sidney took the national depression as a personal vindication. Every banker or broker caught in some kind of dishonesty became an instance to Sidney of his own integrity. He suggested that if he had been prepared to do such things, he too might have enjoyed their success.

And now Mr. Baumann was no longer able to support an idle son, for with the hard times people abandoned their insurance or borrowed on it. The father's difficulties and the son's arrogance made their quarrels more and more desperate. As Mr. Baumann dressed to pay a visit one Saturday night, he was unable to find the pair of shoes he wanted. As always, he was concerned about his appearance, and he became very irritated at being unable to find his shoes, and came into his son's bedroom to ask him if he had seen the shoes, and Sidney, outstretched upon his bed, reading and smoking, was annoyed to be interrupted, and replied that his father ought not to be concerned about such a cheap pair of shoes. The shoes were not cheap, in any case, and this typical judgment of his taste by his son, whose standards were derived from his Christmas jobs in fashionable clothing stores, infuriated Mr. Baumann. He hit Sidney with the flat of his hand, and only Mrs. Baumann's screaming entrance prevented a fist-fight. The day after, Sidney had a black eye which he tried to conceal with powder. It was a Sunday and the Baumanns were going to pay a visit. Sidney wished to go with them, being unable to endure solitude at any time, and having nowhere to go that afternoon. But his mother reminded him of his black eye and his father added that he had no clothes, especially no shoes, suitable for the visit they were going to make. When the Baumanns returned at midnight, they found an emergency wagon and the police in front of the apartment house. Sidney had tried to kill himself by turning on the gas in the kitchen, there had been an explosion, and he had not even been injured. Sidney was taken to Bellevue and kept there for a number of months. When visited by his mother, he told her *she should remember* that it was his father who had driven him to insanity. Hearing this, Mr. Baumann retaliated by saying that his son had been unable to be anything but a failure, even at suicide; and he reported to all that at the hospital, Sidney could not be made to take up any of the forms of occupational therapy. It seemed an epitome to Mr. Baumann that even at this extreme his son should refuse to do anything *remotely resembling work*. It was not customary for Mr. Baumann to be as harsh as this with any human being, but nothing would help Mr. Baumann to forget what Sidney had said to him during the early years of the depression, when Mr. Baumann's income had first begun to be sharply curtailed. He said to his father that *the old oil* no longer worked, and when his father said in perplexity and anger, *what oil? what is this oil?*, Sidney had replied, *banana oil!*, laughing with his whole body at his witticism and then explaining to his father that it was foolish to expect to persuade anyone that insurance was anything but *a gyp* by the old methods of striking up a friendship and paying long visits, *spouting* like the neighborhood sage.

Sidney remained under observation, and Dick assisted his wife in her thriving business. He had a child now. Martha and her husband prospered more and more because the practice of medicine was not as bound to general prosperity as business itself. And after an operation and much nervousness, Martha too had a child. Both grandchildren were daughters, which was a disappointment, but which showed, at any rate, that all disappointments were not financial in origin. As Dick often said,

"Money is not everything," to which his sister always replied, "Money helps," smiling at her own irony.

They were all ashamed of Sidney's *smash-up*, as Dick termed it, but this did not keep them from speaking of it openly with all their friends. Mr. Baumann at seventy was still able to eke out a living for himself and his wife, but he was a disappointed and disillusioned man. He blamed everything on the individual and on his sons' lack of will-power. Mrs. Baumann blamed everything on her husband. She said to Mrs. Fish, however, speaking of Sidney:

"You see: this is what we came to America for forty-five years ago, for this."

Shenandoah was exhausted by his mother's story. He was sick of the mood in which he had listened, the irony and the contempt which had taken hold of each new event. He had listened from such a distance that what he saw was an outline, a caricature, and an abstraction. How different it might seem, if he had been able to see these lives from the inside, looking out.

And now he felt for the first time how closely bound he was to these people. His separation was actual enough, but there existed also an unbreakable unity. As the air was full of the radio's unseen voices, so the life he breathed in was full of these lives and the age in which they had acted and suffered.

Shenandoah went to his room and began to dress for the day. He felt that the contemptuous mood which had governed him as he listened was really self-contempt and ignorance. He thought that his own life invited the same irony. The impression he gained as he looked in the looking-glass was pathetic, for he felt the curious omniscience gained in looking at old photographs where the posing faces and the old-fashioned clothes and the moment itself seem ridiculous, ignorant, and unaware of the period quality which is truly there, and the subsequent revelation of waste and failure.

Mrs. Fish had concluded her story by saying that it was a peculiar but an assured fact that some human beings seemed to be ruined by their best qualities. This shocking statement moved in Shenandoah's mind and became a generalization about the fate of all human beings and his own fate.

"What will become of me?" he said to himself, looking in the looking-glass.

"What will I seem to my children?" he said to himself. "What is it that I do not see now in myself?"

"I do not see myself. I do not know myself. I cannot look at myself truly."

He turned from the looking-glass and said to himself, thinking of his mother's representation of the Baumanns, "No one truly exists in the real world because no one knows all that he is to other human beings, all that they say behind his back, and all the foolishness which the future will bring him."

THE WORLD IS A WEDDING

To Juliet Barrett

ONE: "WHAT DOES SHE HAVE THAT I DON'T HAVE?"

In this our life there are no beginnings but only departures entitled beginnings, wreathed in the formal emotions thought to be appropriate and often forced. Darkly rises each moment from the life which has been lived and which does not die, for each event lives in the heavy head forever, waiting to renew itself.

The circle of human beings united by need and love began with the graduation or departure of Rudyard Bell from school, just at the beginning of the great depression. Rudyard was the leader and captain of all hearts and his sister Laura's apartment was the place where the circle came to full being. When Rudyard graduated, he decided to devote himself to the writing of plays. His aunt had suggested that he become a teacher in the public high school system until he had proven himself as a dramatist, but Rudyard rejected his aunt's suggestion. He said that to be a playwright was a noble and difficult profession to which one must give one's whole being. Laura Bell had taken care of her younger brother since he was four and she said then that Rudyard was a genius and ought not to be required to earn a living. Rudyard accepted his sister's attitude as natural and inevitable, such was his belief in himself and in his power to charm other human beings.

Thus, in a way, this refusal to become a teacher and to earn a living was the beginning of the circle.

The other boys who truly belonged to the circle were also caught in the midst of the great depression. Edmund Kish wanted to be a teacher of philosophy, but he was unable to get an appointment. Jacob Cohen, recognized by all as the conscience or judge of the circle, wanted to be a reporter, but there were few jobs for newcomers. Ferdinand Harrap tried to be an author, but none of his stories were accepted, and he supported himself by directing a business agency. Francis French and Marcus Gross were teachers in the public high school system, although this was far from their ambition, Lloyd Tyler, known as "the boy," was still a student, and Laura made the most money as the buyer for a department store.

The circle was astonished when Rudyard's first long play was rejected by Broadway, for all had been certain that Rudyard would be famous and rich very soon. Rudyard had always been the one who won all the prizes in school and did everything best. Marcus Gross spoke fondly of the day, long ago and far away, when he had first encountered Rudyard in public school. It was the beginning of the new term and after the first hour Rudyard was regarded as a genius by the teacher and the pupils. So it had always been, Rudyard had been the infant prodigy, class orator, laureate, and best student. When Rudyard's plays were refused year after year by Broadway producers the circle was perplexed, for his dramatic works seemed to them delightful and profound when he read them aloud to the circle. Edmund Kish recognized the weakness of the plays, the fact that Rudyard used character and incident merely as springboards for excursions which were lyrical and philosophical, so that the essential impression was dream-like, abstract, and didactic. But he liked the plays for just this reason, and his conversations about philosophy did much to make Rudyard concern himself with the lyrical expression of philosophical ideas.

Laura was disappointed and after a time she concealed her disappointment by speaking of her brother's plays as just trash. Yet she was patient with Rudyard, delighting in the circle as such and hoping that among the new young men whom Rudyard was always bringing to the house there would be one who would want to marry her.

After five years of the depression, the hopes of most of the boys of the circle had faded slowly like a color or were worn thin like a cloth. Their life as part of the circle was their true life, and their lower middle class poverty kept them from seeking out girls and entertaining the idea of marriage. From time to time some of them became acquainted with girls and went out with them briefly, but since no one but Rudyard was doing what he wanted to be doing, marriage was as distant as a foreign country. Disdainful from the beginning of the conventional modes of behavior, their enjoyment of the life of the circle fortified and heightened their disdain.

When Laura began to doubt that she was going to get a husband, she began to drink, hiding the gin in the pantry when Rudyard tried to stop her. She drank on Saturday nights, the nights when the circle came to her house and was most itself, so that some of the boys spoke of "our Saturday nights." When she was really drunken, she became quarrelsome and voluble, and what she said was an incoherent, but blunt utterance of the naked truth. The boys tried to seem indifferent to what she said, but the reason for her drunkenness was clear and painful. When the marriage of a boy or girl who had come to evenings of the circle was discussed, and when the news of an engagement became known, Laura cried out from the kitchen like Cassandra:

"What does she have that I don't have?" Laura uttered this question again and again during the evening, amid other and like remarks.

Laura insisted in vain that her question be answered, and sometimes she placed her hands on her breasts lightly, as if in estimation, although when sober she was ashamed of any mention of sexual desire. Each newcomer or visitor renewed her hope, Laura invited him to come to dinner. Laura was full of great goodness and kindness, a goodness hardly concealed by her disgruntled and grudging remarks. She was unable to understand what was wrong. She lent the boys money and helped them in whatever they attempted, knowing that she was used by them and used most of all by Rudyard. She made petulant remarks, she said that she was a fool, but she always pressed herself forward to be helpful, typing Rudyard's manuscripts which she declared more and more often to be just trash which she could understand less and less as Rudyard's indulgence in lyrical philosophizing grew.

Thus on a Saturday night when the circle had long been in full being, Laura spoke loudly, crying out from the kitchen or uttering her sentences in the midst of a conversation.

"Tick, tick, tick," she said as she carried a dish to the table for the midnight supper.

"What are you ticking about?" asked Edmund Kish, knowing very well that her answer would be an expression of unhappiness.

"O," said Laura, "That's just my life ticking away."

"Can't you stop being human for an evening?" asked Francis French, who did not like to hear of unhappiness.

"No, I can't," said Laura, "I never can, no matter how hard I try. I just keep thinking of the rotten truth, the dirty truth, and nothing but the awful truth."

"We ought to remember," said Rudyard, who was able to enjoy everything, "the profound insight stated in the sentence, *'Joy is our duty'*."

"I don't feel joyous," said Laura, "and I don't feel like forcing myself to be joyous, whether or not it is a duty. I don't like life, life does not like me, and I am unhappy."

"Laura is right," said Edmund, seeking to show sympathy, "she has a right to her feelings. When I used to get peevish as a child, I would say: 'What should I do? I have nothing to do?' My mother always used to have just one answer: 'Go knock your head against the wall' was what my mother always said. She was a big help."

"Tick, tick, tick," said Laura, "that's just life passing away, second by second."

TWO: "HOW MUCH MONEY DOES HE MAKE?"

During the week, Edmund Kish had been visited by Israel Brown, the most admired of all the teachers known to the circle. Israel Brown was a man of incomparable learning. He was lean, tall, hollow-cheeked, and Christ-like in appearance. When he conversed, he spoke with a passion and rush such that one might suppose that the end of his life or of the world were in the offing. He did not seem to belong to this world and this life, although he appeared to all to know about everything in this world. He was a teacher of philosophy, but he touched upon many other subjects, ancient coins, legal codes, marine architecture, the writing of the American Constitution and the theology of the early Church Fathers. No matter whom he met and no matter where he was, Israel Brown rushed to tell his listener whatever his listener seemed to care about. He was able to correct and contradict whatever his listener said to him without offending him. He said hurriedly: "You will pardon me if I point out—," and then told his listener facts about the subject which the listener for the most part did not know existed, or were known to anyone.

Thus on this day when Israel Brown stopped at Edmund Kish's house to get the compendium he had lent Edmund, one of his most devoted students, he was introduced to Edmund's mother and he spoke to her immediately with customary pace and passion, telling her all about her generation, the generation which had come to America from Eastern Europe between 1890 and 1914. He spoke of the causes of the departure of this generation from the old world, the problems and tricks of the ocean liner agencies, the prospects of the immigrants, the images of the new world which had inhabited their minds, the shortage of labor which had drawn them, and the effect of their coming upon social and economic tensions in America.

Mrs. Kish listened to Israel Brown amazed as everyone was who heard him for the first time, amazed and overwhelmed by his eloquence, his learning, and his ravenous desire to tell all that he knew. Edmund as he listened was amused by the dumbfounded look upon his mother's face. She was an intelligent woman who had been a radical in her youth and she was not wholly bound in mind by her middle-class existence.

As soon as Israel Brown departed, Mrs. Kish breathed deeply as if in relief.

"You have just seen a genius," said Edmund to his mother.

"How much money does he make?" asked Mrs. Kish.

This was the story with which Edmund, excited, came to the Saturday evening at the Bell apartment.

He was not disappointed. The circle responded with enormous joy, and immediately Rudyard started the analysis and augmentation of any news which was a loved practice.

"Your mother's question," said Rudyard, in a tone in which gaiety and a pedagogic attitude were present, "is not only brilliant in itself, but it suggests an inexhaustible number of new versions. Your mother has virtually invented a new genre for the epigram. Thus, whenever anyone is praised and whenever anything favorable is said about anyone, let us reply: *'Never mind that: how much money does he make?'*"

"Yes," said Ferdinand, "there are all kinds of versions. We can say: 'I am not in the least interested in that. Just tell me one thing: *What's his salary?*' Or if we want to make him look unimportant: "What you have just told me leaves me absolutely cold. What I want to know is: *What are his wages?*' And then again *'Precisely how much cash has he in the bank?'*"

" *'How much is his yearly compensation?'*" shouted Laura from the kitchen, preparing the midnight supper, but never failing to listen to all that was said.

"It is one of the most heart-breaking sentences of our time," Jacob Cohen declared in a low voice, "and if it brings one to tears, the tears are obviously for Edmund's mother and not for Israel Brown."

"I don't notice anyone refusing any money," said Laura, bringing coffee, tea, and cocoa to the table, "except for Jacob." Jacob had refused to accept an allowance from his father and he had refused a job in the family business in which his older brothers prospered exceedingly. He had explained that he was going to be what he wanted to be or he was going to be nothing.

"It is easy enough to do nothing," said Jacob, seating himself at the dinner table. He did not like to have anyone's attention fixed upon what, in his being, was most intimate and most important.

"The difficult virtue," said Rudyard, "is to disregard the possibility of making money, to live such a life that making money will have no influence upon one's mind, heart and imagination." As he spoke, he was hardly aware that he was thinking chiefly of himself.

"You can't write plays for money, you just don't know how," said Laura, "so you don't have any temptation to resist: that's no virtue." Laura's love and admiration of her brother did not prevent her from attempting to overthrow the attitudes in which Rudyard took the most pride. This was the way in which she tried to defend herself from the intensity of her love and the profundity of her acceptance of him.

Rudyard did not answer her. His mind had shifted to his own work, and he took from the shelf the manuscript book in which his last play was written, seated himself upon the studio couch, and studied his own work, a look of smiling seriousness upon his face.

The other boys were seated at the dinner table, slowly eating the midnight supper and rejoicing in Mrs. Kish's question. Laura pampered each of them in his stubborn idiosyncrasy of taste. Edmund liked his coffee light, Rudyard liked his very strong, Ferdinand would only drink Chinese tea, Edmund insisted on toast, although most of them liked pumpernickel bread best of all. Laura provided what each of them liked best, which did not prevent her from being ironic about their preferences and assuming the appearance of one who begrudges and denies all generous indulgence and attention.

"How beautiful," said Rudyard loudly without raising his gaze from his manuscript book, "and yet no one likes this play, not even my intimate friends. But in a generation or in fifty years, it will be cheered as the best dramatic work of the century!"

Marcus Gross strode in, his entrances being at once loud and founded on the assumption that he had been present all evening.

"The theatre in which your plays are performed," he said, "ought to be named, *Posterity*."

"Very good," said Rudyard, "you may think that you are attacking me, but I regard that as one of the finest things ever said about an author!"

It was felt that this was a perfect reply.

Between Rudyard and Marcus an antagonism had long existed, excited for the most part by Rudyard's open contempt for Marcus, who admired Rudyard very much, but was forced to conceal his admiration.

"You are absolutely safe," said Marcus, responding to the laughter, "you are taking no risk whatever. We will all be dead before anyone knows if you are right or wrong."

"I know now," said Rudyard serenely, never admitting the small doubts which on occasion overtook him and suppressing his anguish at not being recognized as a great playwright.

"The fact is," said Jacob half-aloud, thinking of the life which they lived, "we do not have very much of a choice. It is a question of your money or your life, the Mexican bandit's question. We have a choice between doing what we don't want to do or doing nothing."

"Last week," said Lloyd Tyler, the boy of the circle, and the most silent one, "my father bought his yearly ticket in the Irish Sweepstakes, and it all began again, just the same as every other year."

He told them of the new dialogue between his parents, discussing the Irish Sweepstakes.

"What would you do, if you won one hundred and fifty thousand dollars?" Mrs. Tyler had asked her husband. The cruelest irony was in her voice, for she resented her husband very much because her life had not been what she had expected it to be. What she was saying was that he would not know what to do with a great deal of money.

"What would you do with it?" she said again for emphasis, disturbing Mr. Tyler's careful examination of the evening newspaper.

"I would sleep," said Mr. Tyler flatly and strongly, for he recognized this as a criticism of his powers and his way of life.

"But you sleep now," said Mrs. Tyler, unwilling to be put off, "I never saw anyone sleep as much as that man," she said to Lloyd who was trying to keep out of an interchange in which he recognized twenty-five years of feeling.

"It would be a different sleep," said Mr. Tyler. "If I had one hundred and fifty thousand dollars, it would not be the same kind of sleep."

"No one sleeps better than you do," said Mrs. Tyler, but weakly, knowing that she had been worsted.

"What a triumph!" cried Edmund joyously. "Not even Swift would have made a better answer."

"Yes," said Rudyard, "we ought to strike a medal for your father, Lloyd. He has justified all of us."

"I wonder what he would do with one hundred and fifty thousand dollars," said Marcus.

"He would sleep the sleep of the just and the self-fulfilled," Jacob answered. "What does he have to show for his thirty years of work? He has nothing."

"He has himself," said Rudyard, who often chose to regard all things in an ideal light.

"He does not like himself," said Lloyd, "he does not care very much for himself."

"It is his own fault if he does not care very much for himself," answered Rudyard.

"Is it his own fault?" asked Lloyd sadly, for he liked his father very much, "He thinks that he would see my sister and her husband and his grandchildren more often, if he had money, and if he had given my sister a dowry. He thinks that his son-in-law would think more of him and ask him to dinner more often."

"In my opinion," said Rudyard, using the phrase which was always the introduction of a dogma, "money has nothing whatever to do with the matter. Pardon me for being intimate, but I would say that the real cause of all the difficulty is that your father did not know how to make love, or your mother has never wanted to have your father make love to her. This is the true meaning of the fact that she is dissatisfied with him. Love is always the beginning of everything, that's obvious. And perhaps we may go so far as to say, that *if* there had been satisfied love between your parents, your father would have prospered and made as much money as your mother wanted him to make."

"That's just an *idea*, that's nothing but an *idea*. Money is the root of all good!" shouted Laura from the kitchen, helping herself to one more pony of gin as the visitors arose to depart.

"Everything is mixed in everything else," said Jacob to himself, thinking of how much Laura desired to be loved.

THREE: "NO ONE FOOLS ANYONE MUCH, EXCEPT HIMSELF"

The human beings of the circle and the circle as such existed for Jacob Cohen in a way private to him. The other boys of the circle often discussed each other, but seldom thought about each other when they were alone. They came together in order not to be alone, to escape from deviceless solitude. But Jacob enjoyed the solitude of the morning and the early afternoon, during which he strolled through many neighborhoods, inspected the life of the city, and thought about his friends of the circle. They were objects of his consciousness during his solitude and in this way they existed in his mind like great pictures in a famous gallery, pictures which, however, were studied not merely for curiosity and pleasure, but as if they contained some secret of all pictures and all human beings. Jacob, thinking about his friends and walking many city blocks, was borne forward by the feeling that through them he might know his own fate, because of their likeness, difference, and variety.

This day of September as Jacob set forth was a day of profound feeling because the children went to school again for the first time. Jacob and his friends had prospered in school, and most of all at the university, in a way they never had since then. Now five years had passed and were used. All of them were in some way disappointed as they had not been in school, where each had been able to do what he truly wanted to do. The school had been for them a kind of society very different from the adult society for which it was supposed to prepare them.

Jacob had arrived at Central Park. To the west was a solid front of expensive apartment houses, in front of him was a grove of trees and an artificial lake, next to which were empty tennis courts. Jacob decided to sit down on a park bench and let the emotion inspired by the first morning of school in September take his mind where it would.

He soon found himself thinking, as often before, of the character and fate of his friends of the circle.

Francis French, who now belonged to the circle less and less, had been at first the most fortunate one and the one who impressed the official middle class most of all. He was an extremely handsome young man who spoke English with a perfect Oxonian accent which he had acquired without departing from the state of New York. His presence, his manners, and his accent had secured for him immediately after graduation an appointment as a teacher of English literature in the best of the city universities. He was clearly marked out as a young man with a brilliant academic future.

At the end of the first term, however, the head of the department, who had chosen Francis from among many, found it necessary to summon him and ask him about an anonymous note which accused Francis of immoral relationships with some of his students. In this interview Francis had need only of the good manners and tact which he had cultivated for long and with easy success. But in the shock of the confrontation, he did not reply that the note was untrue and that his friendships with his students had been misinterpreted. Instead of making this nominal denial, which was all that was required, he replied with pride and hauteur. He declared that his sexual habits were his own concern and he said that he refused to recognize the right of anyone to question him about his private life. The head of the department liked Francis very much and he did not care very much what Francis' habits were, for he was an excellent teacher. But he felt that the refusal to make the conventional denial suggested the likelihood of future difficulty, and being concerned about his own position, he felt he had no choice but to dismiss Francis. He tried again to suggest to Francis that a nominal denial would be sufficient, but Francis would not be moved. His stand gave him the pleasure of being self-righteous. For long he had felt strongly that homosexuality was the real right thing, the noble and aristocratic thing, a view he supported by citing the great authors and artists who had been as he was.

To Jacob, looking back, Francis seemed to have been involved in a failure of the imagination. He had been unable to imagine the feelings of the head of the department which were complex and yet also convenient enough. This failure was important because in so many ways Francis had devoted his will to making himself impressive to other human beings.

Now Jacob bore in mind how Rudyard had applauded Francis' stand, although it had cost Francis the status in life he desired so much. Rudyard had declared that no other answer was possible without an absolute loss of self-respect. Yet had Rudyard been confronted with the same choice, Jacob was sure that he would not have hesitated in making the answer which was convenient and profitable. Whether Rudyard knew this to be true of himself or not, he too was involved in the same loss of imagination, for he did not recognize how much Francis had hurt himself. "No one fools anyone much, except himself," said Jacob to himself. "How do I fool myself?"

Francis had soon become a teacher in the public school system, and devoted himself with energy and concentration to his sexual life. For five days each week he taught from nine until three and then from four until midnight his obsession with sexual pleasure took hold of him and in time preoccupied him so much that all the other things which had interested him were forgotten. The drudgery of teaching in a high school was the basis of the intense system with which he dealt with actuality, performing his duties as a teacher with thoroughness because this made him feel secure and full of control when he let himelf go after school.

He let himself go more and more. He came less frequently to the Saturday evenings of the circle, and when he did come, he conferred most often with Rudyard, discussing his adventures and conquests. He told Marcus Gross, who was boisterous and ebullient about his own orthodox desires, that no one knew what sexual pleasure was until he became homosexual. He said also that everyone was really homosexual. Only fear, ignorance, foolishness, and shame kept all human beings from being aware of true passion and satisfaction.

Yet Jacob wondered if Francis did not permit himself passages of intellectual doubt. His sexual preoccupation had become not only a fixed idea which annihilated all other ideas, as one addicted to opium withdraws more and more from all other things; it had become a kind of sunlight: Francis had at first regarded all things in that light and he had come at last to see only the sunlight and nothing else.

"Perhaps one ought not to praise love too much," Jacob said to himself, "what will become of Francis in ten years or when he is middle-aged? He will have no wife, no house and no child. He has made an absolute surrender to one thing and in the end he may have nothing."

Jacob arose from the park bench and began to walk through the park, paying attention only to the movements of his mind.

"On the other hand," he said to himself, "I can't say for certain that anyone else has or will have more than Francis who at least has what he wants most of all."

He thought of Marcus Gross, who like Francis taught in a public high school, but was otherwise unlike him. Marcus was the scapegoat and butt of the circle, a part which he often seemed to enjoy. He was extremely serious about everything, even the prepared jokes by means of which he attempted to show his sense of humor, and he was protected by an impenetrable insensitivity from the epithets and the insults directed at him. In fact, he rejoiced in the insulting remarks made about him and to him, for he felt that such attention showed him as an interesting and rich character. Thus when the story of his visit to a house of prostitution was discussed in his presence, after he had been betrayed by the boy who had taken him, when the very choreography of his visit, his awkwardness, his disrobing, his gestures of affection were enacted before him, he was delighted. And he laughed as at another human being when the comedians came to the moment when the girl was said to have said to Marcus: "You like it buck naked, big boy?" When this quotation was reached, Marcus laughed more loudly than anyone else.

Attacked with a cruelty untouched by pity or compunction, Marcus often provided unbearable provocation. Often in the unpleasant, sodden New York summer, he entered the Bell household and went straight to the bathroom without greeting or explanation, bathed and returned in his bare feet to the living room, unable to understand why his behavior was regarded as boorish and self-absorbed. He was disturbed and hurt only when he was not kept acquainted with all that had occurred in the life of the circle, or when Rudyard attacked him, and even then he was often able to defend himself by answering Rudyard in ways which he regarded as hilarious. When Rudyard looked merely perplexed, Marcus only repeated what he had said, adding: 'The trouble with you is that you have no sense of humor!" To the astonishment of all, he was offended at unexpected times, for no principle or consistent region of sensitivity could be discerned in his hurt feelings. Yet when Marcus stalked from the house at a remark which was no different from many at which he had smiled complacently, and when he did not return for weeks, an effort was made to discover what had offended him. When he returned, he behaved as if he had not been absent, he took part in the conversation as if he had been present all the while, and when Rudyard annoyed, said to him: "How do you know?" moved by Marcus' authoritative participation in the discussion, Marcus replied briefly: "I heard," for he refused no matter what effort was made, to discuss his absences.

Unlike as were Francis and Marcus (they were extremes, the one courtly, the other uncouth) they were also very different from Edmund Kish and Ferdinand Harrap.

"And what about myself?" Jacob asked himself. "And Rudyard and Laura?"

Edmund had for four years been a student of philosophy, waiting to be asked to be a teacher. There were not many jobs to be had, but when there was one, some other student, not Edmund, was given the job. Yet Edmund was clearly superior to the others. The professors, the higher powers who possessed all the favors, at first had been enchanted with Edmund. He was energetic, original and impressive. He was learned and in love with his subject. But he loved to argue and argument excited him always until he betrayed his assumption that the other human being was a fool.

"Yet he does not think that everyone else is a fool," thought Jacob. "Not at all: he only thinks that he is smarter. Then why does he act like that? Perhaps he is trying to prove to himself that he is smart, perhaps he is never sure of that."

Triumphant in his arguments with other students, Edmund sought to be full of deference when he spoke with his teachers, especially after he had been passed by for years. But as soon as a qualification or reservation was suggested, Edmund forgot the politeness he had promised himself. He rehearsed to his teachers the ABC's of the subject and raised objections, which clearly implied that the teacher knew nothing whatever.

His teachers in the end feared and disliked him, and although they were unable to condemn him directly, they spoke of him in letters of recommendation as "a gifted but difficult person." This satisfied them that they were just and was sufficient to keep him from getting any job he wanted.

"What is it?" Jacob asked himself. "Is it something in the darkness of the family life from which we have all emerged which compels Edmund to assert himself like that? Is it his two brothers, his father's tyranny, or his mother's unequal affections? That's just one more thing we don't know."

Jacob paused to have a modest lunch. And the choice of food made him think of Ferdinand Harrap.

As Rudyard sought to be a dramatist, Ferdinand had tried to write stories. He did not lack the gift of experience, as did Rudyard, who found in all circumstances only a backdrop before which to manifest what he already possessed, his charm, his wit, and his delight in himself. Ferdinand was reserved. He held himself back and he was very much interested in whatever was before him. His stories, however, belonged to a small province, the province of his own life with his mother and his mother's family. The essential motive of his stories was the disdain and superiority he felt about these human beings of the older generation, and his stories always concerned the contemptuous exchanges of the characters, the witty quarrels which revealed the cruelty and the ignorance of their relationship to each other.

"You have to love human beings," thought Jacob, "if you want to write stories about them. Or at least you have to want to love them. Or at least you have to imagine the possibility that you might be able to love them. Maybe that's not true. But it is true that Ferdinand detests everyone but his friends of the circle."

None of Ferdinand's stories were published. Unlike Rudyard, he did not persevere, lacking Rudyard's joy in the process of composition and Rudyard's belief in himself. For a time he did nothing at all, and then, in helping one of his uncles, Ferdinand perceived the need of an agency which would arrange matters between manufacturers and retail stores. This perception of the usefulness of such an agency required an acute but peculiar intelligence, an intelligence like a squint. Ferdinand was not concerned about becoming rich, as business men were, and thus in helping his uncle, his indifference and his sense of superiority soon made obvious to him what no one else saw. Soon, with a small office and a girl to handle the mail, Ferdinand was making five thousand dollars a year, and had only to go to the office briefly each day to see that the girl was handling matters properly.

As soon as he prospered, Ferdinand's sense of what was good taste became active. His manners became more stiff and more pointed, and he dressed like a dandy, but strangely, as if he were a dandy of the past. And when he had money to spend, his feeling that he must have the best of everything, or nothing, had to be satisfied. He had to have the best orchestra seats at the theatre and he had to have the best dinner at the best restaurants.

"An only child," said Jacob to himself, "and the child of a mother divorced from her husband since he was four years of age."

The best of anything was truly a necessity to Ferdinand and he suffered very much when he was deprived of it. He insisted also that his friends of the circle join with him, accepting his criterion. This was difficult because they had little money or no money at all. Often Ferdinand paid for them, and he always paid for Rudyard, whom he admired very much. But when he did not care to pay for one of the boys, at dinner or at the theatre, and when they suggested that they come at less expense, Ferdinand strictly forbade their coming. He refused to go or he went by himself to the best restaurant and sat in the best seat at the Broadway play. When he was asked by a stranger the reason for his concentration upon dining well, Ferdinand replied in the curt and stern tone he so often used that dinner was extremely important: if one dined well, one felt good; otherwise, one did not.

A severe, private, hardly understood code ruled Ferdinand in all things. He regarded certain acts as good behavior and everything else, every difference, change, or departure as infamous and to be denounced. It was often necessary to prevent Ferdinand from making remarks of virtually insane cruelty to newcomers and strangers who visited the circle, for if they behaved in a way of which he disapproved or in a way indifferent to what he regarded as proper, he was likely to tell them that they were unpardonable fools. Visitors and strangers did not know what it was impossible for them to know, the strict and personal standard by which Ferdinand judged all acts and all remarks. Fortunately Ferdinand's constraint and stiffness made him speak in a very low voice, so that often enough the most extraordinary insult was left unheard. It was then necessary for Rudyard or Jacob to translate the sentence of final condemnation into a mild euphemism. When Ferdinand said to a stranger: "You must be out of your mind!" Rudyard explained that Ferdinand disagreed with what the stranger had just said, while Ferdinand turned aside, indifferent to the reduction of his insult and feeling that he had made his stand.

Jacob had arrived at Riverside Drive. He looked down on the Hudson River and, feeling the overwhelming presence of the great city, he thought of his friends as citizens of the city and of the city itself in which they lived and were lost.

"In New York," he said to himself, often concluding his slow tours with such monologues, "there are nineteen thousand horses, three hundred thousand dogs, five hundred thousand cats, one million trees and one million sparrows: more than enough!

"On the other hand, there are at least six million human beings and during holidays there are more than that number. But, in a way, these numbers hardly exist because they cannot be perceived (we all have four or five friends, more or less). No human being can take in such an aggregation: all that we know is that there is always more and more. This is the moreness of which we are aware, no matter what we look upon. This moreness is the true being of the great city, so that, in a way, this city hardly exists. It certainly does not exist as does our family, our friends, and our neighborhood."

Jacob felt that he had come to a conclusion which showed the shadow in which his friends and he lived. They did not inhabit a true community and there was an estrangement between each human being and his family, or between his family and his friends, or between his family and his school. Worst of all was the estrangement in the fact that the city as such had no true need of any of them, a fact which became more and more clear during the great depression.

"Yet," thought Jacob, seeking to see the whole truth, "there is the other side, which always exists. They say of New York that it is like an apartment hotel. And they say: 'It's fine for a visit, but I would not want to live here.' They are wrong. It's fine to live here, but exhausting on a visit.

"Once New York was the small handsome self-contained city of the merchant prince and the Dutch patroon's great grandsons. And once it was the brownstone city ruled by the victors of the Civil War. Then the millions drawn or driven from Europe transformed the city, making the brownstone mansions defeated rooming houses. Now, in the years of the great depression, it is for each one what he wants it to be, *if he has the money*. If he has the money! Coal from Pennsylvania, oranges from California, tea from China, films from Hollywood, musicians and doctors of every school! Every kind of motion, bus and car, train and plane, concerto and ballet! And if the luxuries of the sun and the sea are absent, if life in this city seems brittle as glass, every kind of vehicle here performs every kind of motion to take the citizen away from the city, if he has the money! The city in its very nature contains all of the means of departure as well as return. Thus the city gives to the citizen a freedom from itself, and thus one might say that this is the capital of departure. But none of my friends will go away: they are bound to each other. They have too great a need of each other, and all are a part of the being of each."

Jacob Cohen was through for the day. He had said to himself all that he wanted to say. Thus he had conversed with himself during the years that he had dedicated himself to being the kind of a citizen that he thought he ought to be. And if he seldom uttered these thoughts to anyone, nevertheless their feeling was contained and vivid in all that other human being saw of him. This was the reason that he seemed to some, strange; to some, preoccupied; to some, possessed by secrecy and silence.

FOUR: "TEARS FOR THE HUMAN BEINGS WHO HAVE NOTHING TO SAY TO EACH OTHER"

Jacob Cohen for long had been the conscience and the noble critic of the circle. No one knew precisely how this had come about. In school, as editor of the university daily, the students too had felt an incomparable devotion and loyalty to him. It was said that they would do anything for him. And in his family, when he refused to become part of the family business, his father and his brothers were not distressed. They did not think that he was wasting his time when, except for his tours of the neighborhood and the city, he did nothing at all, although in all other families there was concern and anger when the young man appeared to be making no effort to earn a living and to get ahead. It was felt that what Jacob did was right, no matter what he did. No one was surprised when Jacob refused to be a reporter on a Hearst newspaper because he felt that the Hearst newspapers were in sympathy with Fascism. No one was surprised although to be a reporter was Jacob's dear vocation because of which he refused to be anything else.

So too in the circle itself, Jacob's moral preeminence was absolute, although no one in the least understood it. Jacob's judgment, approval or disapproval were accepted as just. It was felt spontaneously that his judgment flowed from principles independent of personal desire or distortion. It is true that all knew a hardly conscious desire that such a person as Jacob should exist, but this did not explain their spontaneous recognition of him as that person.

No one but Jacob knew how much hopelessness and despair he felt at times, emotions bottomless and overpowering which made him lose all interest or power to be interested in anything outside of himself. Jacob did not understand these emotions which persisted for months and made him withdraw from others. Yet these emotions made possible Jacob's noble indifference, an important part of his moral authority.

It was natural that Rudyard and Laura should turn in the end to Jacob for his opinion about an argument which they had disputed for weeks. This argument concerned Rudyard's habit of reading the newspaper at the dinner table when no one was present but Laura.

"You ought to talk to me," said Laura, and there were periods when Rudyard enjoyed conversation with Laura. But often he wanted to read and he did not want to converse when he ate the dinner Laura had prepared when she returned from work. To Laura this seemed an unnecessary affront precisely because she had returned to make his dinner.

"First of all," said Rudyard, to defend his reading, "when I read at dinner it is a manifestation of the truly human. You know very well that if I were an animal, I would take my food somewhere and eat it alone. I would eat it very fast and I would be afraid that some other animal might take it away from me. But since I am a human being and since I have a head," he touched his head as he said this, "eating does not satisfy the whole of my being and it is necessary for me to read."

"How about conversation?" said Laura, disgruntled and knowing that she had no hope of persuading Rudyard since she never persuaded him of anything. "I suppose conversation is not a purely human activity?"

"It is, it is!" Rudyard replied. "But reading is superior to it, in general, as authors are superior to other human beings. And as for me, my being is such that to satisfy the rational part of it, I must regard the great works of thought and literature."

"Half the time you just read the newspaper," said Laura.

"Yes," said Rudyard serenely, "but not as others do, for I read the newspaper to rejoin the popular life of this city."

These grandiose answers, which Rudyard delivered in a tone at once superior and coy, angered Laura, but at the same time impressed her and made her remember that she had long since decided that Rudyard was a genius.

Arriving at the Bell household just after dinner, Jacob was asked his opinion.

"If a brother and sister don't have a great deal to say to each other," answered Jacob, "who does? We might as well be deaf and dumb! As a matter of fact, I'd say that we might as well be dead. Conversation is civilization."

Rudyard bowed to Jacob's judgment in general, making an exception of himself in that his sister was not as all sisters should be. But he did not say this for he was much interested in the idea of the truly human at the moment. As the other boys arrived at the apartment, he took them aside and explained it to them, and they too took pleasure in it, as well as being flattered by the appearance of intimacy which Rudyard conferred upon each of them when he took each one aside.

This discussion, which Rudyard conducted in a comic manner since he did not like to be serious about any ideas, much as ideas were dear to him, was halted when Edmund Kish entered with exciting news about the fate of the marriage of B. L. Rosen and Priscilla Gould.

"They have been seen for two weeks at dinner in the same restaurant," said Edmund breathlessly.

This far-off marriage had first astonished and then fascinated the circle. Some of the boys had been acquainted with B. L. Rosen at school, and they had been contemptuous of the way in which he had continued to be a leader of student political movements long after graduation.

"He wants to be an *official* youth," Edmund had remarked.

"He wants to be a *permanent* youth," Rudyard had added.

B. L., as all who knew him called him, feeling the nascent executive in him, had become in the end the head of all the radical student movements in all the city universities. He spoke for youth and for students. No one, however, knew of Priscilla Gould until her father, a successful Broadway playwright, wrote an article in one of the national weeklies in which he said that his daughter had been taught to believe in Communism, atheism and free love by her teachers at the university. It was B. L.'s task to see Priscilla and to persuade her to defend the university and her teachers. B. L. had succeeded very well. Priscilla had been bewildered and enchanted by the attention she suddenly received. The truth was that she had been a shy and withdrawn student and she had joined the radical student society as a way of being part of the school life, for she was afraid that she would never be anything but a wallflower. B. L. persuaded Priscilla to write an answer to her father in which she said: "My father is dishonest," a kind of choral sentence uttered repetitively throughout the detailed exposition of her father's other shortcomings as a father, such as that he had never given her the attention a child required.

This answer was an overwhelming success and B. L. was credited with a stroke of political genius. But as B. L. had helped Priscilla to write her answer, he had made love to her, almost as if from habit, for he had always absentmindedly courted some girl during his career as a student leader. When Priscilla shyly proposed to him that they get married, B. L. was much too amazed to ask for time to think about such a marriage. His prudence and circumspection had for long been concentrated on matters which were impersonal if not international. His manners and his essential kindness were such that he felt that he had to answer Priscilla immediately. When he saw the fearful and pathetic look upon Priscilla's face, he had assented immediately, telling himself that she might be as good as anyone else and perhaps better. Moreover, if he were married he might have more time for the concerns which truly interested him.

The news of the marriage was first received by the circle as a thunderbolt, but soon it awakened as much passionate interpretation as any other episode of these years.

It was suggested that some pathological feeling had compelled B. L. to marry Priscilla, either sexual feeling for his own sex, or a desire to possess an utterly passive wife. Francis French suggested that Priscilla might resemble B. L.'s mother when he was an infant at the breast. Rudyard thought it far more likely that Priscilla was seeking to escape from an incestuous desire for her father, since B. L. was truly as far away from her father as she could get. Rudyard also dismissed as banal, trite, obvious and hence untrue the view that B. L. might have married Priscilla because he wished to ascend in the social scale. Edmund, on the other hand, declared that whatever motives might have inspired the newly-wedded couple, the marriage was in actual fact an attack on the ruling class. It was somewhat far-fetched to suppose that Priscilla belonged to the ruling class, but the match had an unequivocal symbolic meaning: it was the beginning of the disappearance of the Anglo-Saxon. Ferdinand regarded the union as a striking example of the degradation which overtook all who were interested in social problems and in politics. The underlying reason for all these speculations was that marriage for all of the circle was far-off, and when Laura said: "Maybe she just likes him and he just likes her," she was regarded as superficial.

Edmund's exciting news about the distant marriage was that B. L. and Priscilla had been seen at dinner for two weeks in the same Italian restaurant, and on each night the husband and the wife had been reading two copies of the same newspaper, saying nothing to each other from start to finish.

"It's too good to be true," said Edmund joyously, "after all, they have only been married for six months. But probably they no longer can imagine a period when they were not married."

"Here we see," said Rudyard, declamatory, "in this reading of the same newspaper, a noble effort on the part of a wife to share her husband's intellectual interests!"

"This behavior," said Ferdinand, "is of a matchless vulgarity!"

"If we had any sense," said Jacob, "we would burst into tears for all the husbands and wives who have nothing to say to each other."

"How many months," said the delighted Edmund, "have passed since last they exchanged the time of the day?"

"How about you," said Laura to Rudyard, "don't you read the newspaper at the dinner table?"

"It's not the same thing," said Rudyard, "I did not marry you."

The insensitivity of this remark would not have passed unnoticed, had not Francis French entered on one of his rare visits. He too had a story in which he was very much interested. He had encountered during the previous week-end a youthful teacher and critic, Mortimer London, who was reputed to be brilliant.

"I have long believed," said Francis, "that everyone himself tells the worst stories about himself. London told me (keep in mind that fact that London himself tells this story about himself) that when he was in England last year, he had paid a visit to T. S. Eliot who had given him a letter of introduction to James Joyce, since he was going to Paris also. Now London says that he was confronted with a cruel choice, whether to use the letter and converse with the author of *Ulysses* or to keep the letter in which a great author commends him to a great author. He decided to keep the letter!"

"What a dumb-bell," said Edmund, the veteran scholar, "he should have known that the choice might be forestalled. He might have made a photostat copy!"

"Never mind that," said Rudyard, who did not like to be concerned with practical considerations, "what's really interesting is the extent to which this Mortimer London is insane. For obviously he tells this story because of great pride in himself. He *does not know* that there is nothing worse that he can say about himself: he would rather possess the letter than converse with the great author."

"Never mind," said Laura to Rudyard, "I never saw you hiding your light in a dark closet."

Rudyard did not reply, fascinated by this example of egotism as only an egotist can be.

"I wonder," said Jacob, "what are the worst stories each of us tells against himself."

"Once in a while," said Laura, "just for a change, we ought to try saying something good about anyone. Anyone can run down anyone else, it is as easy as sliding off a chute. What's hard is to love other human beings and to speak well of them."

"You are being sententious," said Rudyard, "it is obviously true that human beings are more evil than good, and thus it would be false to speak well of other human beings very much, although I am willing to try anything once," concluding as often with an irony which, directed against himself, defended him against what anyone else might say.

"The fact is" said Jacob, as the visitor arose to depart, "I can't think of what the worst story I tell against myself is, and that is nothing, if not alarming. We are all living in a world of our own."

"Yes," said Rudyard, chortling because the idea delighted him, "in a certain sense, we are all cracked!"

FIVE: "IT IS GOOD TO BE THE WAY THAT WE ARE"

During the day, after he had labored at his new play in the morning in the glow of after-breakfast, Rudyard participated in a life apart from the circle, a life in which a different part of his being showed itself. This life was concerned with the children and the adolescents of the neighborhood, and it was an intrusion, which annoyed Rudyard, if he encountered an adult. If the adult, the parent of one of his friends, met Rudyard, he said with the politeness and interest of the middle class:

"What are you doing now?" meaning, how are you trying to make a living? How are you trying to get ahead?

"I am helping my father," Rudyard always answered, having nurtured this answer until it was automatic.

"What is your father doing?" the helpless adult often inquired, never having heard of Rudyard's father because he had been dead for twenty years.

"My father is doing nothing!" was Rudyard's stock answer, followed by harsh and triumphant laughter that the questioner had walked into the trap, although in all truth Rudyard was ashamed that he had nothing impressive to announce.

Among the children and the adolescents of the neighborhood Rudyard was at his best, however. In the schoolyard near the apartment house, between bouts of handball, Rudyard conversed in the fall and in the spring with those who were to him the pure in heart and the wise just as he seemed to himself to be to them one of the wise and the pure in heart.

As he sat upon the asphalt court, after a game of doubles, he discussed with his friends Chester and Jeremiah, the star of the school, a boy named Alexander, twelve years of age, who was best in handball, basketball, high jumping, and the hundred yard dash. It was felt by all that Alexander had a great future.

"Suppose," said Rudyard to his friends, "Alexander was at least a hundred times better than he is. Then he would win all the time in all the games. But if he was as good as that, if he won all the time, if every contest was a victory, if he was sure of winning every game, then he would not enjoy the game very much."

Chester suggested that Alexander might then join the New York Yankees and earn a fabulous salary, more than the President's. Jeremiah added that his picture might appear in all the newspapers and he might marry a moving picture actress.

"Yes," said Rudyard patiently, brushing aside these ideas of the glory of this world, "suppose he hit a homer every time he came to bat? Suppose he was sure of hitting a homer? Don't you think he would get bored with playing baseball?"

"Yes," answered Chester and Jeremiah, "but he can't and he won't."

Rudyard was not in the least concerned or disturbed by any pointing to an actual fact.

"This is how we can see," he continued, "that it is good to be the way that we are. It would be no good, if we were unable to play any games at all. But just because we don't know if we are going to win or lose, just because our powers are limited and the other boys have powers not unlike our own, the game is exciting to play. So you can see that we are all what we ought to be."

"Just the same," said Chester, "I would like to hit a homer every time I came to bat."

"Me too," said Jeremiah, "for a year, anyway."

From such interviews Rudyard returned refreshed to his dramatic works. The volley of the conversation, as at a tennis match, was all that he took with him. For what he wanted and what satisfied him was the activity of his own mind. This need and satisfaction kept him from becoming truly interested in other human beings, although he sought them out all the time. He was like a travelling virtuoso who performs brilliant set-pieces and departs before coming to know his listeners.

An old teacher, meeting Rudyard after not seeing him for years, said to him that he showed no little courage in continuing to write works which gained for him neither fame nor money nor production.

"O, no," said Rudyard, "it requires no courage whatever. I write when I feel inspired. When I don't feel like writing, I don't. Thus I am not like other authors. It is not a career, it is like playing a game, and it is not courage, but inspiration, a very different emotion."

This reply was made in the style which Rudyard felt to be noble and necessary. But after this exchange, Rudyard asked himself if he had spoken truly. He knew very well a passion in himself to be applauded and to be famous, the same as other authors. Triumphant and delighted with himself, Rudyard decided that he did not want to be *regarded* as a playwright, he truly desired and enjoyed the activity of writing plays. This activity was enough to satisfy him.

The question and the answer inspired Rudyard to write a play in one act which resembled many of his previous dramas. This play contained only one character, a famous lyric poet, and only one scene, his study, in which he is surrounded by books, photographs, objects of art, and the black souvenir album in which are fixed essays and reviews of his poems which testify to his fame. The shades have been drawn down to bar the light of the living street.

The famous poet holds his head in his hands as he sits at his desk. In a monologue full of blank despair, he speaks of the fact that he has been unable to write a poem for two years.

"What difference does it make if I write a poem or I do not write a poem?" he says.

He holds in his hand a volume of his poems and he says:

"If I have done something worth doing, what good does it do me now? What good if I have drawn from the depths of my mind a good poem, if I do not enjoy now the sense of accomplishment and fruitfulness. One might as well tell a singer who has lost his voice that he was incomparable in all the great parts or equally tell a starving man that he was at a banquet two months before."

He reads aloud passages by critics in which he is awarded the highest praise:

"How can I be sure that they are right?" he says. "Many have been wrong. No poet is ever sure that he has written an important work. The famous in their lifetime are forgotten and nonentities long since in the grave appear as the true poets."

"And if this praise is true," he says, after he reads a new passage of praise from the album, "it does not lessen in the least the pain, the boredom and the emptiness which weigh me down now. If it is untrue, I have been deceived like a drunkard by passing imagination?"

He arises and stands before his long looking-glass:

"I might have acquired a great deal of money. I might have tasted the pleasures of the rich or the satisfactions of the normal. I might have enjoyed myself like a child at the seashore, near the breaking waves all through the glittering day. Instead I have grown warped, narrow and weak in this room at this table."

With his hand, he presses back his brow, looking closely at himself.

"I am too old to turn back and too young to forget my brilliant hopes. I am too intelligent to be uncritical of my fame, and the present is too important to me for me to be at peace because of the laurels I have gained in the past. Praise is worthless, but since praise is worthless, now that I cannot compose new works, I see for the first time, as if this were the first morning of my life, that there is only one reason to write poems: the only reason to write poems is for the sake of the activity of the whole being which one enjoys when one writes poems. This is the only justification."

He seats himself at his desk again, and he says:

"The silence surrounds me like four o'clock in the morning."

He draws forth a sheet of paper and takes a pencil from a cup.

"The silence of the white paper is my everlasting place. There is nothing else for me. Everything else is for the sake of this activity. When I cannot write a poem, when I have nothing in my mind but emptiness, then nothing else is good. When, on the other hand, a blazing excitement leaps in my mind, then I do not have happiness, for then all labor, all hope, all illusion are once more loaded on my back, as I sit here in my solitude surrounded by the silence which is like the night before the creation of the world."

And then, as the curtain falls, the famous poet begins to write upon his sheet of paper.

When this short play was read to the circle, it was received like many other recent plays by Rudyard. They had heard these ideas from Rudyard in conversation and were not much interested or impressed by the dramatic version.

Rudyard was distressed by this reception of his play, for he expected that the admiration of his friends would continue with equal intensity. For some time he had been annoyed with Edmund because Edmund, seeking to please him, would say:

"This new play does not seem to me as good as the first-rate plays you wrote last year."

"It is the best piece I have ever written," Rudyard had declared flatly, to vanquish his disappointment.

And when Rudyard had read aloud two plays and Edmund had said:

"I like the second more than the first," Rudyard also became angry, perceiving the criticism in this judgment.

"Now you can see," he said to Ferdinand, "the reason I have for reading two plays instead of just one. Then it can always be said that the first is better than the second. Perhaps I ought to read three plays each time. Then it will be possible to say, I like the first better than the second, but I like the third better than the first. Meanwhile I have made it possible to refuse to answer the question of whether any of them are any good! To what infinite limits I go for the sake of making my friends full of tact."

But when Edmund said of this new play that it was perhaps the best Rudyard had written, Rudyard was disturbed by this praise also, for it seemed to him to suggest a condemnation of his previous works. It was at this moment of annoyed disappointment, that Marcus Gross entered loudly.

"As for your plays," he said to Rudyard, "what have they to do with anything else? No wonder they are not produced. If you were any good, you would be successful."

"You are just a Philistine," Rudyard replied in fury. "Minute by minute, you become more stupid. You can't tell an idea from a hole in the ground!"

"Your feelings are hurt," said Marcus with solemn calm, as if he had made a discovery.

"You did not hear this play from the beginning ..." Lloyd Tyler began to say.

"It's not necessary," said Marcus, interrupting him, "they are all alike."

"In all the evenings I have been here," said Lloyd because he had been interrupted, "I have yet to succeed in uttering a complete sentence."

Ferdinand was delighted with this remark. "Do you know what

Lloyd just said?" he asked loudly and then quoted Lloyd's remark which seemed to all but Lloyd to be a remark of extraordinary brilliance.

"I have not uttered a complete sentence since 1928," shouted Laura from the kitchen where she was drinking. This declaration caused an immediate uproar.

"Has Laura been drinking again?" Marcus inquired. And when she began to set the table, he regarded her carefully.

"Why don't you get married?" he said to her. "It might do you a lot of good."

Edmund told Marcus to shut up and stop being such a boob, and when the evening was over, Marcus, still astonished by being reproved, asked Edmund what he had done that was wrong and how he had offended Laura. When at last he understood, he said to Edmund pensively: "Do you know, I never thought of that. It never occurred to me."

SIX: "LOVE THE DARK VICTOR WHOM NO ONE
    OUTWITS"

Edmund thought he had made a most important discovery.

Bringing it with him to the Bell household on a Saturday evening, he was hardly able to wait for everyone's attention. And he would not speak until everyone was ready to listen to him.

"A revolution has occurred," said Edmund, "but it is subject to silence, since love is subject to shame. Love has been purified, as never before. Love has been made to be just love and and nothing else but love."

"How?" asked Rudyard.

"By the druggist," said Edmund, "by the sale of contraceptives."

Rudyard and Ferdinand exchanged looks which each understood very well. Was it possible, they said by looking at each other, that Edmund, the withdrawn scholar, had at long last suffered the loss of his innocence, an actual innocence, which existed with complete knowledge?

"The contraceptive," Edmund continued, "has purified love by freeing it from the accident of children. Now everyone with any sense can find out whom he truly loves. Children can be chosen beings, and not the result of impetuous lust or impatient appetite. Now love is love and nothing else but love!"

"Yes," said Rudyard, "a mere material device has utterly transformed the relationships between men and women: a mere material thing!"

"On the other hand," said Francis French, "it also makes possible adultery, and promiscuity, not that I have anything against promiscuity."

"I love my wife, but oh you id," said Ferdinand, who had studied Freud and Tin Pan Alley.

"Yes," said Jacob, "it makes everything too easy, which is always a good reason for suspicion and doubt. Love is more difficult than anything else. Love is the dark victor whom no one outwits."

"Exactly," said Edmund, "this device, so small and inexpensive, assures the victory of love. Love cannot be prevented, love cannot be set aside, no thoughts of utility or shame can intervene."

"There is nothing in it," said Laura, "you still have to find someone to love who loves you."

Jacob, somewhat apart, saw that on this subject opinion was absolute and speculation infinite precisely because they were so far from the actuality of love.

"How far is it to love?" he said to himself. "Love the dark victor whom no one escapes."

Edmund felt that this balloon of an idea, of which he had expected so much, had collapsed. Rudyard, who expected a visitor he had never seen before, was preoccupied, Jacob was withdrawn, Laura was sad, Ferdinand was attempting to produce a new witticism. Yet Edmund felt that he must try again.

"The Pope in Rome," said Edmund, "ought to be told of this. Yes, I will write him an epistle. Does he not know that God looked at Adam, in Eden, and remarked: 'It is not good for man to be alone.' By banning the use of the pure and purifying contraceptive, the Pope misunderstands the word of God which says that the reason for marriage is that man should have children. For it is not necessary to have marriage in order to have children, but if we are not to be alone, marriage alone is sufficient."

Rudyard and Ferdinand again exchanged glances of wonder concerned with Edmund's private life, what was new in it.

Marcus, ever late, entered loudly and demanded to know what was being discussed.

"It is not easy to say," said Jacob, "but on the surface, at least, it is an academic discussion of love."

"Speaking of love," said Marcus, who had need only of a slight pretext to brim over with his own thoughts, "I read a fine story today about Flaubert—"

"The promising French novelist, no doubt," asked Ferdinand.

"Flaubert," said Marcus, ignoring Ferdinand, "made a bet with two of his friends that he would be able to make love, smoke a cigar, and write a letter at the same time. They went to a house of prostitution and found the best girl, and Flaubert wrote the letter, smoked the cigar, and made love to the girl."

"What he really enjoyed," said Rudyard, "was the cigar."

"Speak for yourself," said Marcus, "what I want to know is, What did he say in the letter? And to whom was it written? And what was the tone? and what kind of cigar was it? and did he have time to finish it?"

"Speaking of letters," said Rudyard, who felt that this topic was exhausted, "I am being visited tonight, by a stranger who wrote me a letter."

The letter was from a true stranger, a being from a foreign country, Archer Price, a young man of thirty who directed a little theatre in San Francisco. He had seen two of Rudyard's plays in manuscript, and now that he had come to New York, he wanted to meet Rudyard.

Rudyard was delighted by his letter, but nevertheless made fun of it.

"How can human beings of the Far West understand my play?" he asked. "Their idea of drama is the thrilling final match of a tennis tournament."

Yet Rudyard looked forward very much to the visit of the stranger.

Archer Price arrived at the Bell household with Pauline Taylor, a pretty young woman who lived in New York City, but had come to know Archer during a visit to California. When the strangers entered the house, the discussion of love stopped. In the midst of the introductions, as all were standing up, Archer, who was seldom at ease, said to Rudyard what he had decided to say before he arrived.

"I am very glad to meet you," said Archer, "because I admire your plays very much."

"What a remark!" said Rudyard, who appeared to be astounded by it and who looked to Edmund, as if to see if he too did not suppose this sentence to be outlandish.

"Says he admires two of my plays very much," said Rudyard to Edmund, and then pouted and placed one finger under his chin, as if he were about to curtsey.

"I really admire your plays very much," said Archer, bewildered and offended.

"I know you do," said Rudyard, as if this repetition were unnecessary, "otherwise you would not be here."

Archer seated himself on the studio couch and glanced at Pauline to see what her impression was. She glanced back in sympathy, for she was concerned not with Rudyard, but with Archer, and she knew how distressed he was by Rudyard's way of responding to his utterance of admiration. Neither of the newcomers knew that Rudyard's behavior had been inspired by his extreme pleasure, for he had so long desired the admiration of strangers that his self-possession teetered and he tried to regain his balance by regarding this admiration as peculiar. Both newcomers understood such emotions and attitudes very well, but they did not recognize Rudyard's version, because it was extreme, private, and directed not at the visitors, but at Edmund and Laura.

"What an obnoxious human being," thought Pauline Taylor.

Archer remained curious and open to persuasion. He regarded the apartment and saw that the furniture was worn and second-hand, making a picture of the second-hand and the used culti-vated as an interesting background and decor. Against the wall stood an upright piano, next to which was a phonograph, and upon the wall was a bulletin board, tacked with newspaper clip-pings and letters. Archer had never seen just such a place before, but although it seemed strange to him, he recognized in it the unity which comes of the choices and habits of one human being.

Rudyard seated himself next to Archer to converse with him and Archer remarked upon his surprise that none of Rudyard's plays had ever been produced. Rudyard told him how each month for more than a year he had submitted a new play to a famous com-pany and received each play back before a week had passed.

"I must be on the black list. They hardly have time to get the manuscript from the top manila envelope to the enclosed one, self-addressed and stamped!" said Rudyard, with a joyous look upon his face.

"Soon I will send them a letter of resignation" he said viva-ciously, looking up at the ceiling coyly, "that will puzzle them!"

Archer laughed in relief, for here at last was a remark which he was able to understand as comical.

Edmund and Marcus were full of a story which they wished to communicate immediately. During the week they had heard a debate at Madison Square Garden about religion and Commu-nism. The opponents had been Professor Suss, a famous teacher of Marxist doctrine, and Professor Adam, a theologian. The chief dispute had been about the authority of a socialist state to dictate or deny the teaching of religion to children. Professor Suss had affirmed the right of the socialist state to decide about religious education and Professor Adam had said that this was a denial of freedom of thought and belief, and thus fascist, declaring triumphantly that he was ninety-nine and one-half per cent Marxist, but reserved one-half of one per cent for God, for if one did not reserve anything for God, then the state became the deity.

Rudyard and Edmund were delighted with this story and interested especially in the one-half of one per cent reserved for God.

"How did he decide just how much God deserves?" asked Edmund.

"Perhaps he used a slide rule?" said Rudyard. "Or perhaps he made deductions for dependents, as when one computes the income tax?"

This analysis and commentary continued until Rudyard became aware that no attention whatever was being paid to the visitors who remained silent on the studio couch, looking uncomfortable and perplexed. He arose and went to his room to get the manuscript of a new play for his visitors to read, and when he returned, he placed himself next to Archer again and looked over his shoulder, the while he also cocked an ear to the conversation which remained concerned with the fraction reserved for God by Professor Adam.

"This passage is superb!" Rudyard said suddenly, after Archer had read for some time, and as he spoke, he grinned like a child who has just been given candy.

"Here, in this scene," said Rudyard, after a time, "the ignorance and irony is such that I am supreme among the dramatists who write in the English tongue." And as he spoke, he looked as if he licked an ice cream cone.

"This has not been equalled during the present century," Rudyard said again. Pauline was annoyed by these declarations, but to Archer they seemed to be made with such certainty, such a lack of self-consciousness, such joy and aplomb, that they were delightful. It was clear that Rudyard did not expect his listener to make any comment. He enjoyed uttering such sentences for their own sake. Yet Archer thought also of how such remarks would sound to anyone who heard them apart from Rudyard's gestures, smiles, and look of self-assurance.

"You must take this play with you," said Rudyard, drawing forth a new manuscript, "it is to me the best play in the English language!" And then he giggled.

"To you," said Laura, "and to no one else." She had seen the new look of perplexity on the visitors' faces at this fabulous superlative.

Archer looked at his wrist-watch and arose.

"He lives by the clock," said Rudyard, as if he spoke of one who was absent. "Perhaps I will never see you again," he giggled.

"I don't like Rudyard Bell," said Pauline, as the two strangers departed from the house.

"He is certainly difficult," said Archer, "perhaps it is because he is gifted and has gained no recognition."

But when Archer Price returned to California, he decided that he would not attempt to visit Rudyard Bell when he next came to New York. He felt in the end distressed and perplexed by the visit. It seemed to him that the human beings of this circle existed in a private realm which did not permit the visiting stranger such as himself a true view of what they were and their life. He never saw them again.

SEVEN: "THIS KINGDOM OF HEAVEN IS WITHIN YOU;
BUT ALSO THE KINGDOM OF HELL"

What we need is an Ark," said Rudyard to one and all, "not an island, not a colony, and not a city state, but an Ark."

Once again a play to which he had devoted much thought and hope had been rejected. Silent and angry in the morning, he was full of the future by afternoon, and by night—this was a Saturday night and most of the circle had come to the apartment—he had bounced back to the attitudes he enjoyed amid the circle. But anger and disappointment remained in him like sores and were transformed and expressed by the idea of an Ark.

"It's an ancient and classic expression," said Rudyard, "it's about time that we thought of it. We will get a houseboat or a barge, announcing that this society is evil and we are going to depart."

Ferdinand, ever close to Rudyard, was delighted.

"We will say, *'We're through!'*" he added in a curt tone. "We will have an enormous poster in huge capitals and on it will be printed: *'We have had enough.' 'We do not like this age.'*" His voice became louder and stronger, " *'We find it beneath contempt!'*"

"This is a governing and master idea," said Edmund, equally pleased, "it is a conception so inclusive that by means of it we can make clear our judgment of the past and the future, of experience and possibility."

It was almost midnight. They sat about the midnight supper, drinking more and more coffee, and the idea of the Ark took hold of them like the excitement before a holiday.

"What will we take with us?" Rudyard continued, "I mean to say, what and who will we *permit* to enter the Ark?"

"Precisely," said Francis French, "discrimination is of the essence of this idea. There is no Ark unless we exercise the most pure, exact, and exacting discrimination."

"This is far from a joke," said Jacob, who had remained silent, although moved, "only an absolute fool would suppose that this is a laughing matter."

"Who will be elected," asked Francis, "to this elite?"

"And who will be rejected," Marcus added, "we don't want the riff-raff, the trash, the substitutes, the second-rate, the second best, and the second-hand."

"The best is none too good for us," said Rudyard, "I mean, for the Ark," he smiled with mock humility.

"It is necessary to criticize and evaluate all things," said Edmund.

"What else do you think you have been doing all these years?" said Laura, but she too was enthralled.

"Exactly, this is exactly what we have been doing," Rudyard replied, "and this is the fulfillment which was inevitable."

"And what makes you think," said Laura, "that you're the one to be the judge and the critic? You're no Noah."

"Just the fact," answered Rudyard serenely, "that the conception of the Ark occurred to me. That *such* a conception should have been born among us shows that we are worthy of it. This is not true of *any* conception, but it is true of one so noble."

"Maybe you're just disgruntled," said Laura in vain.

"Noah invented the gong," said Edmund pensively, "and Noah was the first to make wine."

"No wonder," said Laura, "he needed a drink. Anyone would need a drink, after what he went through."

"But for us," said Rudyard, disregarding his sister, "it is not so much what we accept as what we reject that is important."

"You can't have everything," said Jacob, "and you certainly can't have too much."

"We have had enough," said Ferdinand, "and more than enough."

"If you ask me," said Laura, "none of you have what you want, and that's what makes you mad."

"Anger is the vice of gentlemen," said Rudyard, "but the abounding strength of the truly noble. Let us begin with what we reject." He took notebook and pencil in hand.

"We reject automobiles," said Edmund, "I never liked them, anyway. Any boob thinks he is a king when he drives a car."

"An automobile would be useless on a boat, anyway," said Marcus.

"Too many human beings get killed in cars," said Edmund. "A fine thing for a rational being: to die for an automobile!"

"And no more marriage," said Rudyard. "Marriage is the chief cause of divorce and adultery. There are no marriages in heaven and if there are no marriages in heaven, why should we have them?"

"After all, there is something to be said for the family and family life," said Jacob.

"We will have the family," said Rudyard, "we will just not have any marriages."

"How about the phonograph?" asked Jacob, already somewhat apart. "If you reject the automobile, then you can't have the phonograph, and if we don't have the phonograph, how will we be able to hear great music?"

"We don't have to be consistent," said Rudyard, "it is an over-rated virtue used chiefly to defend the fearful from the beautiful possibilities with which their imaginations might become infatuated. We will reject the automobile and accept the phonograph."

Apart from Jacob, it was felt that this was just, reasonable, and full of insight.

"How about the animals?" said Edmund. "Don't forget that we have to have two of each kind, male and female."

"Animals are fine," said Francis, "I like animals. They are interesting, spontaneous, and sincere."

"Animals and also children," said Rudyard. "We will have a new education for them, the education of the Ark. They will not be taught the skills which crush their natures and prepare them to be desperate citizens of the middle class. We will teach them every kind of virtue and vice, and by this true education, they will be made truly free. For in what sense can a human being be said to be free, if he is not possessed by the knowledge of every possibility, famous and infamous?"

"You want the children to be just like you," said Laura.

"I suppose you like the world as it is?" said Rudyard passionately. "Are you happy? Is anyone happy?"

Laura had no answer, but felt that Rudyard was wrong.

"As for me," said Ferdinand, "I spit on this life."

This declaration was acclaimed.

"This life," added Ferdinand, "can go and take a flying La Rochefoucauld for itself."

The addition was also acclaimed.

"Say what you will," said Jacob, when the applause had ended, "there is something that must be said for this life. This idea of the Ark is only an idea, and yet we all hold back. There is no flood of rejections and renunciations. We are all too much in love with many things, whether we have them or not."

"You don't like Arks," said Rudyard, knowing that a crisis had been reached, since Jacob was turning away.

"I like Arks well enough," said Jacob, "although I have never been on one, and can't be too sure. But I like many other things, even if they are not as good as they might be."

"No," said Rudyard, feeling that the emotion was slipping away and that the circle was becoming bored with the idea of the Ark.

"The kingdom of heaven is within us," said Jacob, "but also the kingdom of hell."

"What kingdom?" said Rudyard. "Do you know any kings? Do you know anyone who has found any kingdom within himself? I thought once that I had, but I was wrong."

It was too late. Jacob smiled patiently and in sympathy.

"This is where we are," said Jacob, "and this is where we are going to stay, waiting in hope and fear for what comes next in this life."

"As for me, I am going home," said Ferdinand, and all the visitors arose to depart, for they had had enough of the idea of the Ark.

EIGHT: "PRACTICALLY EVERYONE DOES WHAT HE
WANTS TO DO IF HE CAN"

During a period when Rudyard was absent on a long visit, a celebrated cause and scandal broke out.

The scandal began with Marcus Gross. During the difficult winter of the year, he had paid much attention to a plump and pretty girl named Irene. She was active, efficient, interested in many things, especially radical politics. Marcus met her at meetings of the radical party to which both belonged, and he courted her not only because she was pretty, but also because he had already heard about her from a friend of his, Algernon Nathan. Algernon was a certain well-known type, the perfect student who gets the highest grades in all his classes. He was precise, thin-lipped, tormented by pride, and as humorless as a public monument. He earned a handsome salary and he felt unable to understand why he was not the perfect success in the great world that he had been in school. He had succeeded very quickly with Irene. His parents owned a store and it was simple for him to bring Irene home, either in the afternoon or in the early evening, when his parents were at the store. When his parents came home unexpectedly one day, Algernon left his bedroom, attired himself in his dressing gown, and halted his parents in the hallway, asking them to depart from the house because he was having sexual intercourse. The adoration, and awe of his parents were such that they left the house immediately and hurriedly, supposing that if Algernon, the perfect student, thought that this was right, it must indeed be right.

Algernon provided Marcus with a comprehensive description of his sessions with Irene, who was, he affirmed, "passionate to a satisfactory extent," but with whom he did not like to be seen by his friends. Irene, however, wanted Algernon to take her out and to visit his friends with him. And Algernon found that what he really wanted from Irene, she did not really like. What he really wanted to do when he made love was to whip Irene. He had not gone so far as to propose this exercise to her, but had restricted himself to squeezing her and pinching her while he regarded the pain upon her face. This had been endured by Irene only upon occasion, when she was eager to please him. Her attitude was a blow to Algernon's pride, for he felt that if a girl truly loved him, she ought to want whatever he wanted.

After a time, Algernon decided that it would be more sensible and more efficient to pay for such satisfactions and not to become involved with a girl whom he had to take out and be seen with by his friends. He had made the proper inquiries and found that there were establishments where what he wanted was available, and he had gone to them with system, twice a week, taking with him a book to study on the subway, a book which extended his knowledge about such subjects as some period in history, relativity physics, or mathematical logic.

"Often, however," he explained to Marcus who admired him very much because he was a conventional success, "I merely study the faces in the subway, wonder what lives have produced such faces, and write sonnets about them when I get home."

Marcus blazed with desire when he heard Algernon's somewhat off-hand account of Irene. His own desires were orthodox and straight-forward, and such a girl was just what he longed for. He paid expensive court to Irene and took her to theatres, to the opera and to the ballet, night after night, being impatient. At the conclusion of two weeks, he proposed to Irene that she go to Atlantic City with him for the week-end. She refused flatly, and when he asked if she thought she might feel differently after six months, she said she was sure she would not, she was sorry, but to be perfectly frank, she found him unattractive. Marcus in anger replied that she had a capitalist and Hollywood conception of what was handsome, for he had been told by some girls that he was extremely attractive. He did not add that it was a colored girl to whom he had just paid ten dollars who had said: "Boy, are you handsome!"

No sooner had Marcus stopped seeing Irene than she began to go out with Ferdinand to whom she had been introduced by Marcus. The truth was that Marcus suspected Ferdinand of interviewing and seeking out Irene before his rejected week-end proposal.

Marcus was hurt, as if he had been betrayed. He saw no reason for Ferdinand's being successful where he had failed, and he felt also that such a one as Ferdinand, precious and finicky, had been unfaithful to himself in going with a girl like Irene. He protested long, as if obsessed, to Edmund and Jacob. Both of them, perverted by Marcus' stolid foolishness, provoked Marcus all the more.

Ferdinand hated Algernon and refused to acknowledge his existence when they passed on the street. The year before, Algernon's father had hanged himself because of losses in the stock market, and the circle had had a merry time about this event, for none of them liked Algernon, whom they had known as a student. They had discovered that when they asked most acquaintances if they had heard about Algernon's father, most of them said:

"Yes, he hanged himself!" and broke out laughing. The laughter was directed at Algernon as a prig, and not at the father, a small, quiet, extremely nervous man whom no one knew very well.

The outlandish answer and laughter continued so that as each newcomer was asked the question and broke into laughter, Ferdinand said:

"Look, everyone breaks out laughing," and he was pleased.

And this had also been the inspiration of the most notorious instance of an incapacity to make conversation and engage in small talk, for one day Harry Johnson, an acquaintance of the circle and of Algernon, one renowned for shyness and insensitivity, had encountered Algernon soon after his father's death. After several abortive efforts to make conversation with Algernon, who was no help whatever, Harry tried to break the silence between sentences.

"Say, what's this I hear about your father hanging himself?" he inquired.

This question had been discussed for six months, especially by Rudyard who maintained that it was a direct expression of Harry's hatred of Algernon.

Knowing how Ferdinand detested Algernon, Marcus felt that the one thing which would make him abandon Irene was the knowledge that she had been intimate with Algernon. This would certainly waken the finicky dandy in him.

Jacob was consulted by Marcus.

"Go ahead and tell him, if you like," said Jacob, "but if you tell him, you may not take much pride in yourself hereafter."

"After all, I am a friend of his," said Marcus. "Perhaps it is my duty to tell him?"

"Who do you think you are making that remark to?" said Jacob. Marcus grinned in guilt and recognition. Then he suggested that perhaps Jacob, also a good friend of Ferdinand, ought to tell him about Irene and Algernon, since he had no personal stake.

"You ought to be dead," said Jacob.

Meanwhile the news of the courtship grew. Ferdinand, who hardly ever lent a book to anyone, was lending certain selected works, long sacred to him, to Irene.

"This surely is serious," said Jacob to Edmund.

Stiffly and shyly, Ferdinand was seen bringing Irene to see other treasures and curios of his private cult. It was like the loving son who for the first time brings his intended to see his mother and his father.

"This must mean marriage," said Jacob.

Ferdinand undertook to supervise Irene's habits of dress. He went with her to the dressmaker's and he quickly persuaded her to shift from the garish to the elegant. She was surprised to find that he knew so much about dress and delighted that he cared about such matters.

He explained curtly that he had had several extra-marital relationships which had provided him with an opportunity to learn about such things. He made this explanation because he felt that he must make it clear that he had committed adultery, just as in other periods chastity was deemed a necessity and a virtue.

The two united extremes; it was the union of a brash, bright, full, open, vivacious and buxom girl to a constrained, meticulous, reserved and tormented young man.

The boys of the circle observed that strange changes also occurred in Ferdinand, now that he went with Irene. He had always abhorred politics, especially radical politics. Now he spoke with a venom he had once reserved for discourteous head-waiters of the infamy of the Stalinists.

"What does she have that I don't have?" said Laura. No one answered her although conversation had concentrated upon Irene for an hour. The silence was sharp. Laura thrust her head forward.

"You're no Adonis," she said to Edmund.

"What did I do?" asked Edmund, moved at the same time to sympathy and laughter.

"She has thick ankles and her complexion is rotten;" said Laura.

"Who?" said Edmund.

"*This too shall pass away,*" quoted Laura, departing for the kitchen to get herself a fresh drink.

At that moment the door slammed like a gunshot and Marcus entered.

"Hello, hello, hello," he shouted, the image of abounding good humor.

"What now?" said Jacob.

"What next?" said Edmund.

"I hear that Ferdinand has just married Irene," said Marcus, enjoying the astonishment of this news. He drew forth the engraved card which announced that Ferdinand and Irene would be at home to their friends on Saturday night.

"You will get one tomorrow," said Marcus, "I met Ferdinand in the street and he gave me one."

"What are you so pleased about?" asked Laura. "You're not the one who married Irene."

"I have a very good reason to be pleased," said Marcus, "I know something that Ferdinand does not know."

"Shut up," said Jacob, but vainly.

"What does he know?" asked Lloyd Tyler who had not heard about Irene's intimacy with Algernon.

"This card is very fine," said Jacob, shifting the subject, "it is just like Ferdinand to send a card as well-engraved as this."

"It must have cost a pretty penny," said Marcus, grinning.

Laura returned from the kitchen where she had listened as she drank. She replied to Lloyd's question as if it had just been uttered.

"Marcus has been saying that Irene used to sleep with Algernon and he is going to tell Ferdinand."

"Who says I am going to tell him?" said Marcus, trying to look indignant, but breaking into a fresh grin.

"You had better shut up," said Jacob, all his authority in his tone. To himself he said: "Everyone does what he wants to do if he can, after paying his respects to scruple and compunction."

"I won't say anything," said Marcus, whom Jacob alone was able to persuade to be silent. "But if I drink the champagne that Ferdinand is going to have, who knows what slips of the tongue, what *lapsus linguae* may not leak out? *In vino veritas*, they say!" he chortled, pleased that he had spoken Latin.

"Thank God that Rudyard is not here," said Edmund, and all understood without a word what Edmund had in mind, how Rudyard more than Marcus would have made this marriage the subject of endless discussion until at last Ferdinand would think that his wife's past was always talked about.

Clearly Marcus took pleasure in the fact that now that the marriage was accomplished, Ferdinand was helpless against the infamy unknown to him.

At that moment the absent hero, Ferdinand, appeared in the doorway and was greeted with congratulation which soon rose to acclamation.

"Who said that I am married?" asked Ferdinand, coldly.

"I said so. You said so. It says so on the card you gave me," said Marcus, perplexed.

"I see no reason for making any unwarranted suppositions or assumptions on the basis of an engraved card," said Ferdinand.

"This is stupendous," said Edmund, for he saw that Ferdinand had a trump card up his sleeve.

"The fact is that I am not married," Ferdinand declared. "It is possible that I may marry Irene in the near future, but at present we are merely very good friends who have decided to live together."

Marcus capsized on the sofa. His dismay spread over his face as if he were at the dentist's, his mouth open.

"What do you think of Algernon Nathan?" asked Marcus.

"You know well enough," Ferdinand replied. "He is a knave and a fool. He is a coxcomb and a jackass, and he always will be, if he lives to a hundred."

It was clear then that Marcus was seeking to suppress his own desire to tell Ferdinand about Irene's intimacy with Algernon, for this knowledge was without meaning, if Ferdinand was not married to Irene.

The circle was stunned by Ferdinand's declaration. It seemed to them an incomparable exhibition. The real right thing was not to get married until one wanted to get married and in the meantime to do as one liked, frankly and openly. Ferdinand had often formulated this attitude.

"What do you think of that?" Marcus asked Laura, for she alone often expressed conventional views about marriage.

"How much money does she make?" said Laura. "What is her yearly compensation?"

"Ten years hence," said Edmund, "this evening will still be the subject of discussion and interpretation." No one knew exactly what Laura meant, but it was clear in general that Laura intended to express contempt with the implication also that nothing good would come of such an arrangement.

Laura began to bring in cups, spoons, knives, forks, bread, jam and cheese for the midnight supper.

Marcus, defeated, felt nervous and bewildered. He fell back on a practice for which he had often been denounced, that of drawing upon a store of prepared jokes and epigrams.

"Say, speaking of marriage," said Marcus, "I heard a good one the other day. A girl says to a friend of hers who is getting married soon: 'Is your torso prepared?'"

The others looked at him in a frozen-faced silence.

"What's the joke?" asked Jacob.

Marcus paled. He knew that he was being attacked. But he felt that he must attempt to justify his utterance.

"Don't you see, she says torso when she means trousseau. It is a genuine Freudian *lapsus linguae*."

"Enough of this Latin," said Edmund, "it is a dead tongue, and your grammar would shame a Gaul of the second century."

Marcus, persevering, launched a second effort.

"You are like the Irish," he said laboriously, "it is as Dr. Johnson said, the Irish are a fair people; they do not speak well of anyone."

"Spare us your prepared epigrams and quotations," said Ferdinand, "they resemble canned music."

"The trouble with you," said Marcus, "is that you have no sense of humor. Algernon said you had none and I said that you were hilarious. But I see that I was wrong."

This spontaneous remark was also a success. Everyone but Ferdinand laughed. He did not know why they laughed, but he was too clever to ask that it be explained to him, the trap which had often undone Marcus.

And now they all sat at the table, and ate and drank, and minds and hearts arose as if they danced. Marcus, seated next to Ferdinand, put his hand on his shoulder, and said, still warm with pleasure at the unexpected success of his remark about Ferdinand as humorless:

"You are a fine fellow, Ferdinand. I always admired you and no matter what you say or do, I will continue to admire you."

"Shut up," said Edmund, kicking Marcus under the table.

Ferdinand described his purchase of furniture and how he had imposed his scorn upon the merchants of furniture. It was a very interesting story.

"Say," said Laura, returning from the kitchen where she had just taken her tenth drink, and hurling her lightning-bolt as if she spoke of the weather, "did you know that Irene slept for a whole year with Algernon Nathan?"

"Laura," said Marcus, torn between guilt and the wish to appear to be the reproachful one.

"Yes," said Ferdinand, "I heard all about it the first night I went out with Irene." His tone was matter-of-fact. "What about it?"

"This Ferdinand is without a peer," said Edmund, "he has no equal either in America or Europe."

They all saw that Ferdinand had scored an unconditional triumph. It was impossible to make out if Ferdinand had actually known about Algernon, or with quick wit and perfect control recognized that he must not admit his ignorance.

"Are you going home now?" Jacob asked Edmund. "I have had enough pity and terror for one evening."

"Yes," said Edmund, who did not want to go but who wanted to hear what Jacob had to say about the evening.

"I will go with you," said Marcus.

"You stay here or go by yourself," said Jacob, "we don't want you with us." And on that note of judgment the young men left.

NINE: "A MILLION DOLLARS ARE WORTHLESS TO ME"

After long absence, Rudyard visited the teacher who had most befriended him in school, Percival Davis. After Rudyard had been seated in the study of Professor Davis and questioned about himself, Professor Davis said in a flat, but depressed, tone:

"I am dying."

"We are all dying," said Rudyard, uneasy and trying to find something to say.

"But I am dying faster than most human beings," said Professor Davis, unwilling to permit Rudyard to extricate himself from the fact of his own death. "I may be dead in six months. The fact is, I probably will be."

"I think that it would be boring to live forever," said Rudyard, pleased by this comment, but still uncomfortable.

"Forever, perhaps: but I would like to live for at least a thousand years," said Professor Davis passionately, "I would not be bored in the least. I would learn about every great school of painting, both in Europe and the Orient, and I would cultivate the best wines."

"Yes, you're right," said Rudyard, hoping to shift the subject, "it would be wonderful to live for a thousand years!" He felt that through agreement he was at least polite.

Two months after, Percival Davis died of the heart attack he had expected. After hearing the news, Rudyard went strolling with Jacob and told him of the interview.

"It was not proper of him," said Rudyard, "to confront me with his death. What was there to say? What a pity that we do not have formal utterances for all the important events of life."

"You might have said," Jacob remarked, " 'I hope you are wrong. I hope that you are not going to die very soon.' "

"What difference would that have made?" Rudyard replied.

They passed a church where a hearse and other cars awaited the departure for the cemetery. Jacob, as was his wont, wanted to pause to see the coffin carried from the church to the hearse, for now as ever the joys of strict observation were important to him. But Rudyard refused to stop.

"Who wants to see a funeral, anyway?" said Rudyard, and Jacob, discerning the excess of emotion in Rudyard's voice, yielded to him.

"Two years ago, when a very gifted student died suddenly," said Jacob, "Israel Brown was asked by the family to make the funeral sermon, for the family as well as the student were without religious belief. The sermon was given in the auditorium of the Ethical Culture School. Israel Brown spoke very well, as he always does. He spoke of the gifts of the dead young man, remarking upon his original gift for certain subjects and making clear the difficulty in general of mastering these subjects. Yet all felt that this might have been a classroom and not the ceremony for the death of a young man. Now what kind of a life is this, anyway? Something important and irreparable occurs and we have nothing to say."

Moved by these thoughts, Jacob told Rudyard of a recent effort which he had kept secret. Six months before, in mid-winter when tours of the neighborhood were unpleasant, he had written a short novel, although he had never before thought of being that kind of an author. The short novel had seemed good to him. He had placed the manuscript in his desk "to cool off," as he explained. When two months had passed, he had read his short novel again and decided that it was worthless. It was a Sunday afternoon in April, just before Jacob was due from habit and principle to tour the neighborhood and see what he entitled "the Sunday look."

Depressed and benumbed that his short novel was worthless, Jacob arose from his desk, went to the window, and gazed at the park, full of human beings of each generation, infants, children, adolescents, parents, the middle-aged, and the old.

Regarding them, he said to himself, "I reject one million dollars, the highest prize of our society. For if I had one million dollars, what good would it do me? It would not help me to make this short novel, which is worthless, a short novel which is good. I can say then that I have discovered that a million dollars are worthless to me, since they cannot help me to satisfy the desire and hope which was important, intimate, and dear to me."

Rudyard told the circle of this discovery when Jacob was absent, and they were very much moved and impressed. Often after that, when they were among strangers, they spoke of "the great moment," and "the great rejection." When strangers wished to know what this moment was, they were left unanswered, except that Edmund often said that Jacob had discovered the essential vanity and emptiness of our society. The success of these teasing sentences about "the great recognition," made the boys invent variations, delicious to them, of the enigmatic sentences. It was said that Jacob has renounced a million dollars; Jacob has rejected a million dollars; Jacob has recognized that a million dollars are worthless.

Thus it came about that for the wrong reasons outsiders and strangers suffered the illusion that Jacob was a fabulous heir.

Yet at this time Jacob's feeling about himself and about the circle was undergoing a change.

"We have all come to a standstill," he said to himself, "as on an escalator, for time is passing, but we remain motionless."

"What do I want?" he continued, "Do I know what I want? Does anyone know what he or she wants?"

He decided to visit Edmund, who had once again endured

the period when scholarships and teaching appointments are awarded and who had once again been rejected. In seeking to find motives or reasons to explain his rejection, Edmund let himself go into a kind of hysteria, discussing the matter with anyone he found to listen, speaking of his rare and many labors, and making use of a terminology which no one but a peer in his subject could understand. This had occurred at this time for the past five years and the circle found Edmund's obsession with it boring. Consequently when Francis French had entered in the midst of Edmund's monologue with a piece of sensational news everyone had stopped listening to Edmund, and Edmund, much offended, arose and departed, and he had now been absent from the circle for more than a week.

This was the reason that Jacob, the conscience of the circle, visited Edmund, keeping silent, however, about Edmund's offended departure.

"Do you know," said Jacob, seating himself in an armchair in Edmund's study, "practically everyone is unhappy, though few will admit the fact?"

"Yes," said Edmund, pleased by the renewal of this theme, "that's just what I've been thinking. It would be hard to overestimate the amount of unhappiness in America. The cause can't be just the depression, though I don't want to slight the depression, for obviously the rich are just as unhappy as the poor, though in different ways."

"Yes," said Jacob, "it is not only the depression. The depression is as much an effect as a cause, and the amount of unhappiness was perhaps as great in 1928 as in 1934."

"I know just what you mean," said Edmund, "I saw the other day that ninety-five per cent of the bathtubs in the world are in America. Now if anyone reflects sufficiently upon this interesting fact, he will conclude with the whole story of America."

"Everyone feels that it is necessary to have certain things of a certain quality and kind," said Jacob.

"Bathtubs come from an obsession with personal hygiene, the

most consummate form of Puritan feeling," said Edmund, "but the essential point is that human beings waste the best years of their only life for the sake of such a thing as a shining automobile, the latest model. Since such things are regarded as the truly important, good, and valuable things, is it any wonder that practically everyone is unhappy?"

"The fault is not this desire for things," said Jacob, "but the way in which the motive of competition is made the chief motive of life, encouraged everywhere. Think of how competition is celebrated in games, in schools, in the professions, in every kind of activity. Consequently, the ideas of success and of failure are the two most important ideas in America. Yet it's obvious that most human beings are going to be failures, for such is the nature of competition. Perhaps then the ideas of success and failure ought to be established as immoral. This strikes me as a truly revolutionary idea, although I suppose it has occurred to others."

"It has occurred to you," said Edmund, "as it has occurred to me because we are both failures, and we have to be young men in a time of failure and defeat, during the black years of the great depression."

"Yes, we are both failures," said Jacob, "but I have no desire for the only kinds of success that are available. The other day I heard the cruelest question I ever expect to hear. Two composers met at a music festival in the Berkshires last summer and one of them said to the other: 'Calvin, why are we both failures?' That's more cruel than any other question I ever heard. The other one answered him in a hurry: 'I am not a failure,' he said, 'I am not a failure because I never wanted to be a success.' That's the way I feel too. Nevertheless the fact remains that practically everyone is unhappy. Now if the idea of love supplanted the ideas of success and failure, how joyous everyone might be! and how different the quality of life!"

"You're just dreaming out loud," said Edmund to Jacob, thinking again of how he had failed once more to be appointed a teacher.

The circle altered as the great depression was stabilized and modified. The idleness which had been beyond reproach because no one was successful, because most were frustrated, because the parents' generation had lost so much of its grip and pride, ended, for now there were jobs for everyone, although not the jobs each one wanted. Some had gone to Washington to take the new Federal jobs made necessary by the New Deal, and in New York too it was no longer difficult to get a job. Rudyard refused to be employed in the Federal project for playwrights, authors, musicians, and other artists, and he defended his refusal, as from the first, by speaking of his principles. Laura was angry at this refusal, but after a time she declared once again that Rudyard was a genius and he ought not to have to earn a living.

Soon all who belonged to the circle except Rudyard and Jacob had jobs which enabled them to pay for the modest round of luxuries upon which Ferdinand insisted. The theatre began to be for Ferdinand a kind of ritual. No matter how poor the play was, the ceremonial of going to the first night of a Broadway play had for Ferdinand the rigorous and expensive qualities he had desired since he put aside his desire to be an author. His marriage became by imperceptible degrees of which no one dared to speak, a recognized union, but this did not change in the least Ferdinand's participation in the circle or his mode of life. Irene was accepted by the circle as being just like Marcus, and the circle's judgment of her was formulated by Rudyard when he said: "Personally, I like her," a statement which meant that he understood very well all the reasons for not liking Irene, and which was understood by all to mean that Irene was detestable.

Marcus went to Bermuda for the Christmas holidays, and at Easter he went to Cuba, trips paid for by his labors in the public school system. After his trip to Cuba, he spoke of the *Weltanschauung* of the cabin cruise and of the nature of time and duration on a luxury liner. Rudyard declared that Marcus had become a beachcomber and an idler. When Marcus replied that Rudyard was in no position to accuse anyone of being an idler, Rudyard told him that he was being ridiculous. "Don't be *too obvious*," said Rudyard to Marcus, "it is expected that you will be obvious, but please draw the line *somewhere*." Roaring, Marcus answered: "Obvious, obvious! what do you mean, obvious? If I say that the sun is shining, I suppose you will say that I am being obvious." "Yes!" said Rudyard in triumph and joy. "Who discusses the weather? Who discusses sunlight? We are not peasants. The weather is an old story, it is old hat."

Soon after this exchange, Rudyard was asked if he wanted to teach the drama in a girl's school in Cleveland, Ohio. The job was excellent and Rudyard was extremely pleased. "Such is the mystery of this life," he said. "The secret missions and visits of Milady Fortune, a well-known lady of the evening, are invariably surprises. Had I sought this job, I would not have received it. Just because I did not strive for it, it was given to me. All good things are given, not gained by the effort of the will."

No one paid attention to this comment and interpretation, because more interesting by far was the topic of the effect of Rudyard's departure on the circle as such. Edmund declared that Rudyard ought not to become a teacher, since he had dedicated himself to the writing of plays. Edmund quoted some of Rudyard's best past arguments in defense of his mode of life, and concluded with the statement that Rudyard would feel unhappy and estranged when he was so far from the circle. Laura was affected the most. She was excited and pleased for a moment, and then she was terrified. She said to Rudyard repeatedly that she might well ask to be sent to Cleveland by the department store which employed her. But Rudyard felt that he had had enough of life with Laura. He told her that he did not consider such a move a wise one for her, and he suggested that she secure a smaller apartment, for he did not intend to return to the city in the summer, he was going to be in the country. Ferdinand agreed with both Rudyard and Edmund. They were both his friends and whatever they said or did was right.

Edmund and Jacob discussed the fate of the circle after Rudyard's departure. Jacob felt that the circle would continue certainly and some of the others, overshadowed by Rudyard's energy, might now realize new possibilities in themselves. He observed how year by year Rudyard's authority had diminished so that now Ferdinand truly dictated the circle's mode of life more and more, as he earned more and more money. When he said this, Jacob explained as before that he himself did not truly belong to the circle. This was a necessity to each of them, to maintain that he himself was but a visitor or stranger, although the others truly belonged to the circle.

As Rudyard prepared to depart, he said again to his sister that she surely ought to move to a smaller apartment, since it was unlikely that they were ever going to live with each other again. The other boys said nothing, but they felt it cruel and unnecessary for Rudyard to dictate to Laura. Edmund suggested to Ferdinand in private that perhaps Rudyard did not want the circle to exist when he was absent. Hearing Rudyard say petulantly to Laura for the fourth time that it was senseless for her not to move elsewhere, Lloyd said with naiveté that then they would all be deprived of their community. "Yes, that's just it," said Rudyard, his face full of annoyance and distaste, "I don't want Laura to provide a clubhouse anymore." Laura became furious. "You were willing enough for me to do that until now," she said. "Never," Rudyard replied, "I never wanted you to provide a second home for the boys." He spoke with a self-righteous tone because he was sensitive now about the fact that he had been dependent upon Laura.

The week-end before Rudyard was to depart for Cleveland, Ohio, it was decided that a farewell party ought to be given for him. Ferdinand immediately declared that as a matter of fact he was going to contribute a case of champagne to this party. As his prosperity mounted, his gestures became more and more of a systematic extravagance. Laura wanted to make dinner for the whole circle, but Edmund dissuaded her. The question of who was to be invited to this party among those on the edge of the circle, the visiting strangers and the accepted newcomers, became the subject of intensive discussion.

The whole circle dined at the best restaurant in the neighborhood and Ferdinand insisted upon paying the check. "He is beside himself," said Edmund to Jacob, "this departure means more to him than he knows."

By the time everyone had returned to the Bell household, Laura was drunk. This was no less than was expected, for Laura had been drinking every night for weeks. But no one expected the speech she began to make as soon as the champagne was opened.

"Five years ago, just about the time when we all began to see each other," said Laura, rocking and gaining the attention of all by the loudness and shrillness of her voice, "I read a story by Rilke. I think it was Rilke. It was just a very short story. It was just a page and a half, and it may have been less. It was very good. I don't remember all of it, but what I remember was very good. The story is about wandering Siberians. They are hunters and they hunt wild cows on the Siberian steppes or tundras, or something. Anyway, they hunt for wild cows."

Rudyard, annoyed, said: "Laura has established the fact that they were hunters. She has made that clear." He was obviously impatient with Laura.

"Never mind," said Laura, "the main thing is that the Siberians spear the wild cows like cowboys on horseback. And when the poor cow is bleeding to death, the hunter lays down on one side of the cow and chews big pieces of meat from the side of the cow. This is just like many other stories so far. The different part is that on the other side of the cow, the horse also lays down and chews out big pieces of meat."

"The story," said Rudyard, "is by Kafka, not Rilke, and you have distorted it." He took a book from the shelf, turned to the proper page and read aloud, pausing after each sentence.

"'Their very horses live on meat. Often a rider lies down beside his horse. Then both feed on the same piece of meat.'"

"The story," Rudyard continued in a critical voice, "is about nomads, not Siberians. It is nomads who come to the capital. They eat butchers' meat, which they have stolen from butchers' vans. The meat comes from the slaughter house and nothing is said about eating living cows who are bleeding to death. You have changed the story in a way familiar to me because I know how your memory distorts many things, making what has happened more brutal and more cruel than it was in actual fact."

"Never mind," said Laura. "Let's say that I wrote the story then. I wrote the story from my knowledge of life. But I am the cow, and you," she said pointing at Rudyard, "are the nomad, the Siberian, and you," she said, pointing to the other boys, "are the horses, chewing on the other side."

"I am not a horse," said Marcus, who was amused and thought this a witticism.

"Shut up," said Edmund to Marcus.

"If you expect too much from human beings," said Jacob, "you are bound to be disappointed."

"I never expected anything unusual," said Laura, "all I ever wanted was what everyone else has."

"This is getting hysterical," said Marcus, who was always slow. "What a party!"

"Can't you think of anything good to say about any of us?" asked Jacob in a kind voice.

"I can," said Laura, "but if I lean backwards anymore, I will fall down and injure my spine, to coin a phrase." Laura reached for a glass of champagne, which Rudyard tried to keep her from getting. But he was unsuccessful.

"I don't have what I want," said Jacob to Laura, "and I don't think that many of us have what we want."

"Yes," said Rudyard, returning to his own kind of rhetoric, "I too may say that I am disappointed. My plays are not performed, although many of them are masterpieces, if I may say so. I think I may say without immodesty that I am superior to the age in which I live. I pay for my superiority to Broadway by leading this life of obscurity. Yet I do not seek out a scapegoat, as you do, Laura. Furthermore, we ought to remember that this life is a mystery in which each of us is given by God his own gifts and shortcomings. To live is better than anything else! Let us take pleasure in life!"

"Never mind," said Laura, "if you like, go ahead and say that God gave me a plain face and made me full of self-pity. What am I going to do about it? Do you think I ought to take pleasure in it? I want a husband like all the other girls. I don't want to be left alone."

"In my late adolescence," said Edmund, "life seemed to me to be Shakespearean. But now as I get older I see that life really resembles the stories of Dostoyevsky."

"Enough of these literary allusions," said Laura. "You're no Karamazov."

This new version of Laura's famous sentence, "You're no Adonis," drew forth reminiscent laughter lacking in vigor because Laura stood before them, cold-faced.

"Marriage is not so important," said Irene, who had been silent and who, as a newcomer, had not really understood what Laura was saying.

"*What do you have that I don't have?*" said Laura to Irene, quoting herself again.

Jacob arose and it was natural that all should accept this moment as belonging to him.

"The fact is," said Jacob, in a low and careful voice, "we all have each other and we all need each other. Laura's story was a very good story, whether it was written by Rilke or Kafka. All of us consume each other, and life without such friends as we are to each other would be unbearable. The best pleasure of all is to give pleasure to another being. Strange as it seems, I see this truth every day when I give my cat his dinner, and I see how unbearable solitude is when I come home and he is pleased to see me, and I am pleased that he is pleased."

99

"I am not a cat," said Laura, unwilling to be consoled by mere analogy, "I am a girl."

"Each of us," said Jacob, "has been disappointed and most of us will continue to be disappointed. It would be foolish to try to say that the disappointment is not painful or that it is good for us or that it is necessary. Yet, on the other hand, which of us would really like to be dead? Not one of us would prefer that his life had ended in childhood or infancy, and that he had not lived through the years he has lived. Since this is true of the past, it is likely that it will be true of the future, and in the same way. By the same way, I mean that we will not get what we want; our desires will not be richly satisfied; but nonetheless we will be pleased to live through the years, to be conscious each day and to sleep every night."

"Not me," said Laura, "speak for yourself." She took another glass of champagne.

"You do not know what you are saying, Laura," said Edmund. Taking a book in his hand, he too read aloud:

"'When one is upset by anger, then the heart is not in its right place; when one is disturbed by fear, then the heart is not in its right place; when one is blinded by love, then the heart is not in its right place; when one is involved in anxiety, then the heart is not in its right place. When the mind is not present, we look, but do not see, listen but do not hear, and eat but do not know the flavor of the food'."

"I am wearing my heart on my sleeve," said Laura, unmoved, "all the sentences in all the books will not do away with my disappointment."

"How about your love?" asked Marcus.

"I don't have any love," said Laura.

"*How much money do I make?*" said Edmund.

"We can't just run on like this," said Jacob, "and yet nothing seems to do any good."

Laura had begun to cry and those who saw her tears tried to make believe that they did not see them.

"I just don't like it," she said, sobbing, "I am going to get out of this house." She started for the door. Edmund and Ferdinand took hold of her and dissuaded her.

"Have some more to drink," said Marcus in an effort to be helpful.

"I am going to try again," said Jacob, "since there is nothing else to do but try again." He said this as to himself and then he spoke loudly and clearly:

"*The world is a wedding.* I read this sentence in an old book last week. I had to think for two days before I had any conception of what this sentence *The world is a wedding* was supposed to mean. Does it mean anything? Yes, and it means everything. For example, it means that the world is the wedding of God and Nature. This is the first of all the marriages.

"It was natural that I should think of Pieter Breughel's picture, 'The Peasant Wedding.' Do you remember what that picture looks like? If you look at it long enough, you will see all the parts that anyone and everyone can have. But it is necessary to belong to a circle of friendship, such as ours, if one is to be present at the wedding which is this world. "

"The world is a marriage of convenience," said Laura drunkenly, "the world is a shot-gun marriage. The world is a sordid match for money. The world is a misalliance. Every birthday is a funeral and every funeral is a great relief."

"I only went to a wedding once," said Francis. He spoke in a low voice but with an intensity which made everyone listen. "It was the wedding of my older sister at the age of thirty-six.

"The bridegroom's mother, who was eighty-five, was brought in a taxi to the ceremony. She paid no attention to the ceremony, but kept telling my mother how, at the home for the aged where she lived, she was persecuted and other old men and women pampered; but my younger sister and I listened to what she said because it was more interesting than the ceremony itself. One thing we kept noticing was that the bride was at least a head taller than the bridegroom.

"Then the old lady was sent back to the home for the aged in a taxi, after getting my mother to promise to see her. After her departure, the wedding party went to the big downtown hotel where the bride and bridegroom had taken a room for the night. My younger sister and I kept getting more and more disappointed because we had never been to a wedding before, and we thought that all weddings must be like this. Up in the hotel room where we had been sent to wash, we looked at the twin beds and giggled. Then we stopped giggling because the room looked as depressing as everything else. We had dinner in the big dining room downstairs, the bridegroom, the bride, my mother, my younger sister and myself. No one had very much to say to anyone else. It was just as if we were having dinner on a rainy Sunday. After dinner ended, we said goodbye to the bridegroom and the bride, and we went home in the subway. I had homework to do and my sister had to practice her piano lessons. We asked my mother if in honor of the occasion we might not postpone the homework and the lessons, and she said the wedding was all over."

Francis paused. He had become almost breathless as he continued his story.

"I want to ask all of you this question," he said. "Do I agree with Jacob that the world is a wedding, or don't I? What do all of you think?"

"You're right," said Laura, "and he is wrong."

"In the beautiful picture by Pieter Breughel," said Jacob, disregarding what Francis and Laura had just said, "you can see a squatting child on the floor, sucking his thumb which is sticky with something sweet. Standing by the table are two musicians, bearing bagpipes. One is young, handsome and strong; he is dressed in brown and his cheeks are puffed out. The other musician is unkempt and middle-aged. He looks far away as if he were thinking of his faded hopes. The serving men are carrying a long tray full of pies. The bride is seated beneath the red-white mistletoe and on her face is a faint smile, as if she thought of what did not yet exist. The bridegroom is leaning back and draining down the ale from a fat stein. He drinks as if he were in the midst of a long kiss. Nearby is a dwarf and at the head of the table a priest and a nun are conversing with each other. Neither of them will ever have a husband or a wife. On the right hand of the bride, an old man looks ahead at nothing, holding his hands as if he prayed. He has been a guest at many wedding feasts! He will never be a young man again! Never again will youth run wild in him!

"Opposite the bride are the fathers and the mothers, all four. Their time is passed and they have had their day. Yet this too is a pleasure and a part for them to play. I can't tell which is the suitor whom the bride refused, but I know he is there too, perhaps among the crush that crowds the door. He is present and he looks from a distance like death at happiness. Meanwhile in the foreground a handsome young man pours from a jug which has the comely form of a woman's body the wine which will bring all of them exaltation like light. His bending body is curved in a grace like harps or violins. Marcus, open a new bottle."

Marcus obeyed, and after the pop, the puff, the foam, and the flow, he poured the wine in glasses.

"I suppose everything is all right," said Laura, "I suppose everything is just fine."

"No," said Jacob, "I don't mean to say that this life is just a party, any kind of party. It is a wedding, the most important kind of party, full of joy, fear, hope, and ignorance. And at this party there are enough places and parts for everyone, and if no one can play every part, yet everyone can come to the party, everyone can come to the wedding feast, and anyone who does not know that he is at a wedding feast just does not see what is in front of him. He might as well be dead if he does not know that the world is a wedding."

"You can't fool me," said Laura, "the world is a funeral. We are all going to the grave, no matter what you say. Let me give all of you one good piece of advice: *Let your conscience be your bride.*"

NEW YEAR'S EVE

To Edna Phillips

The evening of the profound holiday drew much strength and unhappiness from such depths as the afternoon, the week, the year of unhappiness, and the lives that long had been lived. This secular holiday is full of pain because it is both an ending and a beginning. In this way, it participates in some of the strangeness and difficulty of both birth and death.

On this memorable evening and at this New Year's party, the idiom which prevailed might perhaps be said to be that of unpleasant cleverness. The party had not been the object of careful thought, nor had it been inspired by the emotion of celebration. Hence some of the guests hoped vaguely until the afternoon darkened that they might be asked to come to some other party. This hope communicated itself like uproarious laughter as some of the guests spoke to each other during the winter afternoon. Each in his tone of voice unknowingly communicated the sense that this party was not the party which, in the depths, the psyche desired like first prize.

Grant Landis was the only human being who did not have this feeling about the party. He labored all afternoon in the office of

Centaur Editions, a small publishing house of which he was one of the owners, and when anyone called him upon the telephone or visited him, he invited each one to come to the party too. He was a human being who possessed an infinite interest in other human beings and an inexhaustible energy, an energy so great that it triumphed over reality when it was dismal by moving forward to fresh arenas of frenzied activity.

Early in the afternoon, Shenandoah Fish, a youthful author of promise, entered the office and Grant immediately invited him to the party. Shenandoah had come to the office because he had little else that he wanted to do, because he wanted to converse with Grant Landis, and because he hoped to hear more praise of his small book, which Centaur Editions had published in October.

Eager to hear more about his small book, the invitation to the party came as a major pleasure. However, he tried to conceal his delight, saying that he had promised to spend the evening with two of his friends, Nicholas O'Neil and Wilhelmina Gold.

"Bring them too," said Grant, as Arthur Harris, the other owner of the press, entered the office, returning from lunch. Since nine o'clock in the morning Arthur had heard more and more strangers invited to the party. Hearing of this fresh addition, he had difficulty in concealing the annoyance which rose to his face. However, he greeted Shenandoah with a warmth which broke through his annoyance, asking the youthful author what he was writing now? Another dialogue?

The mixed and complicated character of this question, as it struck Shenandoah, can be understood only by mentioning the nature of the youthful author's first work. It was a satirical dialogue between Freud and Marx in which Freud comes to agree that capitalism is organized anal eroticism when Marx agrees in return that the oedipus complex is an oppression rooted in the ownership of the means of reproduction. In asking Shenandoah if he was writing a new dialogue, Arthur did not intend to make an ironic remark. But it was ironic. And the irony, though inspired by Arthur's annoyance at the new additions to the New Year's party, had an objective foundation in the fact that the youthful author's first work might well be an accident and not the proof of a lasting gift. Although Shenandoah recognized the irony, and sought to disregard it, he misunderstood its true cause. He thought that Arthur supposed him capable of composing nothing but satirical dialogues, a misunderstanding inspired in him by the deep fear that it might be true.

Nonetheless Shenandoah said nothing in reply and decided to return to the rooming house where he lived. When he had closed the glassed door of the office, Arthur criticized Grant for his indiscriminate invitations. Since both of them were intellectuals, both resorted to theories about the nature of a party and about each other's characters. A party at which too many of the guests are strangers is likely to fall flat, Arthur argued.

"There is enough alienation in modern life," he said roundly, "without installing it in the living room."

"Everyone is interesting," Grant replied and it was true that he found everyone interesting.

"Everyone is interesting to you," said Arthur harshly, "because you talk all the time—"

"Spontaneity," said Grant, recognizing with laughter this description of his character, "strangers bring spontaneity to a party."

The argument continued thus, full of abstractions, but motivated nonetheless by a conflict which was founded upon two different feelings about life. And as they argued and as they irritated each other, elsewhere in other boxes of the great city old conflicts were renewed and new ones quickly engendered. Grant's wife, Martha Landis, quietly quarreled with her mother-in-law upon the telephone. Frances Harris, Arthur's wife, became more and more angry because Arthur had not come home on time.

"He is holding a theoretical conversation somewhere," she said to herself.

Meantime Shenandoah was visited by his friend Nicholas O'Neil, who was unhappy and who suffered from a cold, the outcome perhaps of the fact that this was his birthday, or the outcome of his depression that he was twenty-five years of age and not yet famous. Nicholas and Shenandoah had become annoyed with each other, arguing about the merits of a poem. Nicholas in his annoyance and depression declared sullenly that he did not want to go to Grant's party. He said this repeatedly, although the prospect of being at home with his family during the New Year evening was unbearable.

And meanwhile Grant Landis returned from the office to his apartment and found his wife Martha pale with annoyance because of her mother-in-law's remarks, remarks which were made unknowingly to a successful rival who had scored an overwhelming victory. Hearing Martha's version of these remarks, Grant became very angry with his mother, an anger in which the thirty-six years of his life were revived. Thinking of these remarks, Grant became more and more angry until his anger was such that he might have still been unmarried.

During the sooty afternoon, a light rain began to fall. The weather was not cold and shining, as it should have been for the winter holiday. The weather was boring and gray. Nevertheless in the streets of the first capital of the world, the capital of the accessibility to experience, there was some gaiety, leftover gaiety from the Christmas holiday. Christmas trees shone with a toytown brilliance in apartment house windows, as evening slipped down. Few human beings looked at the trees, however, and fewer were aware of them, for they had been present for more than a week.

And at the same time Wilhelmina Gold argued with her parents as she prepared to go downtown to meet Shenandoah. The argument concerned the fact that Wilhelmina was going to meet Shenandoah downtown, instead of his obeying the manners of the middle class and coming to call for her. This kind of behavior had been the cause of many disputes between the parents and the daughter. The parents were not sure that Shenandoah was more than a mere friend of Wilhelmina. He did not behave like a suitor or prospective son-in-law. But then he did not behave like any one they had viewed in almost fifty years of life. This made them suspect every possibility. Apart, however, from any concern with marriage, they found Shenandoah's behavior inexplicable. For example, his self-consciousness was so extreme that he stumbled whenever he thought that anyone was looking at him when he crossed the room.

"Some day he will fall flat on his face," said Mrs. Gold, enjoying the idea and yet fearing this young man.

He was incapable of saying, How do you do? with the least aplomb, although on the other hand once he began to speak it was difficult to interrupt him. He never dressed well and although he seemed to them to be smart and to know many things, when he spoke, he spoke with such passion and contempt and with so many speech defects that it was difficult to imagine that he would ever be successful and well-to-do. Worst of all, from the point of view of the Golds, he was not the kind of young man who, when married to Wilhelmina, would come with her for dinner every Friday night after taking an apartment not far from the Golds.

The argument in progress between parents and daughter went back to the old and estranged past. The parents had objected grievously from the beginning because Shenandoah did not always come to call for Wilhelmina, but she met him on a street-corner or if it was cold in a cafeteria. It was useless to explain as Wilhelmina had tried to explain to her parents, poor souls who had known youth at the turn of the century, that a girl was not of necessity a loose woman merely because she waited for a young man on a street-corner. Yet such is the capacity of the human heart to accustom itself to infamy, they had come to accept the fact that Shenandoah did not always come to call for her because there were times when, in an effort to ease her difficulties, he did call for her.

Mr. Gold blamed his daughter's acceptance of this peculiar young man, if acceptance it was, upon the university she had attended for four years, and where she had met Shenandoah. He forgot that before going to the university Wilhelmina had rejected with violence and contempt the *mores* and ethos of her parents.

Mr. Gold felt that she might have altered and become sensible if she had only met the right young man.

Wilhelmina's sensibility was that of an only child who for twenty-four years has been adored, tended, and nagged by her parents. As Mrs. Gold helped her pretty daughter to dress, she made remarks which shifted between ruthless criticism and infatuated admiration. She observed once again that her daughter had the legs of a Ziegfield Follies girl and a face as refined as those she studied on the Sunday society pages. But, given such native gifts, why, at the age of twenty-four, a late age for an unmarried girl, did she have to go out only with this strange author in unpressed pants? Mrs. Gold was unable to penetrate this unpleasant act. Her disappointment with her husband, who was not rich and hence to her mind a failure, united with her hope and her disappointment in her daughter, and all these feelings, which had their beginning in the first week of her marriage, arose to the point of compulsion. She made remarks which she knew would enrage her daughter because they had enraged her many times before.

"Why," she asked her daughter as she helped her to adjust her dress, "did you discourage Herman like that? After all, he wanted to marry you so much."

The fantastic character of this question will be understood from the fact that Herman had been married for four years now and was the father of three children, all girls. But more than that, Herman was a dentist, extremely prosperous. During his suit, he had argued long and stubbornly with Wilhelmina about her disdain for *Collier's*, which he read with passion from week to week, impatient for the appearance of each new number because of the unbearable excitement which the serial inevitably inspired in him. And he had pointed out to Wilhelmina that if she married him, she would have no dental bills, and when Wilhelmina had said, "What a vulgar argument to make to a girl," he had observed that what she regarded as vulgarity now would seem merely good sense to her when she had begun to cope with "the facts of life," a phrase which made Wilhelmina wince as if it were a dental drill.

Wilhelmina's detestation of Herman had a general and representative character to such an extent that the mention of his name was enough to annoy her. When her mother, forced by a compulsion she did not in the least understand, once more regretted Wilhelmina's rejection of Herman, Wilhelmina donned her coat quickly and left the house, declaring that once she was married she would have nothing whatever to do with her parents. Consequently, Wilhelmina's ride downtown in the subway was one in which she was sickened by her sense of guilt, while Mrs. Gold spent New Year's Eve in tears, tears interrupted only to renew her quintessential criticism of her husband, who quietly damned the day that he had decided to send his daughter to the university.

And at this time, Shenandoah and Nicholas travelled crosstown in a street-car, standing up in the press and brushing against human beings they would never see again. They continued their argument which on the surface concerned the question, should Nicholas go to a party where he would for the most part be a stranger? This was a type of the academic argument, since the street-car slowly went crosstown, bearing the young men to the argument's conclusion. Yet the dispute had come to the point where each young man, oppressed, cited and bore in mind only the other's faults of character, and Shenandoah was becoming aware that the other passengers were listening in amazement to their virtually ontological discussion of character when the street-car arrived at their destination, and they dismounted. Immediately they saw Wilhelmina on the street-corner, angry at her mother, Shenandoah, and chiefly herself. But her anger vanished as he arrived and there was no longer any reason to be impatient.

Nicholas, Wilhelmina and Shenandoah entered the remodeled tenement in which Grant lived just as the drizzle of rain turned into a downpour.

"Hello," Grant cried loudly to them from the top of the stair after the antiphonal buzzes and the shoving of the door. He shouted down the stairwell at them from sheer love of the act of greeting. But this was complicated by another habit, just as frequent, that of crying down a question in a troubled or virtually mystified voice.

"Shenandoah?" he cried down the stairwell, as if some pressing problem had been uttered. And when the question was answered by Shenandoah in an unclear voice, unclear because he was always uneasy in formal matters, Grant then shouted back a greeting, a greeting in which his voice sometimes broke or grew hoarse, while his visitors ascended, unseeing, and unseen, and unable to shout back at him because they did not enjoy his temperament or his pathological excess of energy.

As soon as the visitors arrived at the head of the fourth floor, they found that Grant, Martha, and another couple, Oliver Jones and his wife, Delia, were in their coats and about to depart. Grant explained that Arthur had called and asked them all to come to his house because he could not come uptown to Grant's.

"Arthur thinks he has a cold," said Grant in a tone which plainly implied that this was one more manifestation of hypochondria. To Nicholas and Wilhelmina, Grant said, "I am overjoyed that you decided to come," a remark inexplicable and so much in excess of any real need of the moment, that Nicholas and Wilhelmina were left tonguetied, and Nicholas became anxious with the fear that somehow Shenandoah had communicated his doubt about coming to Grant.

As they left the house, and looked for a taxi, Grant resumed his argument with Oliver Jones, trying at the same time to signal a taxi and to enlist Shenandoah in the argument. In the background, pale, thin and nervous, stood Delia Jones, wishing that one of them would speak to her. She was sure that no one was aware of her presence. Nicholas suffered from precisely the same feelings.

"That is the only possible explanation," he said to himself, still preoccupied with Grant's greeting and Shenandoah's betrayal of him. Since no one paid any attention to him, he decided to become active, useful and prominent. He went out into the middle of the street to hail a taxi, and finally stopped one, but at the same time his feet became soaked as he stepped into a black puddle near the sewer. Consequently Nicholas lost interest in everything but his wet feet and his cold. As they seated themselves in the taxi, Delia Jones became very self-conscious about the pressure of the bodies of the other human beings, and she wished again that she had stayed at home.

When these guests arrived at the apartment house where Arthur Harris lived, Nicholas was disturbed so much by the possibility of pneumonia that immediately upon being introduced to Frances Harris he asked her if he might please have a pail of hot water in which to bathe his feet. Frances was thunderstruck by this request, but since it seemed to have been made with the utmost seriousness, she gave him a pail for hot water, making no comment, for she was one of perfect tact.

The party had not become a unique kind of being as yet. One reason for this was that not everyone had arrived. Yet it was already clear that the great psychological *place* of the party was the sense of having-nowhere-better-to-go.

In general, the guests already present suffered in one or another way from the emotions which had distorted the newcomers. Some felt that they were not wanted before they arrived, and when they arrived they saw that this view was incorrect, since no one seemed to care very much who was present. Thus, corrected by incontestable perception, some of them felt that they would not have been invited if this had been an important party, the kind of a party they had supposed it to be when they felt the emotion of flattery upon being invited.

Soon after their arrival, a long and important conversation began between Shenandoah and Oliver Jones.

Oliver was an interesting and unfortunate human being. Shenandoah liked him very much and was ashamed of liking him, for the only reason for liking him was personal charm. Oliver wrote fiction in which his desire to be a circulating library success was at war with his desire to be a serious author. He had a true talent for fiction, but he was unaware or unsure of this fact, and this made him dishonest in a variety of ways. This dishonesty might not have mattered very much, had he remained able to be honest with himself and honest in the activity of authorship. But his sense of guilt pressed him to the point where for relief it was necessary for him to deny to himself that anyone was honest and that honesty had any real existence. Consequently, his native gift for understanding other human beings was often annulled by his need to deny that other human beings were unlike himself; and thus he suspected everyone of everything because he suspected and convicted himself of many wrongs. He had recently shocked his already overworked conscience by writing a review of stupendous praise for a work by an extremely influential and foolish literary critic who had befriended him and who might befriend him many times again. This review went so far in false praise that the critic himself was embarrassed as well as pleased. But before writing the review Oliver had read passages of the book to many of his friends to show them how foolish the book was. He had done this because he suffered, like so many other human beings, from a desperate desire to be honest some of the time. He bore in mind these occasions of deprecation and consequently apologized too often for the extreme praise he had given the book, forgetting that no one cared very much whether he was honest. And all this behavior would have been unnecessary to Oliver, had he only known that he was really a gifted author! Unsure of his gifts, Oliver was ashamed of his wife Delia, and they had what Oliver assumed to be an understanding that each was free to become involved in amorous interludes. Delia did not understand this understanding, she suffered very much because her husband had not made love to her for years, and she tried very hard but without success to become involved in what Oliver termed amorous interludes, concerning which he had stipulated only that she be discreet and keep them a private and personal matter.

As Shenandoah conversed with Oliver, Delia surveyed the living room, wondering against intelligent doubt if tonight might not be the beginning of an amorous interlude.

Shenandoah and Oliver were discussing Gide's *Journal* which both had lately read. Shenandoah did not know French very well and he may have been mistaken in his comments, which concerned Gide's jealousy of Proust. This jealousy did not show itself directly, but it seemed to Shenandoah to express itself in Gide's sentences about Proust's grammatical errors and his irrational resentment that Proust had chosen to conceal or invert the homosexuality of the protagonist in *A la Recherche du Temps Perdu.*

"... How foolish jealousy is, among authors," said Shenandoah, after he had spoken of Gide, "Proust, Eliot, Rilke, Mann and Valéry all produced great works and received the recognition they deserved. Literature is not like space and business. One great work does not displace another great work ..."

This view irritated Oliver. Had he been in better health and had he drunk less, he might have concealed his irritation. He was irritated both because he thought that what Shenandoah said was untrue and also because he wished with all his heart that he were able to believe that it was true.

"Don't be naive," said Oliver, "it's obvious that authors compete for fame. Not only that, Proust wrote the work which Gide should have written and he took from Gide his hold upon the rising generations of intellectuals ..."

"I don't mean to deny the *hallucination* of competition," said Shenandoah, intoxicated by the benevolence of his idea, "and I certainly don't deny the existence of jealous feelings. But consider how, after twenty years, both Gide and Proust are studied as great authors. They do not get in each other's way and the rising generation reads the works of both with the same attention and admiration."

Oliver said nothing for the moment. He was trying to restrain his irritation. We are probably both wrong, said Shenandoah to himself, for this had often been true. Oliver passed to the possibility that Shenandoah was denying the actuality of competition because he feared the feelings of his rivals. Next, Oliver felt that what Shenandoah had said was an attack, however unknowing, upon his own acute sense of rivalry. He had to decide that Shenandoah was right and he had been foolish for years, or that he was right and Shenandoah was ignorant and innocent. The latter view immediately triumphed and his irritation took hold of him and he felt compelled to wound Shenandoah.

"How old are you?" said Oliver with a beautiful hardness upon his face.

"Twenty-four years of age," said Shenandoah. He knew very well that the question was an affront, but he did not want to quarrel with Oliver.

"You are just an infant," said Oliver, determined to hurt Shenandoah's feelings, "you have just not lived long enough." Thus, with this sentence, he declared that Shenandoah did not know what he was saying and he won the argument.

"How old are you?" said Shenandoah with awkward constraint. His determination not to be angry had quickly broken down.

"You know how old I am, thirty-four," said Oliver in fury, "I've told you a dozen times."

"Well for that matter," said Shenandoah, "you know how old I am, but I was too polite to mention the fact." He knew that this remark was self-righteous an instant too late to halt himself.

"O never mind," said Oliver, for his mind had shifted to the much more serious irritation he felt because he was thirty-four years of age, a thought which became most urgent and most productive of feelings of anxiety and despair on a birthday or on New Year's Eve.

Shenandoah moved away as Oliver looked at the carpet and then at nothing at all. Oliver felt a pang of guilt as Shenandoah departed and consequently he sought to remember all that was wrong with Shenandoah.

Shenandoah expects everyone to be as interested in him as he is interested in himself, Oliver thought, as he sought self-extenuation; he has decided that competition does not exist because it makes him uncomfortable, which is one form of egotism, and because he thinks very well of himself, which is the worst form of egotism.

Shenandoah had departed ostensibly to freshen his drink, but actually to hide his despair at his inability not to get into arguments with other human beings, especially those he liked.

He was overcome by a convenient self-pity as he reached for cold ice to put in his highball glass. His self-pity was convenient because it made it unnecessary for him to engage in further thought.

All I ever wanted, he said to himself brokenly, was to have friends and to go to parties. Shenandoah had for long cherished the belief that if he were an interesting and gifted author, everyone would like him and want to be with him and enjoy conversation with him.

He criticized the self-pity which wept in him, he criticized it and repudiated it from the top of his mind, for all the good it did.

In other cages of the room, other human beings were trying without success to get along with each other.

Nicholas O'Neil sat on the bathtub rim, his feet in a pail of hot water, full of self-pity and self-absorption, wondering what disease would take him to an early grave.

Arthur Harris remarked to Wilhelmina Gold that much might be said of the truth of the remark that drinking was an inexpensive form of mysticism. Wilhelmina replied that it was far from inexpensive. The party bored her because she did not like to drink.

Martha Landis looked across the living room at Delia Jones and regarded her gown, which was intended to suggest to many minds the delightful possibility of taking it off. Martha knew of the domestic agreement of the Joneses, since Oliver was unable to hold his tongue about matters interesting to him, and she saw both the intimacy and the pathos of the gown. Delia, who was beginning her second drink, was still unhappy and uneasy, for no one had spoken to her very much, a silence which often occurred at parties. Because of her uneasiness, Delia tried to down her drink quickly. She began to feel miserable because she had not married the man who had courted her for two years before she encountered Oliver. She had refused him because, when they went out to dinner, he filled his pockets with granulated sugar, a habit contracted during a poverty-beslummed and unsweetened childhood. During the courtship he was earning a great deal of money and there was no reason for any hoarding of sugar: it was merely a tic which continued from childhood, and absentmindedly, yet compelled by the whole being. He had other such habits, although they were less public. Thinking about these habits, Delia felt that she had regarded them as being too important, for she forgot, after these years, how expressive and significant they were. And after all, why should anyone have to pay for another human being's childhood? One has to pay for one's own, and one is in debt as it is because of the continuous expense. The pain of these thoughts was so keen that Delia went to get another drink, and drank it down quickly in the hope of false serenity and false joy.

Delia was attractive and intelligent. She was unable to understand why no amorous interludes occurred, for certainly Oliver was not in the least at a loss, and she heard everywhere of extramarital episodes of other human beings. She did not understand that it was not a question of a defect in her, but of the difficulty of direct communication in modern life, the difficulty of making clear her willingness. At times she entertained this explanation, but the passing recognition was ineffectual and melted away because more powerful by far was her fear that she was not attractive. By attributing her poverty in love to an unattractiveness which did not exist, she arrived at a picture of her plight which was coherent and which required no activity on her part, but merely sorrow. This view permitted her an uneasy acquiescence in continuous unhappiness.

And now the party had become an entity and an event like a snowfall in a metropolitan city. Everyone had had enough to drink, just enough to make them amiable. Everyone shone. The charms of each human being sparkled like theatre marquees. The conversation seemed, in the warm subjectivity of choice spirits, to be as brilliant as Mozart. In some ways, the exchanges resembled a ballroom dance. In other ways, they were like the moment when the silent and everwondrous snow has overcome the great city and made a new thing of it, full of innocence, freshness, and unexpected marvels of whiteness.

The stories which were told were not lacking in malice, but the malice was gentle, it was apologized for, and it was introduced only because, as everyone knows, it is very difficult to be funny without attacking some other human being for whom one has, as a whole, some admiration and affection.

Frances Harris told the story of the Polish schoolgirl who, when asked what her religion was, replied that she was an antagonist.

"We are all antagonists," said Shenandoah to himself in easy despair, looking across the room at Oliver.

Wilhelmina looked at Shenandoah, saw his unhappiness, supposed that he had had an unfortunate conversation, and knowing Shenandoah, thought he must have said something utterly without tact.

"He always tells other human beings what he regards as the bitter truth about each one of them and then he is astonished that they get angry."

In another room, Grant Landis was making telephone calls without pause in an effort to secure signatures to a petition which protested against a suppression of civil liberties in the activity of labor leaders. His purpose was noble, but on the other hand he spoke in the same way, with the same intonations, giggles, and implications of intimacy to each of the different human beings, and this suggested that perhaps each of them existed for him only in a limited sense as a unique individuality.

Delia Jones was now free of the inhibitions which had tormented her so much. She had had four strong highballs. She began to look about at the men of the party whom she did not know and wonder what it would be like to have them make love to her. It is different with everyone, one of her female friends had told her. It is the same with everyone, Oliver had reported. Delia did not look at the men she already knew, deluded by the view that they had already decided against her, since she was not attractive enough.

Nicholas O'Neil remained outside of the zone of false or specious well-being. He still sat upon the bathroom rim and left only when someone else wanted to enter. This became more and more frequent as the drinking continued. Since Nicholas had had nothing to drink, he was alienated from the party in every sense. Finally he decided that it was useless to remain in the bathroom any longer, for he was discommoded so often by the tide of events. Hence he donned his wet socks and shoes again, returned to the living room, and looked with a critical eye at the happy people.

Wilhelmina regarded Shenandoah as he sat relaxed and thus free from the distortions of self-consciousness. He seemed almost attractive now, but not at other times, for he was so self-conscious that he was unable to sing with thousands when the Star-Spangled Banner was played at Madison Square Garden. Wilhelmina told the story of the labyrinthine bureaucracy of the Emergency Relief Bureau where she was employed. St. Francis himself, she explained, would be regarded as difficult by the Bureau, if he were on relief, because he gave food away to the birds.

Hearing Wilhelmina and suffering from echolalia and a banal association of ideas, Nicholas exclaimed:

"Jesus, Mary, and Joseph!" for the idea of St. Francis as unable to get relief in the Irish Catholic city of New York struck him as being as inconceivable as the Immaculate Conception.

Oliver Jones, disturbed more and more because he had hurt Shenandoah's feelings, tried to renew conversation with him. But Shenandoah was lost in the thought of how happy he might be, were he but able to believe in the divinity of Jesus Christ.

"God in a girl's womb! it is inconceivable," he said sadly and half-aloud.

Oliver, being unable to gain Shenandoah's attention, looked to see what Delia was doing. She was sitting next to Horatio Lapin, a limited person who came to parties only to drink. But Delia was not acquainted with this fact. At other and less decorous parties Horatio Lapin had often been accosted by young women of some beauty. He had looked at the young lady, scrutinized his drink, and then invariably decided to have another drink. It was less trouble.

Oliver knew that Delia might soon begin to behave amorously and conspicuously. He decided to do nothing, however.

"Let her have a good time," he said to himself warmly.

His eyes fell on the bookshelves and he saw a copy of *Axel's Castle* by Edmund Wilson. He drew down the book, brushed through the pages, and his eye and heart were caught by the following passage, which he arose and recited as if it were blank verse:

"It is at the death of Bergotte that Proust's narrator, in what is perhaps the noblest passage of the book, affirms the reality of those obligations, culminating in the obligation of the writer to do his work as it ought to be done, which seem to derive from 'some other world,' 'based on goodness, scrupulousness, sacrifice,' so little sanction can we recognize them as having in the uncertain and selfish world of humanity—those 'laws which we have obeyed because we have carried their precepts within us without knowing who inscribed them there—those laws to which we are brought by every profound exercise of the intelligence, and which are invisible—and are they really?—to fools'."

Oliver dropped his exalted tone of voice. He was in all truth devoted very much to the sentiments he had quoted, but he did not think that many others felt like that. Hence, after some hesitation, he made a remark which was intended to diminish or discount his allegiance to Proust's words:

"These noble sentiments," he said in a tone of unpleasant cleverness, "would be more becoming, if Proust had not been homosexual, dishonest, insincere, a snob, a literary politican, and a pet Jew."

Although some had been oppressed by the rapture with which Oliver recited the passage, all were offended by his facile cynicism and attack on Proust.

"He is the last one to cast the first stone," said Arthur to himself, "especially after writing that review."

"His overworked conscience," said Shenandoah to himself, "has just enjoyed some relief by spitting itself in the face."

In the other room, Grant Landis continued to devote himself to the making of phone calls which might help the lot of the jailed labor leaders.

In general, Oliver's cynicism was the end of the period of good feeling, which might have ended anyway because of the progress of the drinking.

Then the telephone pierced everyone's ears. Grant had ceased his calls for a moment in order to look up a number in the directory. As Arthur went to answer the phone, everyone forgot about Oliver's remark, though the sourness of the emotion remained like dregs.

Leon Berg was on the telephone. He was detested or disliked by everyone at the party because his chief activity was to explain to all authors that they were without talent. From what Arthur was saying in reply, it was clear that Leon wanted to come to the party, and had sufficiently downed his resentment at not being asked to the party to humiliate himself by asking if he might come.

At the party a discussion of Leon's character began, and in this discussion, the truth was used as a form of falsehood, since bias, like a squint, selected only his unpleasant and evil traits.

Meanwhile Leon left the room in which he lived and stopped to exchange a word with Claude Kagan, a minor poet who admired and feared him, impressed by the fact that he wrote nothing at all and condemned everyone, including Shakespeare. Leon told Claude where he was going and when Claude asked without much hope if he might come too, Leon replied that such an addition would be quite impossible. He then remarked quickly that all modern poets were worthless because they did not have the effect upon History of John L. Lewis and Bing Crosby, and concluded by saying that there would be no new world war because so many human beings expected a war and so many human beings had never been right about anything.

At the party the conversation continued to be a discussion of Leon, and Oliver revived the rumor that Leon's second name had been Bergson, shortened by him because he was unable to endure the rivalry between his own ambition and Bergson's fame. In fairness to Leon, some of his best stories were quoted, in particular the one about the man who visited the World's Fair and said that the one thing lacking, the one important thing, was a screamatorium, a place where everyone who wished might go to scream because of the quality of life in this period.

Leon was walking crosstown and losing his feeling of pleasure that he was going to the party. He stopped to have a drink, but this did not help him very much. Resentment mounted in him and he wondered if they were laughing at him because he had asked to come to the party. He decided that this was an untrue view inspired by his sense of persecution, but he was none too sure.

As these thoughts went through Leon like swords, Delia Jones at the party was going from one man to another, making amorous proposals which were regarded for the most part as efforts at wit.

"Who are you?" Delia cooed at the strange men, staring deeply into their eyes. Shenandoah, regarding this action from a distance, saw that Nicholas would be the next candidate, and then, fearing perhaps wrongly, that Nicholas might welcome the overture far too well, moved forward to prevent his friend. He tugged his sleeve and said as softly as possible:

"Don't be foolish, she's very drunk."

Since there was no immediate justification for the fear that Nicholas might welcome Delia, Nicholas turned on Shenandoah in silent fury.

Shenandoah's move was observed by Oliver and he was upset by it. He decided that something must be done. But he was afraid that an open scandal might occur.

"Who are you?" said Delia to Leon as the door opened on his face.

For a split second, Leon thought that he had rung the wrong bell. Then he saw Arthur, who had just opened the door and was standing at an angle to it. Leon was grossly taken aback. He had not counted on much of a reception, but he was so uncertain as to being welcome that this seemed to be a direct attack.

But all the wit and fury in him rose in inspiration.

"Who are *you?*" he cried back at Delia.

Her face fell. All looked, for Leon had spoken loudly. Two laughed. No one knew if Delia's consternation was the consequence of Leon's triumphant and leering face, or the result of her actually being unable to think of who she was.

Oliver saw the relaxation and defeat in her. He decided that this was the best moment to correct her or to send her home without an outbreak of recrimination. He drew her into one of the bedrooms and asked her to behave herself. Unfortunately he was unable to keep the irony in his mind from entering his voice, though he had tried to be gentle and reasonable in tone.

"Everyone feels as you do," he said foolishly, "there is no need for this self-indulgence."

Her hysteria became positive again.

"I am not self-indulgent, you are!" said Delia in overflowing hatred.

"All right, you are not, *I* am," said Oliver, "but please try in any case to behave yourself."

"Why?" screamed Delia in fury, "Why? Why should I behave myself? *What does it ever get me? Everyone is against me, anyway. No one cares for me and no one ever will.*"

Oliver agreed with her, but was unable to endure the shame of her screaming, audible all over.

"Why?" she continued to scream without adding any explanation.

"Behave yourself because I brought you here," said Oliver curtly.

"Why?" she screamed more loudly than ever.

"This is what I get for bringing you here, out of a misplaced sense of pity," said Oliver.

She slapped him in the face and said that she was going to kill herself. He held her arms and she struggled against him. Arthur entered.

"Come now," he said in a friendly way which Delia misunderstood, "everything will be all right."

"Who asked you to come in here?" she said screaming again.

"After all, I live here," said Arthur, astounded by her attack. Delia broke loose from Oliver's hold and slapped Arthur, who now regretted profoundly his entrance, as well as what he had just said.

And then Frances came into the room with a cold compress for Delia. Frances had been kind to Delia, and Delia felt that at last she had an ally.

"Go away," said Frances to Oliver, and Arthur.

"You are my friend," said Delia to Frances, weeping and once more limp. And thus, after a time, Frances succeeded in quieting Delia, who became very ashamed, although Frances sought to assure her that no one regarded her behavior as anything but an attack of illness.

Meanwhile the unseen scene was discussed in the living room. And then Wilhelmina noticed that they had not marked the moment of the New Year, when the party horns are blown, whistles peal, everyone kisses, and sings "Auld Lang Syne." The radio was playing that they might know the exact moment of passage and unbearable beauty. But Delia's screaming had made them unaware of everything else.

They all went to the window to make sure that it was already the New Year; and they saw that the rain had turned into snow, the most beautiful of all the illusions of the natural world. Yes, it was 1938. How strange that it should be 1938, how strange seemed the word and the fact.

No one knew that this was to be the infamous year of the Munich Pact, but everyone knew that soon there would be a new world war because only a few unimportant or powerless people believed in God or in the necessity of a just society sufficiently to be willing to give anything dear for it.

As Shenandoah, Nicholas, and Wilhelmina parted in emptiness and depression, Shenandoah was already locked in what was
soon to be a post-Munich sensibility: complete hopelessness of
perception and feeling.

"Some other world," he said to himself, "some world of goodness; some other life; some life where the nobility we admire is
lived; some life in which those who have dedicated their being
to the examination of consciousness live by the laws they face at
every turn."

"What are you babbling about?" said Wilhelmina.

"I am sorry for the whole world, said Sadie Thompson," was
Shenandoah's reply. But he knew well enough that he was chiefly
sorry for himself. But he shrewdly decided not to admit this to
Nicholas and Wilhelmina.

"I wish I had not come," said Wilhelmina, "I will never have
any children."

"I won't marry you, unless we are going to have children," said
Shenandoah stupidly.

"I don't want to marry you," said Wilhelmina.

"I wish everyone would drop dead," said Nicholas as they descended into the subway.

"*Why?*" asked Shenandoah.

"Who are *you?*" replied Nicholas, deciding to have nothing
further to do with Shenandoah and going home by himself.

THE COMMENCEMENT DAY
ADDRESS

It was truly a perfect day for such an occasion, even for the events which later took place, for the day too was fitly transformed at the proper time. Large florid clouds, scalloped or foamy at their edges, calmly sailed the sky and merely emphasized the sky's serene dominion, while the foliage about the campus fluttered mildly in the silken breeze. The campus itself was deformed by the rows of temporary wooden seats, by the speaker's platform, and mostly by the grandstand, a temporary construction also, where the graduating students had to be seated because there were so many. Yet the grave buildings which guarded the campus protected the scene from such insinuations of a garden party as might have been caused by the summery gowns and parasols of the ladies. Everything was as expected; nothing more could have been asked of the June afternoon.

The Commencement Day Address was to be given by a speaker substituted at the last moment because of the sudden illness of the first choice. This substitute speaker was Dr. Isaac Duspenser, who had recently become famous, after a lifetime of obscurity, for his "History of the United States," in eight volumes. He was, it seemed, a curious character, having astounded the reporters who interviewed him upon his great successes with many extremely cynical or passionate remarks which made good copy and were widely publicized. It was this newspaper fame which had gained him the invitation to speak, for the President was always interested in publicity and knew that the metropolitan reporters would pay more attention to this commencement with such a speaker present, especially because the university was itself in the metropolitan area.

Having been introduced, the chubby, round-shouldered old man (resembling Clemenceau or Whitehead in old age) began to speak:

"No one," he began, "will forget this occasion. So complex, so moving, so much of these times, it may lapse from your attention, but will stay in your consciousness, like a tinge of ill-health, part of the underworld in which we really exist."

What astonishing presumption, thought everyone, and as we did so, the old man plainly giggled, to astonish us even more.

"You lovely boys and girls, or, if you will, ladies and gentlemen, gaze today toward the invisible flower of the future. That is why I shall speak to you about the past."

Someone tittered. He went on: "How shall I interest you? How shall I interest you in the past which is so much of the future? I know what interests you usually. If I am witty or if I am salacious or if I tell riddles, you will listen to me, and give me your wanton attention. A jokebook or blackout or conundrum, such are the staples of your attention. Well! believe me when I say that I have come to speak to you in the guise of a travelling salesman!"

The audience laughed frankly, very much intrigued.

"I have spent my days in taking time seriously. Now, as you see, it has taken me—seriously!" and he extended a wrinkled hand, as if to show his age. The titters recurred.

"A travelling salesman indeed! For I intend to sell you my idea of time. Have any of you thought seriously of time? I know you have not. It would be well, then, to begin with your ignorance, for there are many things, such as the air we breathe, with which we are well acquainted and yet of which we are ignorant.

"Such an occasion was the August evening of 1897, in Cincinnati, Ohio. My two friends and myself were drinking beer, long past midnight, in a restaurant's open air garden near the banks of the Ohio. Everyone had left, but one couple holding hands and very sad; the waiters, who wished we would go too, were extinguishing the Japanese lanterns and cleaning up. One of my friends said, in the warmth of his mild intoxication: 'All men are my brothers'; 'All men are my fathers,' I said, merely by way of rhyming and for the poor joke, which the other friend took up, saying: 'All men are my sisters,' and we all laughed happily, so that he said again: 'All men are my sisters,' and then I knew what time was: 'This is no joke,' I said, trying to stop their laughter, 'All men are my fathers!' Think now! Each of you carries in his heavy breast a stupendous weight, the generations of men!"

The audience was profoundly shocked by the speaker's extreme transition; a bomb could have exploded without disturbance, so rapt was our attention.

"Last night, in my hotel room near Broadway, I went to bed early, wishing to think of what I am now to say. In my naked bed, in Plato's cave, I watched reflected headlights slide the wall. What rules History? I asked myself, as I have, again and again, through the examined nights of my existence. Everyone knows that History has many causes, efficient causes such as great men, kings, heroes and philosophers, material causes such as climate and geography, final causes such as Progress, the Kingdom of Heaven on Earth, the classless society, and lastly formal causes, human nature, the relations of production, dialectic."

Here a fit of coughing took the old man, and while he composed himself conversation sprung up all over. Everyone felt that the promise of the first moments of his speech was not going to be fulfilled, but a tedious discourse, as indicated in what he had just said, was under way.

"Which of these causes is most important? I have asked myself that question many years. Is one of them the most important one? And often the problem has seemed as enigmatic as the blue sky overhead."

"Seeking this first mover of time, an incredible number of my nights have been sleepless. And always, between sleeping and waking, while the rain beat and the wind troubled the window curtains all night long, I could always hear carpenters hammering nails in repeatedly below the window. Always, then, I would watch the unreal gray of morning melt softly in, seeping into and fathoming the fallacy of night, lifting the clothes on the chair from underseas, kindling the mirror on the wall. Still unable to sleep, I would always hear the milkman's chop-chop, hear him striving up the stair, hear his bottle's chink; and I would rise from bed, light a cigarette, go to the window and observe the street lamp's vigil and the horse's patience. And always, going back to bed, I would hear a fleet of trucks straining uphill, grinding in second gear, and I would be sure that their freights were hooded by tarpaulin. This has happened many nights for many years, the travail of early morning, the rumors of building and movement, the mystery of waking with the same self, always, always, from the ashes of sleep the phoenix with eight hundred thousand memories!"

By now the audience was completely mystified, for the old man had gradually adopted a tone of the utmost tenderness, and it even seemed that he was moved to tears, for he hauled out an enormous handkerchief bordered with black, and dabbed at his eyes.

"What was I but a sleepwalker?" he suddenly cried out, and the audience laughed frankly again, relieved that he had abandoned his embarrassing intimacy. And now the President of the university arose and asked in his official voice, loudly, so that we all might hear, whether or not Dr. Duspenser was ill. "I am not, I am not!" he replied, seeming to brush the President aside like an interloper.

"No! I understand now, I am no longer blind, and I intend to tell you what I know.

"Some say that History is ruled by the lonely men who, in their cells, conceive the ideas whose beauty and lure is so great that societies are newly formed and reformed. Thus it is said that everything which exists was first an idea in some intellect: the discovery of America was an idea in the mind of Columbus.

"Others say that History is ruled by the different ways in which goods are made. *How*, by hand, or by machine, *by whom*, by the guildsman or by the wage-laborer, and *for whom*, the lord of the manor or the millionaire, how, by whom, and for whom, foodstuffs, clothes, and instruments are made, this, this structure is said to be the prime mover of History. Thus the discovery of America took place because a trade route to the Indies was required.

"Both of these versions are right, *in a way*. They are two sides of the truth, which is terrifying. I, an old man, must utter this truth, terrifying because so precarious, so dangerous, to you, who are children."

Part of the audience found this tedious, part found this fascinating.

"For many years, on a birthday, on an anniversary, on New Year's Eve perhaps, in the midst of celebration, suddenly and without effort, recognition has come, and I have understood what has given my existence its color, its motive, and its pain. Then, in horror, I have felt as if I had been asleep for years, while my existence happened to me, and had awakened, but only for a moment, and must soon sleep once more, a remorseful Van Winkle. This emotion is like that of the husband who discovers his wife's inconceivable adultery. It is the sentiment of having lost one's will and fallen, will-less, in the middle of traffic. It is the terror I have often known looking from some 57th story down to the street below, the miniature avenue hastening to and fro in complete irrelevance."

He paused once more, drawing out his handkerchief and wiping his brow. A hum rose through that portion of the audience which was composed of parents and visitors. The graduating students in their grandstand were not listening. An airplane gnawed overhead, bare, abstract and geometrical in the cloud-flowered sky; and its tone accented the passage of the afternoon. One listener had a firm sense of the narrow metropolitan city, its ribs bound by deep, narrow rivers, narrow on all sides, narrow in its tall towers, full of thousands of drugstores and apartment houses, full of thousands of narrow avenues, all of which stood in back of the idyllic campus scene and showed its falsity.

"What, then, is the ruler of History? Think of the first morning of American History. For weeks, Columbus has been haunted by premonitions. 'We dreamed of a nightingale, singing,' he says; and on October 9th, 'All night heard birds passing,' and then, at last, land. But why had he come? What after all was the reason underneath of his arbitrary and perilous ambition: Gold, gold, gold! Not gold the metal, but that gold which was what he regarded as valuable above all other things, the gold of the drawn desire in his heart. And from the very outset, there was an exchange of goods: 'I presented the natives with some red caps, and strings of beads to wear upon the neck, and many other trifles of small value, wherewith they were very much delighted, and became wonderfully attached to us.' What could be more natural, since all voyages travel like arrows towards that which seems to be valuable."

Those who still listened grew more and more amazed at the speaker's obscurity and the unmistakable passion of his speech. And now the day was shadowed, for the sky had clouded over and darkened. A cool quiet slipped upon the campus, and the audience looked about with concern.

"Columbus looks about and sees everywhere that which is regarded as valuable. He sees trees on the shore: 'These groves, the most beautiful I have seen in my life, have abundant springs of sweet water, and trees of a thousand kinds, so lofty that they seem to reach the sky. And I am assured that they never lose their foliage; as may be imagined, since I saw them as green and as beautiful as they are in Spain during May. And the nightingale was singing, and other birds of a thousand kinds, in the month of November.' But he has one other preoccupation, and asks: 'Are there gold mines in this island?' An incalculable amount of gold, they tell him, which he repeats to Luis de San Angel, and to their

Spanish Majesties. 'This is a land to be desired, and once seen, never to be relinquished,' because, he says, there is so much gold here, which the natives surrender for worthless fragments, 'fragments of broken platters, pieces of broken glass, and stray buckles.' Let us, then, not deceive ourselves. Columbus came for gold, and History moves towards whatever is supposed, by the heart of man from time to time, to be gold.

"The ruler of History is the thick-grained working heart longing for one kind of money or another. History moves in a direction desired, sometimes chosen! in the direction desired or chosen by the heart sensitive, sensitive to many goods, some goods, or too few! It was what was desired that moved medieval Europe to the Holy Land; it was what was desired that created the machine in the West, not the East, where they desired something else. The anxious care in the rising and falling breast, the anxious care under sleep, beneath what we say, below the watching mind, focusing itself upon some money, which comes to seem the sum of good, fashions the misshapen form of the societies of men. I see all History as a lovesick boy fumbling his sex in the darkness."

The President hurried forward: "I must beg you to restrain yourself, Dr. Duspenser! There are ladies present." The audience was dumbfounded, an enormous hubbub spreading. It looked for a moment as if some would rise and answer the speaker, or booing would break out. But the old man went on:

"Some want enough to eat and a small garden. Some want to sit by the fire and read long novels. Some want to swim the English Channel. Some long for an estate in the country and the deference of servants. Some wish to drive automobiles at enormous speeds. Some dream of Japanese prints and delicate girls. Some desire the poise of the acrobat and the assumed egotism of the millionaire. Some dream of ecstasy with a chorus girl or courtesy among the well-bred or a racing stable. Some care only for good tobacco."

The audience did not readily adjust itself to this sequence, and there were mutters of disapproval.

"Some care for animals, some think of the other world, some study Kant. Some wish to understand. Some carve soap sculpture, some dream of the Middle Ages. Some would be learned, some would be generous, some would be dignified, some would be witty. Some seek an unborn son and some a father ten years gone. Some would like to have attention paid to them, some merely wish to be allowed to stay. Some are proud of their first editions, some are proud of their gold teeth, for teeth are nearer the ego. Some are drunk, some are ill, some are without hope, but none without desire for goods, because that is the mover of time. Some merely wish to go to sleep.

"All spend much time before the looking glass. All are afraid of death. All can be hurt by laughter because the self is a wound. The greatest terror, the greatest abomination, is the death of the will which desires and chooses. All go their separate identical ways led by the longing in the obsessed, obscene heart."

A storm was definitely threatening, to judge by the darkened sky and the chill which ran the campus.

"But why do I trouble to tell you this? You are not interested, this does not concern you, you would prefer to be doing something full of immediate enjoyment, such as eating. Why, then, do I take the trouble?"

But the old man had gone too far. An angry young man, apparently one of the instructors, arose, looking like a camera in his cap and gown:

"You're a tired old man and an intellectual exhibitionist. There is such a thing as propriety and you have violated it, insulting the ladies present. And the learning which we work hard for, studying, weighing, checking, criticizing, you pretend to proclaim, with a few half-truths, many commonplaces, and several melodramatic courses."

"My poor boy," the old man replied, "did you envy the bright one capable of recitations at the birthday party? did you resent the drum major at the dress parade? do you often seek anonymity at the theatre? Must *I, too*, pay for your childhood?"

This did not mean very much to the audience, but the protestant seemed disturbed, and the old man seemed to regard this as a sensational retort.

"Whatever my reason for speaking thus to you (and I have just mentioned the place where it is to be found), I will now remind you of *your* reason for listening to me and trying to understand me.

"You, as you sit here and listen, are going on in time. From minute to minute your existence is falling away from your breathing side. For your existence is, in a way, a finite totality which can be computed. There are 60 minutes to an hour, 24 hours to a day, 365 days to a year, and perhaps 70 years to an existence. You are very well aware of all this. But have any of you ever stopped to think that this gives you a mere 36,792,000 minutes in which to exist, a sum which is melting away as I speak, like ice under a terrible sun!"

The audience took this as amusing.

"What you do with your time is not wholly your choice, for you are only half-free, and not at all free so long as the movie of night surrounds your head. For even when you are no longer in ignorance you are half the serf of the time and place in which you live, which is History.

"But inasmuch as you have choice, think now! Is it wise to spend Sunday afternoon lost in the *New York Times*, considering politics in the Balkans, the major league batting and the letters to the editor? Is it just to regard so highly your vacation in Bermuda, your diversion, three times a week, at the neighborhood cinema, your amusement at contract bridge? Is it proper to spend your treasure of time in the revery of a fine cigar, in discussing politics with the barber, in shooting for double or nothing with the tobacconist? Is it really best to buy sleep at the drugstore, evade work with a novel, enjoy grandeur at the band concert, gain integration with tobacco, and Asia upon the screen? Is this wise, is this just, is this proper, is this, above all, thrifty?"

A few fat drops of rain fell, but the storm had not yet arrived.

"No! you will learn nothing from what I say. But I have regarded the sky, which is a grave blue crystal, and I suppose that I have seen the time to come.

"This is the time after the wars and revolution. The proletariat has won its just dominion, God be thanked. The age of plenty has arrived: everything is streamlined, everyone is comfortable, everyone has enough. Medical science has prolonged existence and afforded us the most precise control of the body.

"Now all interests have become aesthetic. Ethics and aesthetics have identified, and the highest learning is aesthetic. Ceremony and ritual occupy everyone: such virtues as self-denial, chastity and charity have been replaced by wit, skill at ballet dancing, *savoir faire*. Self-control and patience remain virtues, however, because they are necessary to the profound ballet in which every human activity takes place. Etiquette is of infinite detail, and there are delicate codes for every act from morning to night. All problems, too, are aesthetic. The reigning school of philosophy, whose ideas have permeated even the cinema and the daily newspaper, has long since convinced everyone that only that is meaningful which can be reduced to sentences about time and place: thus all problems are soluble or without meaning. Cooking has become a major art, and everyone is a gourmet. All conversation is versified, and the popular taste prefers rhymes with feminine endings. There is no interest in the past, although a school of comic dramatists has attempted to use history as the source of the naive and ludicrous.

"But what a priceless enlightenment dialectic affords this society. Everyone now becomes infinitely bored. The listlessness of the populace is followed by the greatest indifference on the part of the administration. Suicide waves of increasing frequency occur. No one wishes to do anything about this; the few who are troubled are accused of supposing that an objective morality exists. Soon this society faces death as a whole: only then do many awaken. What a marvelous dialectical ordeal this is! Who would say that it is not best to have its experience, once freed of the present economic hell which is infinitely worse and also threatens us with death?"

A student arose in the grandstand and began to speak with great passion:

"You're a tired old man, who would like peace. Whether you know it or not, you are merely attempting to provide one more intellectual justification for a dictatorship in which the present structure of society is maintained by force and repression!"

"Wait!", the old man replied, "hear me to the end. Then you will see how untrue what you say of me is. But only if you try to understand me."

The rain began in earnest now. Drops spat and pelted; in the West lightning defined itself like a set of nerves; soft mutters of thunder arrived, and the audience looked about in dismay. The President arose and said: "I fear, Dr. Duspenser, that we will have to terminate your address at this point because of the weather. We have all listened with great interest, and, I am sure, great profit" (a polite deal of applause fell, as the audience began to move).

"No!" said the old man, "wait!"; the exodus ceased immediately, some seated themselves again. The rain too seemed to soften and slow down its patter. "I have not finished. Do me the courtesy of remaining until I have concluded my idle remarks," he said, bitterly. A tall and spinsterish woman was tugging at the old man's sleeve, as lightning darted in broken branches towards the Western sky.

"I have come, as I said, as a travelling salesman, and I still have several things to sell you." He lifted up a big suitcase to his speaker's stand, and drew forth, to our final astonishment, a machine gun, what seemed to be a slice of bread, and something smaller.

"Here is a machine gun, a piece of bread and butter, and a bar of chocolate, all of fine quality. As a matter of fact, I obtained them quite cheaply and can let you have them for very little. Think now! regard your own heart and mind. How much will you give me for this darling machine gun, a substitute for the barber and the hangman, capable of making anyone serious? Bread and butter too, how much is that worth to you, is there indeed a limit to the price you would pay for it? A bar of chocolate, full of immediate pleasure, a dainty thing, the aesthetic thing, without responsibility! You there!" he said, pointing to a student in the grandstand, "What price would you be willing to pay for a bar of chocolate? How much?"

The student, at first embarrassed, replied: "No sale!" and everyone laughed in great relief at this pleasant note.

Then the old man drew forth an oval looking glass. "I cannot understand your conduct, Dr. Duspenser," said the President, stepping up again. "I cannot understand yours," the old man shouted back, and the amazed audience laughed nervously. And the rain's fury came, lightning jetting the sky, and rolling thunder, riding immediately afterward. And now the old man held the looking glass before him, as if coquettishly tidying his hair.

"Ah!" he said, "How much will you pay for *this*, this wonderful thing which gives you back yourself? How much? How much do you care for yourself as seen?"

Some student called out: "Fourteen Confederate dollars!" and the audience giggled, once more relieved. The old man paused, as if trying to control irresistible anger. The audience was by this time entirely fascinated, although the rain continued.

"But a looking glass is dangerous. It is a menace about the house, and the dog does not know enough to watch it. You might really see yourself in it, although all the lies in your dirty hearts will usually protect you. You might really surprise yourself one day and see how hideous you are. Or the children! the children might see you as you watched yourself in the mirror and recognize that your eyes are focused on excrement!"

"This is obscene and intolerable," the President cried out, and then, making himself more ridiculous, blew his whistle, a flute-tone, to summon the campus police.

"You have eaten what pigs eat, you have existed on that by which pigs exist, until now an old man looks with terrorized eyes at the society in which he must live and die. You are beyond insult. I rise like Isaiah, saying, *Ye are confounded for the gardens ye have chosen!* History is moral through and through! Everything has its price!"

Lightning darted in great broken branches to the West. The campus police came upon the platform and led a weeping old man from the campus. The middle-aged daughter who had attempted to stop her father before was now trying to explain to the President that her father had been ill for some time and was scarcely responsible for what he said, but had insisted on accepting the college's invitation. The audience moved out, exhausted, puzzled, and wet, speaking from all possible standpoints of the historian's derangements. One had a returning sense of the metropolitan city, narrow and tall on all sides, full of traffic, accident, commerce and adultery, of a thousand drugstores, apartment houses and theatres, its belly veined with black subways, its towers and bridges grand, numb, and without meaning.

Meanwhile the mouse-gray evening entered imperceptibly above the street lamps going on and the sizzle of the taxis' tires on the wet avenue.

THE TRACK MEET

My only other encounter with the problem of showing a visiting Englishman the sights had been very jolly, you might say, although full of minor and trivial complexities. This first visitor was a chap named Edwin Reynolds, and he found anything and everything in American life fascinating. Indeed, he enjoyed and was excited by everything so much that he thought he understood everything, too—as if excitement were insight. In the course of showing him around, I suggested that we go to a baseball game, since it was a purely American phenomenon, and he was delighted. We went to see two excellent minor league teams play a double-header. As we were going down the runway to the inside of the stadium, he said that he did not know the rules of baseball, so I explained them briefly, moving through the turnstiles, looking for good seats along the third base foul line.

"The pitcher," I said, "is trying to get the ball past the batter. The batter is going to try to hit the ball between the infielders, or over their heads, or between the outfielders, or over their heads, or bouncing in front of them. If he can hit the ball over their heads and into the stands, it's just plain wonderful and known as a home run, or a homer for short." I saw that we had to hurry, because the game was going to begin very soon; the pitcher for the home team was already on the mound and making his last few warmup throws to the catcher. "The infielders are trying to get hold of the ball and throw it to first base before the batter gets to first base. The outfielders are trying to catch the ball before it bounces, or if it does bounce, to get to it, and throw it back to the infield as soon as possible."

"What about that chap with the mask on his face?" Edwin asked. "And the peculiar jacket or what have you?"

"Oh, the chest protector," I answered. "That's the catcher. He wears the mask and chest protector because the ball may hit him hard and injure him. He is trying to catch the ball if the batter misses it or lets it go by, and he is also trying to tell the pitcher how to throw the ball so that the batter will have a hard time hitting it well—not hitting it so hard or so far that the infielders will be unable to get it and the outfielders will be unable to catch it."

I must say, I was rather pleased with my elucidation at first, and it took a little time for me to perceive how numerous were the shortcomings and omissions. However, I took care of them one by one as the game continued, and by the seventh inning practically everything was cleared up except for two somewhat important points. The first was the double play. For a time, it seemed that this would remain for Edwin a mystery, involving what might even be called antinomy; for he found a contradiction in the fact that if a man was on first, the infielder had only to touch the second sack to put him out, but if the batter hit a ball to the outfield, rounded first, and tried to make it a double, then the infielder had to tag him out. Edwin thought it rather unfair that he should have to tag the runner in the second instance but in the first only had to touch second base. Finally, I said to him that this was one of the rules of the game, and light shone immediately in the darkness. I still don't know why this was so utterly and quickly illuminating, except that perhaps if anything is a rule, and, moreover, a rule of the game, it is as lucid to an Englishman as trial by jury. However, this did not entirely dispose of the difficulty, for Edwin had no little trouble understanding why a base runner must tag up before running if a fly ball is caught but is allowed to run if the ball is not going to be caught. This, too, seemed unfair to him; so, after other attempts had proved vain, I just said that it was one of the rules of the game, and that settled that. Lastly, Edwin would not believe that the game was played with passionate seriousness by the players and regarded with equal seriousness by the specta- tors. He thought that the roar of the crowd and the booing at the umpire was either a kind of ritual or the fulfillment of an obliga- tion. Nothing I said dissuaded him, and it was useless here to invoke the rules of the game, for he mistook emotions for rules.

As we left the ballpark, moving among disgruntled and down- cast fans (the home team had been beaten), Edwin declared that it had been a most refreshing and charming experience, and "quite typically American."

Because he was the kind of person he was, his gazing politely at America was very pleasant, and interesting, in a mild way, and did not bring about any emotional strain. Thus I was not at all prepared for what happened when I was visited a second time by a touring Englishman. However, it is difficult, if not impossible, to conceive of how anything would have served to prepare me and help me to behave with propriety and dignity during the painful incidents that occurred during this second visit. Perhaps if I had been sent to a concentration camp, or if I had lived my childhood and adolescence in a jungle, I would have been less innocent and better prepared; but perhaps not.

The visit was curious from the very beginning. The doorbell of my apartment woke me up. I did not want to answer, but the ringing was persistent, and it stopped but started again, as if my visitor had paused to make sure he was ringing the right bell.

I answered at last, annoyed and feeling sure that this was the only way to stop the ringing. It was just six, and although it was spring, a chill drizzle was falling. I heard the little dripping and the sliding sound of a passing car. And when I opened the door, my visitor told me that his name was Reginald Law, and I asked him to come in. He did not apologize for his persistent ringing.

He sat himself down in an armchair and explained that a mutual friend whom he had encountered in Japan had suggested he look me up when he came to New York. The mutual friend was Hippocrates Pappas, and I was astonished to hear that he had been to Japan, for he was the kind of person who did not even like to leave his house. But perhaps during the war....

Reginald Law did not respond to my effort to make conversation by discussing the friend we had in common. I thought I recognized in him a type—the kind of person who makes no effort to sustain a conversation and who appears to be not at all disturbed by the painful silence that occurs when strangers meet and find that they have little or nothing to say to each other. In these circumstances, I have often said foolish, and indiscreet, or intimate, or tactless things, merely to revive conversation, being made panicky by painful silences and feeling wrongly that the responsibility is always mine.

This time, I decided immediately that the responsibility was equally his and that I would not say anything, if he did not. We glanced at each other, and I thought he was regarding the fact that I was in my dressing gown and pajamas.

"You *are* Frank Lawrence?" he said at last.

I said that I was, and he told me that he had two tickets for a track meet, which was to begin in half an hour. I argued mildly with him that it couldn't start so early in the morning, and I had no desire to go to a track meet. It all seemed quite strange to me; it was as if I were dreaming. There was a curious lack of sequence in what had occurred since I had been awakened, although the cloudy spring light that appeared in the windows was real enough.

The telephone began to ring, and I was astonished again, for it was extraordinary for anyone to call me at that hour in the morning. I answered the telephone, which was in the bedroom, and heard the receiver at the other end being placed back on the hook. I thought, It must be that crank again.... I had been for the past year an editor of a new encyclopedia, and a hack who had been fired, after turning in several poor and inaccurate articles on subjects he knew worse than nothing about (he cribbed from older encyclopedias, and even his cribbing was mixed up, inaccurate, and disjointed), thought that I was the person who had been the cause of his losing his job. So he had called me at three o'clock in the morning, and attempted to hold a genial and intimate conversation, and when I told him I was trying to sleep, he wanted to know if I had a woman with me! I hung up in anger, and he kept calling, night after night, until at last I told him how unkind he was to wake me up at that hour, and he replied, "My hatred of you has turned to pity," but he had continued to call and then hang up without speaking. That was why I thought it was him again, although he had been silent during the past two weeks.

Anyway, I got dressed and decided to go with Reginald Law and see whatever there was to see. Outside in the street he hailed a cab, and then explained that he was travelling on an expense account.

"I say, do you mind if I call you Frank?" he said, as we sat back in the taxi.

"I wish you would," I answered, but I was struck again by how curious his behavior seemed. It was quite natural for an American to use my first name immediately, but it was not at all natural—at least to me—on the part of an Englishman.

We were soon at the high school stadium where the track meet was to take place, and again, when I saw the crowds entering the stadium, which looked like a small or diminished version of the Polo Grounds, I really thought that I must be dreaming.

I pinched myself as we went down the runway, and then I asked Reginald to shake hands with me. He did, raising his eyebrows, and his hand, slightly moist, was real, not imagined.

"Do you want to be sure that I don't have a gun or a knife up my sleeve?" he asked.

"I just want to be sure I am not dreaming!" I replied, troubled by the irony and dislike in his tone.

As we moved to our seats, I was sure that something was wrong, for I saw in the distance, in a box seat, my mother. What was she doing at a track meet? And I was displeased that she was present. I did not want to greet her, and I hoped that she would not see me.

Around the baseball diamond there was a cinder track, concentric with the stands, and with a starting line, hurdles, a finish line, and the like. And yet the field still seemed very much a baseball diamond and not a track.

An official who looked like a baseball umpire was firing a gun idly into the air. He's practicing, I thought, to start off the runners. But it occurred to me that this was not the kind of thing which required practice. All over the field, young men in track suits were jogging up and down, limbering up, stretching, and turning somersaults. The crowd, as it continued to increase, became more and more tense with excitement.

And then among the track men I saw my five brothers, Edward, Nicholas, Leopold, Alphonse, and Carolus. We had been named after the crowned heads of Europe (my own name was actually Franz Joseph, not Frank) and this not only affected us all very much but showed the infinite and foolish hope our parents fixed upon us. And I knew then that something must be wrong; something must be very wrong. If I was not dreaming, certainly I was in a state of hallucination, for this was not the real world.

"You see those young men jogging up and down near first base?" I said to my English visitor. "They are my brothers. We were named after the crowned heads of Europe." Now, if I am not dreaming, he will not reply, I told myself.

"Really?" said Reginald Law. "I was informed that you had no brothers, and were an only child."

What was I to make of this? I shrank from asking him who said that I was an only child, knowing that it might have been Hippocrates Pappas, who had often told me—but in a friendly way that kept me from becoming angry—that I was a hardheaded egotist. The idea seemed to amuse him; he seemed to think that I enjoyed being a hardheaded egotist.

I called out to my brothers, and they stopped, turned, and

looked at me and then looked blankly at each other, as if they did not recognize me, or as if I were some crackpot who was pretending to be a friend of the performers.

I yelled again, and they turned to look up at me again, but they just shrugged their shoulders. I thought of going down to the field and insisting that they speak to me, but then it occurred to me that perhaps this was some gag they'd thought up. One of them—it was Carolus—waved finally. It was the vague gesture one makes to a stranger.

"Everything happens to me," I said to Reginald Law, letting the sentence slip out before I knew what I had said, and then I was ashamed of myself.

"You're all right," said the reticent Englishman. "You're doing very well. As you Americans say, you have no kick coming."

"How do you know?" I said to him in anger. "What do *you* know about me?"

"I judge merely by your appearance," he answered. "You're looking very well."

"Appearing is not reality!" I shouted at him. "How do you know what is happening to my head, or beneath my shirt, in my pounding heart?"

And now I saw that my shouting had made people turn and look at me, among them my mother. She, too, looked at me coldly and without recognition; then she looked back at the field.

"I don't care," I said to myself. "What difference does it make, anyway?"

I shouted once again at Nicholas, whom we all called the Czar, and who had once been very devoted to me.

"Nicholas!" I shouted. "I am one of the Lawrence boys. I'm Frank. What is going on here, anyway? Why won't you say hello to me?"

He looked at me and then turned away, jogging.

"Hey, Nicholas!" I cried out, when I saw that he was not going to answer me. "You used to like me very much. When I die, you will be silent," I said desperately and passionately.

Silence except for the murmur and excitement of the crowd, munching peanuts and gazing avidly.

"Really, the advertisements are quite charming," said Reginald Law.

I looked at them. A billboard on the outfield wall advertised the overwhelming merits of an ale. A tarpon, swordfish, or some kind of fish leaped from the sea, as if to show his eagerness. A spiral of words declared the Purity, the Body, the Flavor in every glass.

"Look," I remarked idly, "fish don't drink beer. Or do they?"

Reginald Law ignored this facetious remark. I recognized the mood I was in, of trying to work off my uneasiness and shake off my nervousness by making poor jokes.

Another billboard boasted about a cigarette — "Travels the smoke further, further" (I did not know for sure what this meant) — and showed a smoker's fat and grinning face.

Still another billboard showed a scene at a masquerade party. A sad-looking, frowning young man was by himself in the foreground, dressed as a clown. His mask was up, and his face showed his humiliation. Behind his back, a girl dressed as a peasant was laughing at him, and a character attired in the red tights of Mephisto was holding a pitchfork toward our hero, and gloating and sneering. A foursome near the punch bowl, one wearing a horse's head as a mask, were also staring and laughing at him. The pretty girl was saying to Mephisto, "Maybe it's something he did not eat." Elsewhere, in neat paragraphs, the prose elucidated the theme: "It's nothing to clown about. Maybe that dull, logy feeling comes from a diet lacking in pep. Why not try America's super breakfast food?" The panacea for every form of melancholia and social failure, this matchless cereal is represented by a vivid box that ascends at the edge of the poster, while under it is a little poem which expresses incontestable insight: "LIFE IS SWELL — WHEN YOU KEEP WELL."

"At least it's not his teeth, his tooth powder, or his lack of an expensive automobile," I murmured.

Nearby, a poster showed a girl looking lasciviously at a man who had a well-combed head of hair. She was a very pretty girl, I thought, and dressed as if she were rich.

"A wise jury," I said to Law, "would convict her of fornication or adultery for a look like that."

"You make too much of these matters," he said in an offhand, deprecatory tone. "You are too serious. What difference does it make, anyway?"

"What difference does anything make?" I replied in irritation. "You can prove anything or doubt anything. Some people think that nothing exists, or that the earth is flat. Just try to prove to them that they are wrong."

I realized that I was jumping about foolishly, so I turned back to the billboards. The fact is that, to be honest about it, I knew very well how many of my comments were expressions of personal disappointment.

By the right field foul line was a big garish billboard that showed a young man standing in back of a beautiful young lady to whom he has just given a radio. She is smiling sweetly, her blond hair is set in an upswept hairdo, and she is wearing a low-cut gown. His right hand, as he stands behind her (his smile is an innuendo), is resting on her shoulder, and his fingers point down, as if he wanted to touch her breasts—as if he would soon touch them. In flowing letters the poster broadcasts the big phrase "My Own *Personal* Radio," and she holds her small set as if she were holding a little child.

"The radio draws upon the empyrean just like the oversoul," I remarked, "or am I wrong?"

"Righto," said Law.

"You know about Kierkegaard, don't you?" I asked.

"The Norwegian playwright?"

"You are thinking of Sibelius, the Lithuanian general. Kierkegaard is the George Washington of Denmark. At least, that's what he seems to be to the Danes I encounter in New York. They admire him very much as a national hero and never read anything he wrote, although he is just as entertaining as Bob Hope and perhaps more so. But anyway, what I wanted to tell you was this: he thinks there are three fundamental attitudes to existence—the aesthetic, the ethical, and the religious. Probably as good an illustration as any other would be a situation in which you wanted to kiss the wife of a friend. If you were aesthetic, you would kiss her without compunction, and like it very much. If you were ethical, you'd take a sedative, an aspirin, or a barbiturate, and, by thus pacifying yourself, free yourself from the desire to kiss another man's wife. If you were religious, you'd neither kiss the lady nor take the sedative!"

"Yes?" said Law. "At what point, if any, would the husband's feelings be considered, or the wife consulted? Look here," he continued, "these things are in the end a question of taste."

"Righto," I said. What was the use of talking to him? I did not know why he felt as he did, nor did I know why I said what I did. Meanwhile, one of the runners had jogged up to the last billboard and was kissing the handsome girl who had just been given a radio. He was kissing with the intensity of one who drinks water after five sets of tennis in July, his throat pulsing, his Adam's apple bobbing.

"How foolish," I said. "What good does that do him? The girl does not exist. And New York is full of real girls."

"Perhaps he prefers the poster image to the difficult actuality," said Law. "He cannot be rejected, and he does not have to take much trouble to win her favors."

"But that's ridiculous," I said, and then became silent, thinking that since everything was utterly ridiculous, it was pointless to harp on any one thing.

Two umpires were now firing pistols repeatedly. The sharp sounds were like thin pieces of wood being split.

The hundred-yard dash was about to begin, and ten runners crouched tensely at the starting line. Two of my brothers, Leopold and Carolus, were in the race, and appeared just as tense as the rest. The pistol cracked out, and they leaped forward, obsessed. As I had expected, Leopold and Carolus were very fast, and ran almost even with the first runner, a tall, gangling young man. As they came toward the tape, the first runner moved ahead, his legs kicking up at the knee, like pistons. But then Carolus threw himself forward and knocked the tall young man aside, making Leopold the winner of the hundred-yard dash.

The crowd rose to its feet and went wild, clapping and roaring as when, in the ninth inning, with two men out and the bases loaded, the home town slugger hits a homer, bringing his team from behind and winning the game with one powerful swing of his shoulders.

"That's nepotism," I said, rising to my feet to see what was happening. "I mean that's not fair—that's against the rules of the game."

"Nature is unfair," said Law, "and existence is also unfair. There is too much pointless pretense. That fellow who you seem to think is your brother behaved according to the dictates of his heart, clearly. Most human beings behave like that and don't admit it—not even to themselves."

As for me, I must admit my feelings were mixed; I was touched by Carolus's brotherly action, however unfair.

The amplifier in center field announced the winner and cited Carolus for conspicuous honesty and distinguished action, which struck me as a most curious choice of words.

Leopold, the winner, was led, like a horse, to the box where my mother was seated, and Carolus came with him. She congratulated Leopold, but she kissed Carolus fervently twice upon his cheek. "You have brought honor to the family," she said, and she looked tearful with pleasure and happiness.

Whether this is dream or hallucination, I said to myself, something is certainly wrong with me.

The drizzle had long since stopped, and now the sun was trying to break through the cold, cloudy light. Reginald Law bought two morning newspapers from a vendor of pop, peanuts, score cards, and other forms of reading matter.

He read the news to me in a soft, indifferent voice. A housewife had killed her husband after finding two letters from another woman in his pocket. He had given her a mink coat that cost five thousand dollars for her birthday two weeks before, but she had stabbed him to death with steak knives, recently purchased. The couple had two children, twelve and nine. The husband had been very devoted, the neighbors said.

"She shouldn't have done that," Reginald Law remarked. "Now he's dead. Is she better off now?"

He then read a story about a husband who had killed his wife, a bride of two months, because she had come home fifteen minutes late. Insane jealousy, the newspaper explained. "I killed her," the husband told the police. "Boy, how I loved that gal!"

Law's next choice was the story of a bus that had crashed through the railing of a canal bridge, drowning the sixteen children in it and the driver.

"Somewhat pointless," he said. "Don't you agree?"

He continued to read aloud. A Chicago schoolgirl had admitted that her accusation of rape was false. She had entered the youth's car willingly, she told the police captain. A girl in Massachusetts had committed suicide because she had no date for the weekend and had had none for four previous weekends. She had left a note which said that she was sorry for the trouble she had caused everyone. A faulty gas heater was responsible for the death of three persons in a suburban two-family house.

"You're making a selection," I said, "and it's extremely one-sided."

"Perhaps it is one-sided," he replied, "but these things did in fact occur. You would not be able to console any of the victims by telling them that what had occurred was not by any means representative."

He looked at me with a faint smile. Then he took from his pocket a small volume, which I saw was the *Book of Common Prayer*, and read aloud, but softly:

"Keep me as the apple of thine eye; hide me under the
    shadow of thy wings,
"… mine enemies compass me round about, to take away
    my soul.
"They are inclosed in their own fat, and their mouth spea-
    keth proud things.
"They lie waiting in our way on every side, watching to cast
    us down to the ground …"

The mile run—the feature event—was about to start, and I
saw that my five brothers were in a huddle, as if they were playing
football, near the starting line, and I wondered what underhand
trick they were planning now.

As the starter's gun cracked out, the crowd uttered a low roar.
A runner broke forward, ahead of the rest. I would have been surprised by what happened then, had I not exhausted the surprise
in me, for a very pretty girl dressed only in a bathing suit climbed
over the railing (low whistles accompanied her, but the runners
jogged patiently and indifferently, as if they did not see her) and
crossed the path of the pace setter and tried to stop him, and when
he would not stop, she hit him over the head with a pop bottle.

This action was received with a kind of studied applause—the
polite but vigorous handclapping the hometown crowd awards
the pitcher for the visiting team who has been shutting out the
home team.

"That kind of thing is the kind of thing which is not done," I
said to Law, using the phrase "is not done" in an effort to appeal
to the English mind.

"What makes you think so?" said Law, without turning his
eyes from the track.

"It spoils the game," I said weakly and without conviction.
"There is no contest if you do not play fairly. And the winner
does not feel pride but guilt."

"You are interested in platitudes," said Law, "but I am interested in reality."

The reality that interested him at that moment was the sight of the stricken runner stretched out on the grass of the infield and coming to consciousness as the pretty bathing suit girl kissed him with tenderness and sympathy. A moment after that, they were sprawled out on the grass.

"All the world loves a lover," I remarked, but Law paid no attention to my feeble essay at irony.

Meanwhile, the runners, who had been holding back were now moving forward with determined energy. I saw that my five brothers were among them and that they were close to each other, and I hoped that they would not try any tricks again. A spectator threw a pop bottle and hit one of the leading contestants on the head, and this time the applause was unanimous, full-throated, and full of conviction.

The race, as it came to the final quarter mile, had become a contest between seven runners, and I was struck by the fact that all five of my brothers were among them. Just then a fight broke out. Leopold hit Carolus, slapping him hard in the face, Edward turned and knocked Leopold flat with a quick left hook, Carolus kicked Edward in the groin, and when Leopold rose and tried to continue in the race (although he no longer had any chance of winning, barring more interventions), he was tripped up by Nicholas, who in turn was slapped hard by Alphonse, who had just stopped and watched until then, and who was himself knocked down by a hard blow to the head delivered by Edward. In a moment, they were mixed in a scrimmage, as if the runner had just been tackled in a football game, trying to break through the line, and the crowd was roaring and I stood up.

I told Law that I couldn't sit by when this family riot was going on, and started making my way down to the field. He followed me. The bell that marked the end of the mile run clanged, and some of the spectators rushed out to congratulate the winner and carry him on their shoulders, but he darted away from them like a clever halfback and kept on running, as if the race were not yet over. The crowd was very much moved and pleased by this, and they applauded him, but their applause turned to laughter as he continued in deadly seriousness and ever-increasing speed. At last, an official who looked like a senator or the governor of a state—florid, heavy, and histrionic—signalled with a limp hand to two policemen with rifles, and they raised their guns and shot the winner down.

I halted when I saw this. "I don't want to be killed," I said to myself, drawing back.

"Don't you want to join your brothers?" asked Law, for the boys were still struggling on the ground, kicking and punching, and straining to get up. "Don't you think you should?"

"No," I said, in answer to everything.

Five girls dressed as drum majors pranced forward, shaking their hips, and came to attention in front of the wrestling heap. The girls, who now looked like a chorus line in a musical comedy, drew forth pistols and shot my brothers to death, as if they were shooting horses with broken legs. The struggle subsided immediately, the boys collapsed like punctured balloons, and I was terrified, and started to run away. Law caught up with me, seized me by the shoulders, and punched me in the nose, knocking me down.

I cried out, "What have I ever done to *you?*"

At first he didn't answer. When he saw that I was going to get up and try to run away, he said to me that it would do no good, I would not get away, and I said to him that I knew this was just a dream, nothing more than a dream, and I was running away to awake into the ordinary day, and the little things and small actions of early morning, since this was just a dream, as he knew very well.

"What difference does it make if it is a dream or it is not a dream?" he said coldly and sternly as I burst into hysterical, grotesque, and unmanly tears. "It is worse for you—it is far worse for you if it *is* a dream. I should think that by this time you would know that."

He stood above me, glaring and looking as if he still intended to keep me from getting up from the ground where I sprawled. The dusk was growing above the empty stadium, and the cold sky looked like a distant lake ringed by black and leafless trees.

"How is it worse for me if it is a dream and only a dream?"

"I detest explanation," said Law. "Do you insist on one? Are you really sure that you don't understand?"

"I often feel that I know little or nothing," I said, in a pleading voice, fearful that I would soon awaken, and that the moment of awakening would occur just as he began to tell me what I wanted to know so much.

"The things I read you out of the paper were, if anything, more shocking than what has just occurred down there on the field. You don't escape from nightmare by waking up, you know. And if what occurred on the field were merely imaginary and unreal and merely your own private hallucination, then the evil that has terrified you is rooted in your own mind and heart. Like the rest of us," Law said scornfully, "you not only know more than you think you know but more than you are willing to admit. Look at yourself! *Just look at yourself!*"

I tried once more to stand up, and awoke, and found myself standing up, staring, in a sweat of confusion and dread, not at the sky but at the looking glass above the chest of drawers next to my dishevelled bed. The face I saw was livid and swollen with barbarous anger and unbearable shame.

THE CHILD IS THE MEANING
OF THIS LIFE

Samuel Hart was the youngest child in a family of four children. His father, who had been a strong ambitious man, died of overwork, that is to say, of trying with too much passion and intensity to become rich. At the time of his death his younger daughter, Sarah, was already married and his older daughter, Rebecca, had already begun a career as a designer of dresses. Leonard, the young man of the family and the third of the children, was studying to be a doctor and supporting himself by helping to run a cigar store at night. Thus the death of the father left the family intact as a family, especially since the mother Ruth Hart was a powerful human being who lived through her devotion to her children.

Samuel was a spoiled child and his mother felt that he was willful. But she felt that this was his nature and no one could change a person's nature. Being much younger than any of the other children, Samuel was also spoiled by his two sisters and his big brother Leonard. Thus one might say that if the fact of being the youngest child was the most important trait of his being, the fact that he had two older sisters and an older brother was also very important in him.

Samuel did not like to go to school and he did not like to work. He liked to hang out with the boys on the block and he was infatuated with games and with gambling. At school, the only subject in which he did well was mathematics, perhaps because his interest in gambling had made calculation interesting and important to him.

He wanted to quit high school because he did not succeed as a student, and though his brother Leonard sought to persuade him not to stop before he had finished, after a time his mother felt it was foolish to force a boy to study when he disliked school so much.

"He will never be a student, anyway," she said, "it is not his nature."

She was consoled by the brilliance of Leonard, a brilliance which did not, in fact, exist, for Leonard succeeded in getting from one step to the next step on the long journey to becoming a doctor only by deadening drudgery and forced striving, since he was like his father, intense, passionate, ambitious, and without imagination.

Samuel admired his brother and took pride in the fact that he was going to be a doctor as he took pride in his family as a whole, whenever pride was possible. And Samuel also admired Leonard because his mother loved Leonard so much. It was accepted in the family as a natural fact that the mother should love Leonard most of all. Perhaps the girls felt some resentment of this preference, but their resentment never became strong while on the other hand there had been a sharp obvious rivalry among the girls for the affection of the father.

Leonard was loved very much not only by his mother but also by his older sister Rebecca, for Rebecca in many ways, and especially in the depths where the emotions begin, followed her mother. Consequently Samuel was the pet of his sister as well as of his mother. The indulgence granted him was endless. One reason he did not like to go to school was that it was very difficult for him to get up in the morning, the result of his dislike of going to sleep or of coming home from his evenings with the boys. His mother became angry when he stayed out late, but hated to wake him up in the morning, and she did not become angry when he would not get up because as a mother she felt that sleep was very important to a boy's health. Leonard's health was delicate and she wished that he too would sleep late instead of getting up in the early morning to study just as his father had risen at five and waited impatiently for the time when his store would be open for business.

Sarah was somewhat critical of her mother's attitude to Samuel and she felt that a boy ought to have an education. But it was thought by the family that Sarah was too critical of everyone. When Sarah argued with her mother that she was spoiling Samuel by "waiting on him hand and foot," the mother merely became angry. She pointed out Leonard's habits as a justification of her belief that it was a question of a boy's innate nature, the character he had at the moment of birth.

"You are not a good mother," said Sarah, "it is not good to pamper a boy like that. What will become of him?"

"I want my children to be happy, that's enough," said Ruth Hart, angered by her daughter's criticism.

Sarah married Michael, a successful young man, when she was nineteen and departed from the bosom of the family, much to her brother Samuel's relief, for she was the only one who nagged him and tried to get him to behave himself. Soon after Sarah's marriage Samuel quit high school and took a job with a neighborhood storekeeper. But since this job required that he get up early in the morning, it was not long before the storekeeper decided that Samuel was, as he explained to one of the girls, "too unreliable." Samuel went from job to job and sooner or later his passion to be with the boys and to gamble made him lose the job. In fact, to the extreme shame of his family, Samuel gambled with the money he had collected for a newsdealer who delivered newspapers, and it was necessary for Rebecca to take money from her own salary and hush up the whole affair. Sarah remarked that Rebecca was permitting herself to be used when Samuel gambled with the funds of his employer a second time, and Rebecca defended herself by saying: "I suppose you want me to let him get sent to reform school. How would Mamma feel then?"

"He ought to be taught a lesson," said Sarah. But the only result of Sarah's criticism was a feeling of dislike on the part of Rebecca, her mother, and Samuel, who were united whenever the pride of the family was involved.

Two years after the death of the father occurred the most shocking event ever to affect the family circle: Leonard died suddenly, just after he had graduated from medical school. His mother was inconsolable and some thought that she might die too, so extraordinary was her grief. She had taken the death of her husband with the equanimity of a strong, courageous, and instinctive being, and she had resisted the efforts to persuade her to marry again. But the death of her son left her in a state of impenetrable silence and apathy.

"It's as if she had turned into a statue," Sarah reported to her husband six months after the death of Leonard. "She sits by herself in her room, looks at Leonard's picture, and sometimes tears roll down her face, but she never makes a sound."

By this time Sarah had had her first child and friends of the family suggested that Ruth's first grandchild might console her. Hence, Sarah made a habit of bringing the infant in his baby carriage to her mother's house. The little boy, who had been named after his grandfather, was rocked, fed, and diapered in front of his grandmother, who paid no attention to him, although his birth had pleased and excited her six months before Leonard's death. Sarah told her mother of the advice of friends of the family, for she was always one to suppose that explanation was the proper means of attaining any end.

"Mamma, Jasper will be just like Leonard," said Sarah, "you wait and see."

The mother regarded her daughter and her grandchild with an absent-minded politeness. She was too kind a person to resist these efforts at consolation and she was too kind to say how ridiculous it was to expect a mere infant to take the place of a grown man who had become a doctor.

"I would like to be alone," she said politely, and she said nothing when Sarah insisted that it was not good for her to be alone.

Leonard's death disturbed Samuel a good deal. He was fifteen years old at the time and he had been impressed but disturbed when family visitors had said to him, "Now you are the man of the family." The funeral was the most serious event of Samuel's life, and he behaved in a subdued and official way, but this did not prevent him from getting the evening paper when the family returned from the cemetery and studying the final scores in the major league pennant races. Actually Leonard's death made Samuel very much afraid, but he concealed his fear that he might die in early youth like his brother. He concealed his fear most of all from himself by means of his devotion to professional sports, major league baseball especially, which were not only the basis of much of his gambling with the other boys, but also as interesting to him as the ancient epics must have been to the classical world.

After Leonard's death, when his mother slowly took hold of herself and rose from her stony mourning, Samuel had his own way in all things. His mother spoiled him as never before, she was undisturbed when he lost or quit his jobs, and she never disturbed him when he slept late in the morning. She was particularly concerned about his meals, this was the one part of life about which she forced her own feelings, she insisted that Samuel eat well and she watched him eat with an intensity which was needless, since Samuel usually ate very well. He preferred sharp dishes, pickles, and delicatessen, and sweet dishes. It was for Samuel and not for Rebecca that his mother went down to the store in the cold early mornings of winter to get fresh rolls and coffee cake.

"This is rotten," Samuel said often of what his mother gave him, for he had come to expect to be pleased at every meal.

Meanwhile Rebecca, the good daughter and the one who supported her mother and her brother, went to business with two sandwiches and an apple in a brown paper bag, thus saving money. She gave most of her salary to her mother each week, and her mother put as much as possible in the bank, so that Rebecca would have a handsome dowry to give her husband.

When Samuel again and again gambled and lost the money he had collected, mother and daughter did not need to confer. Money was withdrawn from Rebecca's hard-earned savings, and without hesitation the money was returned to the rightful possessor.

"You support your brother as a gambler," said Sarah. "He is not even a good gambler. He always thinks he is going to win."

"It is my money," Rebecca replied. "I don't want to see Mamma miserable."

"Mamma is your weakness," said Sarah.

"Who is *your* weakness?" Rebecca replied. And it was true that Sarah was hard on everyone, especially hard on her husband, a difficult man in many ways.

But after this exchange, Sarah, insulted, sought out a motive for Rebecca's generosity. She decided that it was fear that when the proper husband came along for Rebecca, he would be repelled and perhaps driven off by the knowledge that the brother of the family was a scoundrel and a crook.

"That's true," said Rebecca when Sarah accused her of being thus motivated, "but that's not the only reason."

Rebecca then went to Samuel and told him what Sarah had said. "You see, not only do you make your mother miserable, but you make me look like a fool. Who ever heard of a sister who had to pay her brother's gambling debts to be sure that she would get a husband?"

"Why do you do it, if you don't want to?" asked Samuel, bemused in the abstract by his sister's behavior. And when Rebecca was enraged by this query, Samuel said that she was a crank and left the house.

Having arrived at early manhood, it was now possible for Samuel to get jobs in the garment district where his sister was employed and where he was liked by everyone. But these jobs also involved getting up early in the morning and when he was late to work day after day, he was fired, though not without a polite apology by the boss to Rebecca. Each time he was fired, Samuel lost his temper and told the boss what he thought of him, what a cheap skate he was; and he was sure that he was in the right. Only when his sister had to pay his debts did he become contrite for a time.

Sarah's marriage showed no sign of improvement, on the contrary everything became worse, as Michael became more successful. Michael allowed only one thing to interfere with his infidelities. He would come home in the evening to watch his infant son be fed and then departed again on some transparent pretext. Sarah's feeling of humiliation reached a new intensity when the husband of a girlhood friend saw Michael going into a downtown hotel when he was supposed to be in Pittsburgh on business. Hearing of this, Sarah went to her mother and said that she wanted to leave her husband and return to the household. Ruth Hart insisted that she stay with her husband. Rebecca entered the argument on her mother's side.

"Lots of women get used to that kind of behavior," said Rebecca. "No one thinks any less of you because Michael behaves like that."

It was more difficult for Sarah to take criticism from Rebecca than from anyone else. She turned to Rebecca and said:

"You'll see how you feel when your husband goes off for a week end with some cheap woman."

Samuel also admired Michael because he was a successful businessman.

Until he was twenty, Samuel showed no real interest in girls, and he did not seek them out, although when he was with the other boys he enjoyed the discussion of making love and made believe that he too had women on the string. When he was twenty, he was seduced by the stenographer in the office in which he worked. She was a girl of thirty who had been beguiled by her perception that Samuel was indeed innocent. Samuel had found the experience a strange one. It was not the exciting or overwhelming experience it was supposed to be, and he wondered that the boys made such a fuss about it. However, he took pride in the fact that the girl had gone after him, and he bragged to the boys of the gang about the occasion.

"I did not have to do a thing," he said, "it was handed to me on a silver platter."

"That's the way some girls are," said one of Samuel's friends, "they want to be like men, they want to start everything."

"Don't forget," said another interested young man, "some of them like them young. Samuel looks just like a big baby."

In his own mind Samuel compared the excitement of gambling, of playing poker or betting on a ball game, with the mild experience of love he had just known. When he bet on the outcome of a contest, he became very nervous, he waited impatiently for the results, he smoked cigars and was unable to sit down, and when he won he was penetrated by an extraordinary calm and joy, an emotion succeeded soon after by easy and imprudent spending. He did not win very often, but when he did, he bought himself what he considered the best shirts, neckties, and hats. The pleasure of entering a store and buying whatever he liked seemed like a kind of drunkenness.

Rebecca suggested in vain that when he won he ought to make some attempt to give her back the money he had taken from her. And then, seeing that he was not going to pay her back, she tried to persuade him to keep some of the money so that he would not be broke all the time.

"There must be something wrong with me," Samuel said to her on the occasions when it was necessary for him to be penitent. "I don't know what it is that makes me throw away money like that. I get the feeling that I am always going to win and that my luck has changed once and for all."

This feeling that he might some day break through and make a lot of money made Samuel declare that one day his sister would be repaid.

"You're going to get it all back," said Samuel, "every last nickel and with interest."

His mother continued to regard Samuel's behavior as unpleasant but inevitable. After all, there were many misfortunes which were far worse, and she thought that some day Samuel would change. It was foolish to expect too much from a young man, and there was little that could be done to alter a person's character or the nature of things. She became angry again with Sarah when Sarah, intervening as before, criticized Samuel; and when he told her to keep her big nose out of his affairs, Sarah, who would say anything when enraged, shouted.

"You were the one who should have died instead of your brother. Your brother was trying to make something of himself."

"Don't say that," said the mother sternly, for she felt that it was unfair, since it was not Samuel's fault that Leonard had died in early youth.

As the years passed and Rebecca did not find a husband, her mother became more and more troubled. And the unmarried state of her daughter disturbed her much more than Samuel's shiftlessness and gambling. At first it seemed that Rebecca was too particular, and there were friends of the family who felt that the success of Sarah's husband was the reason that Rebecca had so high a criterion of a suitable husband. There was no question but that an acute rivalry existed between the sisters, although curiously enough it was Sarah who suffered from it more than Rebecca. Yet perhaps it was not curious, for Rebecca had been her father's pet as a child and now it was clear that her mother preferred her to Sarah.

During the first World War, during prosperity, Rebecca's salary increased and by the end of the war she was made a designer by her employer, partly because he liked her very much, and partly because she was dependable, although uninspired. She had no genuine gift for design, but she was very good at following the fashions and imitating the inventions of other designers. As a designer, her salary was so high that the question of whom she would marry became more difficult, for she felt that she did not want to surrender her pay check of one hundred and fifty dollars a week merely for the sake of some struggling salesman who made perhaps a third of that amount. But her mother was impatient. Rebecca was already thirty and her mother became embarrassed when she heard of the marriages of other and younger girls. As a mother, Ruth Hart felt in the depths of her being, where the family life dictated her emotions, that it was utterly wrong that Rebecca should be unmarried.

"Don't worry, Mamma," said Rebecca, "the right man will come along one of these days."

Ruth Hart, however, did not depend upon this belief, and she studiously saved as much money as possible from Rebecca's salary so that the right man would be tempted by the money Rebecca had to give him. Rebecca obeyed her mother in all things, but she pointed out to her that many girls married with out giving any money to their husbands.

"This is America, Mamma," said Rebecca. "You left Europe twenty-five years ago, but you think about everything as if you were still a girl in Europe."

"Money is money," said her mother, "it is just as important in America as Europe."

Rebecca was fairly content and she joked about being an old maid. But her mother's will prevailed. It was decided that if an investment were made in a better apartment and in better furniture, if mother, daughter, and son moved to a better neighborhood, Rebecca's chances would improve. When these shifts had been accomplished, it was decided that Samuel's name was vulgar and that it might be a good idea to call him Seymour. This was Rebecca's idea, and Samuel was indifferent.

"You can call me whatever you want," he announced, "but it will take some time before Mamma calls me anything but Sammy."

The shift from Samuel to Seymour took years to complete, but Seymour went forth to a new job with his new name and for a time it seemed that the new name might mark the beginning of a new life for him. He was given a job by a real estate dealer who admired his mother and his sister, and he went to work promptly each morning to collect the rents and the installments on real estate purchases which constituted this business. He played poker on Saturday nights, but his luck was good for a time. But this reform lasted only until the end of winter and the beginning of the baseball season. Three months of good behavior made Seymour think that his luck had changed. He went to the opening game of the National League pennant race and bet the money he had collected that morning on the team he wanted to win. Thus he lost more than he had ever lost before, and once again the money had to be made good from Rebecca's bank account.

"How did I know I was going to lose?" he said to Rebecca when she told him that he must stop being dishonest. Seymour believed that since he was sure he was going to win, he had not been dishonest in betting his employer's money.

"You will always lose," said Rebecca, "can't you understand that? You're not the type of person who makes a good gambler."

This seemed an irrational argument to Seymour. After all, he might have won the bet.

"I can't lose all the time," he said with some meekness, knowing that as soon as Rebecca was involved in an argument about the nature of gambling her first anger was over and she would resign herself to paying the boss back.

"This is the last time," said Rebecca, "the very last time. I am not going to do this again. You can just go to jail."

Seymour knew very well that his mother would never let him go to jail, not as long as there was a cent in the bank. She became angry with him too and shouted at him and told him that he was good for nothing, but when he stalked from the house and did not return for dinner, she became so upset that she sent Rebecca to try to find him.

The bet and the loss were concealed from Seymour's employer, but Seymour fell back on his old habits of sleeping late and staying up late. The employer began to call up each morning to ask Rebecca when Seymour was coming to work, and he told her that this was unheard-of behavior.

"You know that it is only my respect for your mother and you that makes me stand for this kind of thing. Who ever heard of a boss ringing up to find out if one of the men in his employ was coming to work?"

Rebecca pacified the boss and Samuel's mother shouted at Samuel in the morning when he did not get up, but he merely turned to the wall and tried to sleep some more when she shook him and yelled at him. He knew that however she shouted at him, she would return to the devotion and attention to him which was so much a part of her conscious being. She would let the water in the tub for his bath, she would hand him his socks and his underwear, she would press him to eat more at breakfast, even though he had slept too long.

During this time of great prosperity five years after the first World War, it was easy to get jobs and Seymour did not remain unemployed for any length of time. But he became ashamed of not being one of those who prospered, and when friends of the family visited the house, Seymour shut his bedroom door or moved about the house as if he were not a part of the family. He had a native shyness and a native bluster, but the bluster showed itself only in the intimacy of the family circle or among the boys at the drugstore.

His mother told Seymour that he ought not to be like that, he ought to come out and greet friends of the family.

"You are shy," she said, "I know what it is. I was shy until I was fifty years old and then I decided that it was foolish to be shy."

Yet Seymour suffered from an overwhelming curiosity about everyone who came to the house and everyone the family had ever known. No sooner had the visitors departed than Seymour came forth from his self-chosen exile and questioned his mother and sister like an inquisitor about what had been said and what events had occurred in other families.

"What are you, the district attorney?" Rebecca said to him, worn out by his tireless questions, which were often resumed the day after, for Seymour turned over in his mind what he had been told, and found it incomplete, inconclusive, or contradictory. He suspected lying and dishonesty in everyone, and most of all he suspected the distortion or the bluff.

"How can I tell you when they don't tell me," said Rebecca, impatient that Seymour should require an account so exhaustive.

"What's the matter with you," said Seymour, "can't you answer a civil question?"

And often Rebecca and his mother found that only by answering all of Seymour's questions was it possible to bring his curiosity to an end.

It was natural that Seymour should be very much interested in the careers of other young men. When he heard of the misdeeds of some of them he manifested a scorn and a contempt which arose from the intensity with which he really believed in a middle-class morality. When Sarah, or less frequently Rebecca, remarked that he had no right to judge other young men, since he was virtually a black sheep himself, Seymour felt that they were unreasonable and personal.

"*Don't do as I do*," said Seymour, "*do as I say*." This was a quotation from some minister who had been reproached for misconduct. Seymour had long since forgotten what the nature of the misconduct was, but the sentiment seemed to him a complete justification for his judgments. Moreover, he took no little pride in the righteousness of these judgments and he felt that they showed that his heart was really in the right place, however often his own behavior was worthless.

"Naturally," he said, when his sisters told him that he ought to obey his own precepts, "naturally, it would be better if I practiced what I preach. But what do you want me to do, preach what I practice; would you like that better?"

Seymour felt triumphant, but Rebecca shook her head. She was unable to answer him, but she felt that he was wrong.

"You're just using words," she said, "you have no right to condemn other human beings the way you do."

By the time Sarah had two big children, Nancy and Jasper, her marriage was hopeless. Her mother suggested that she take a large apartment and that Sarah come to live with her and Rebecca and Seymour. Sarah accepted this proposal because Michael, who wanted a divorce, gave her only enough money to support the children, declaring that he would give her a monthly sum proportionate to his prosperity only when she gave him his divorce. But Sarah was determined not to give him a divorce, and her mother supported her in this determination. Mother and daughter believed that after a time Michael would return to his wife and children.

The new life in which Rebecca, Seymour, and the mother lived with Sarah and her children was a peculiar one. Rebecca was devoted to her nephew and niece just as she was devoted to her mother and brother. When they went to school she gave them a nickel each day until Sarah found out and became very angry, for Sarah herself gave Nancy and Jasper only a penny for spending money and she felt that this gift of a nickel subverted her own arrangement with her children.

"Whose children do you think they are, yours or mine?" said Sarah. "Who is bringing up these children?"

Seymour too became close friends with Nancy and Jasper. He teased them mercilessly, but he also played games with them. He invented a version of baseball which could be played with an old football given to Jasper by his father. Seymour was one team and Nancy and Jasper were the other, and the game was played in the long hallway of the apartment. The game was played with an extraordinary passion both by the children and by their young uncle. Meanwhile the racket was such that the people who lived in the apartment below knocked on the ceiling and finally complained to the superintendent. Sarah objected because her hallway carpet was being ruined.

"You ought to be ashamed of yourself," said Sarah to her brother, "you ought to be ashamed to play games with children."

She did not understand that the fascination of the children for Seymour was profound and the motive was Seymour's desire to be a child himself. This was the reason that he teased Nancy and

Jasper in the way that he did. Nancy proved to be sturdy enough to answer back in kind when he sought to make a fool of her, but Jasper was sensitive to the point of illness and he wept when his uncle said that he was a baby or he tried to hit him.

"Let the children alone," said Sarah and Rebecca, "play with someone of your own age."

Seymour preferred the children. He had a strong hold on them because he had newspapers all the time and the children wanted to see the jokes. When displeased with them and when he wanted them to run errands for him, Seymour used his ownership of the comic strips as a kind of capital which made it possible for him to give the children wages and rewards. He also used the jokes as a means of turning the children against each other, for it often became a question of who was to see the comics first, Nancy or Jasper, and Seymour tantalized the children, exacting concessions and promises from them by raising the question of which of them was to get the comics first. When he was displeased with one of them, he announced that the object of his displeasure was not to see the comic strip at all, and although Rebecca, who was always moved by a strong sense of justice, undermined Seymour by promising the punished child her own newspaper when she came home at night, this hardly served to reduce Seymour's power. He had more newspapers, for he bought most of them during the day, and he was at home more often than Rebecca.

There were soon many quarrels between Sarah and Seymour because of the children and because of Seymour's habits. Seymour left wet bathtowels on bedspreads, he left an egg-soiled newspaper on the kitchen table, and he wet the bathroom floor when he bathed. It was also difficult to get Seymour to depart from the bathroom because his baths were of such long duration, he enjoyed them so much, and he read the morning newspaper while in the tub. In these quarrels between the brother and sister, the mother and Rebecca always defended Seymour and soon there were periods of silence when Rebecca and Seymour would not speak to Sarah. Sarah then told her children not to speak to their uncle and aunt, and though Nancy disregarded this request, Jasper, who was pathetically sorry for his mother while at the same time he disliked her, obeyed her request and tried to avoid his aunt when he went to the school. His aunt saw that he paused on the stair, waiting for her to depart, so that he would not encounter her and she was wounded as seldom before, for she did not know that Jasper took his mother's part only because he felt that his mother was an unfortunate woman who had been abused by his father. Rebecca liked Jasper very much and during such periods she was disturbed by the illusion that he did not like her.

The worst conflict came when, as if inevitably, Seymour took sixty dollars from Sarah's dresser drawer, bet it on a ball game, and lost it. Discovering the disappearance of the money, Sarah immediately accused Seymour of having taken it. Rebecca said that this was not true, for Seymour had never taken any money in direct theft before. When Seymour came home, Rebecca went into the bedroom with him and extracted the truth from him, although Seymour yelled his innocence at first. Then she acted quickly, she went into Sarah's room and asked her if she had looked carefully in the dresser drawer, for perhaps the money had been misplaced. It was after eleven and Sarah had already gone to bed. She was angry that she had been disturbed and she said that her sister knew her well enough to know that she would not omit any corner of the dresser if she thought her money might be there. Rebecca had moved quickly to the dresser and begun to make her own search, speaking conciliatory words to her sister. Jasper, who at that time slept on a cot near his mother's bed, had been awakened by the light and he blinked at the scene, knowing what argument had preceded it. Swiftly Rebecca drew her hand from the open dresser drawer.

"Look," she said, holding up a handful of dollar bills, "it was here all the time!" and she gave her sister the money.

Sarah took the money and said, "You put it there yourself," for she was not one to permit anyone to get away with anything.

"It was there all the time," said Rebecca, looking with hatred at her sister, and conscious that her money, as Sarah knew, was being given to her although Seymour was Sarah's brother as well as Rebecca's.

"She does that because she is ashamed that her brother is a thief," said Sarah to her son Jasper when Rebecca had departed. "She is afraid that she will not get a husband if anyone knows that your uncle is a thief. But everyone knows that he is a good for nothing, anyway."

Jasper felt so much sympathy and pain for his mother and his aunt that he was unable to fall asleep for a long time and he felt like crying.

Meanwhile Rebecca damned her sister as she spoke to her mother in the bedroom they shared. Ruth always defended everyone and she defended Sarah by reminding her sister of Sarah's lot, how cruel her husband was to her, and how she needed money, now that Michael gave her just a bare subsistence.

"I need money too," said Rebecca. "I don't have any husband."

"Money is the reason for all the trouble in the world," said Ruth speaking with a sense of all the years she had known.

When the incident was passed, and all were friendly again, Jasper was sent with Seymour one day to get a haircut. Seymour gave the barber a dime tip, and Sarah became outraged once again, and said that she had no money to give barbers tips, she was a woman deserted by her husband.

"That does not mean that I have to look like a cheap skate," said Seymour. "You told me to take the kid to the barber: next time take him yourself and see what happens when you don't tip the barber."

"I never tip him," said Sarah. "You're just a big sport on your sister's money."

And in fact, Sarah never tipped the barbers for the children's haircuts and she disregarded the gestures of contempt and anger which sometimes occurred just as, when a storekeeper refused to sell her a grocery which was on sale because she was not a steady customer and had entered the store just to save a few cents on the one item, Sarah departed from the store with an untouched dignity, not in the least distressed by what the storekeeper had said. She was extremely proud and given to extraordinary anger when her pride was penetrated. She was not moved by such incidents because she began with the idea that she was smarter when she saved money by such devices and she took pride in the fact that Michael, though he seldom praised her, had said:

"That girl can make a dollar go farther than anyone else in the world."

Michael did not know that it was precisely this ability, in which her whole being participated, which made her the kind of a wife she was. Nor did he know that this desire to save money was the same emotion, in all truth, that made Sarah so jealous of the other women her husband went after. Ruth Hart, however, illuminated by her years and her intimate experience of goodness, perceived the complicated truth when she said to her daughter that it was strange that she drove a man who was making so much money from the house and yet at the same time was so concerned about the expenditure of money.

Ruth Hart pointed out that the suitors who came to see Rebecca from time to time were all men who would never be as successful as Michael, Michael was really one in a million. But Sarah justified herself with the hope that Michael would return one day as he had returned before, exhausted by sensuality, pleased to have a home, and in love with his children, if not with his wife. She would then have everything she wanted, a husband who was rich and who was faithful to her, too.

Seymour never spoke with Sarah about her husband, but he questioned his mother like a detective about the latest events in the unhappy marriage. He admired Michael, he detested Sarah, and he felt that he and Michael were men of the world. When he heard that Michael had moved from a hotel to the apartment of his latest lady friend, he was disappointed, for he felt that Michael would have more freedom in a hotel to seek out whatever new companion he wanted.

"Look at you," said Ruth Hart, "you like to have a woman take care of you: why do you think that Michael does not feel like that too?"

"If I had the money that Michael has," said Seymour, "I would have a man servant."

"I am better than a man servant," said his mother.

Soon there was a new quarrel between Sarah and Rebecca about the children. Sarah again referred to the fact that the children were hers and not Rebecca's, and that she was not going to let the children be spoiled by an old maid aunt who was overdevoted. Rebecca often referred to herself as an old maid and for this reason Sarah, who did not know or wish to believe that other human beings were as proud as she, thought that it was all right to speak of Rebecca as an old maid.

"Shame on you," said Ruth Hart, "to say such a thing, such an insulting thing! You pick out what your sister is most ashamed of in the whole world and you throw it in her face!"

Sarah cited her sister's own references.

"She says herself that she is an old maid."

"You're smart," her mother replied, "but you have no feelings." It was then necessary for the mother to explain that she did not mean that Sarah had no feelings about herself, she had no feeling for what occurred in other human hearts. Sarah denied this and stopped speaking to her mother. She decided to get a new apartment and to live by herself with her children.

Her mother tried to stop her and she resumed conversation with her daughter as if nothing had occurred. But it was useless. Sarah declared that she would consent to stay only if the amount of rent paid by Rebecca was increased, for Rebecca paid only a third of the rent on the premise that Sarah too was helping to support her mother, and Sarah, as Michael's wife, was really more prosperous than Rebecca.

Sarah moved to a new apartment and Ruth Hart looked with Rebecca for a new apartment and in the end it was the mother in Ruth Hart who decided that she and her daughter and her son would take an apartment in the same house as Sarah. Sarah had been installed for a month on the fourth floor when her sister, mother, and brother arrived on the second floor, and soon Ruth Hart was constantly passing from the second floor to the fourth floor and back, supervising her family. Sarah was not really displeased to have her mother so near, although she concealed her satisfaction. She liked to be alone where no one could tell her what to do or criticize her actions, but it was a comfort to have her mother near her and it made it possible for her to make visits and leave the children alone at home. By this time Sarah's hope that her husband would return began to fade. A separation between Sarah and Michael had been arranged by lawyers and Sarah received a monthly stipend which was adequate to all of her expenses and even her desire to save. Sarah felt the amount was unjust because it was not proportionate to Michael's earnings, but when a lawyer advised her to sue Michael for a divorce and thus secure alimony based on Michael's wealth, Sarah refused because she still tried to believe that Michael would return to her and also she knew that what Michael wanted most of all was to get a divorce. His desire for a divorce made Sarah suspect that there was some woman he wanted to marry. Michael when he visited his children mentioned the divorce and on one visit he stopped to see Ruth Hart, asking her to use her influence on her daughter to persuade her to the sensible action of a divorce.

"What makes you think I have any influence?" asked Ruth Hart.

"I know you have a big influence on her," said Michael. Between the son-in-law and the mother-in-law there was an admiration for each other which often made Sarah indignant.

"How can you like anyone who behaves like that to your daughter?" said Sarah. She felt that Michael deserved moral condemnation and she was incensed by her mother's admiration of Michael's masculinity and worldly success, although she herself took pride in the fact that her husband was more successful than the husbands of any of the girls she had known.

"I would rather have a poor man," said Sarah, "who was good to me."

This was not true, but Sarah had no way of knowing that it was not true, because she had so many reasons of mind and of heart for not divorcing her husband. The reason she mentioned as sheer justification was her children's benefit. But her mother told her with tact that her real reason was her fear that some woman would become Michael's wife, if she divorced him. In her own circle the prestige of being Michael's wife remained strong, even though Michael had left her.

During these years, Seymour's idleness became more and more of a burden to his sister Rebecca and his mother. He refused to make any effort any longer to get a job because he had been discouraged so much by his failures.

His friendship with his nephew and his niece increased. He played poker for nothing with them and he took Jasper to the ball game once, in a brief week of affluence. Nancy had already begun to go to high school and Jasper was old enough to have long and serious discussions with his uncle, whenever they were on good terms. The one occasion on which Jasper had been taken by Seymour to the Polo Grounds served to make Jasper hope for years that he would be taken again, a hope that Seymour used to secure personal services from Jasper, such as getting him newspapers and cigars downstairs at the stationery store.

"Some day I will take you again," said Seymour.

"What day?" said Jasper hopefully, for he had become as passionate a baseball fan as his uncle.

"I don't know what day," said Seymour. "On the day that I make a lot of money which I never will."

"Yes, you will," said Jasper who at this moment of early adolescence did not like to think that anyone was not going to be successful and rich.

"Don't you think you're going to be rich some day?" Jasper asked his uncle.

"Maybe I will," said Seymour, "but probably I won't. It's just one of those things: I am not the successful type. I've been a failure all my life"—Seymour was now twenty-eight—"and that's the kind of thing that does not change."

Jasper was shocked. At the age of thirteen he was appalled to hear anyone speak of himself as a failure. He was unable to understand the indifference with which Seymour spoke of being a failure.

At this time too Seymour discussed with Jasper Sarah's harshness of nature.

"When you get older," said Seymour, "you will understand that a woman without a man gets that way. She can't help it. Of course, Sarah never had a good heart. But if your father had not left her, you and Nancy would not be nagged all the time."

And then at last Rebecca had a suitor whom she was able to take seriously. Her mother was delighted and impatient. Rebecca too bloomed freshly, although she was no longer the thirty-five years of age she admitted. Her suitor was James Mannheim, a middle-aged dentist who had been married before and who seemed to all a very well-educated man. Seymour did not like James and he said that James was always making speeches. But Jasper was delighted that such a well-educated man might become a member of the family, and Sarah, though she was critical of James, was also impressed. Sarah observed that James was a head shorter than Rebecca and the two made an incongruous couple, and her mother, though she agreed that this observation was true, remarked that such things made little difference in the long run. Rebecca and James had met through the mediation of a friend of the family, a man who had made a fortune in dental supplies and who had told James that if he ever wanted to get married again, he knew just the right girl for him, a girl who had a fortune to bring as a dowry and who would make an excellent wife, for she had made an excellent daughter as everyone knew. James was interested in the dowry and he wanted to settle down again. But he feared marriage because his first marriage had been a humiliation. He visited Rebecca and was pleased with her and especially pleased by the extraordinary dinners he was given, dinners which Ruth Hart had labored from early morning to prepare. At these dinners he held forth and explained his views on many subjects to the Hart family, impressing everyone but Seymour, and impressing Jasper more than anyone.

"Just big talk," said Seymour, who did not come to dinner but heard about it from the bedroom where he had secluded himself.

The courtship continued for a full year. James took Rebecca to plays and to the opera, he brought her his books to read, he made much of young Jasper who had long wanted to know an intellectual human being, although he was not yet acquainted with the term, intellectual. Rebecca loved her nephew Jasper and she was touched that he should be fascinated by James at the same time as she felt that her sister's child, a good-looking and well-behaved boy, showed James what kind of children she might have.

As this courtship continued, Ruth and Sarah became impatient for James did not come to the point of asking Rebecca to marry him, and after all, James was fifty if he was a day while Rebecca was closer to forty than anyone really admitted. If she was to have children, she ought to get married soon. James, however, was perfectly content to be a suitor and Rebecca glowed as never before, excited by the many things that a courted girl did. When the couple finally reached the stage of mild petting in the living room, Ruth in the kitchen listened with a mixture of pleasure and distaste. This was what she wanted, she wanted her daughter to get married, but the pair seemed a grotesque version of the romance of courtship which Ruth believed in at sixty just as she had when a girl of sixteen. And Seymour was displeased without any admixture of joy in his sister's courtship. When Jasper sat with him in his bedroom one Sunday afternoon, having come down from his own apartment to discuss the major league pennant races with his uncle, the two heard the sound of loud smacks succeeded by giggles.

"I never heard anything as disgusting as that," said Seymour to Jasper. And Jasper too felt that the sounds of petting were unpleasant, although like his grandmother Ruth he was impatient that his aunt Rebecca get married.

When summer came, a crisis occurred. James proposed marriage at last. But it turned out that he wanted Rebecca to continue to work at the job which paid her such a big salary. Rebecca refused. She explained that one did not get married except to change one's life, and this would be no change for her. More than that, Rebecca wanted her mother to live with her, at least for a time, and James wanted a home of his own. The proposal fell through and James departed, leaving Ruth Hart in tears in the kitchen from which she had overheard the discussion. Her strong will showed itself immediately and she told her daughter that she did not want to live with her, she wanted her to get married. As for Rebecca's job, Ruth told her daughter that they could argue about that after the marriage, for James would change his mind, he would like having his wife at home all day. But Rebecca was immovable. She was not going to work, if she married, and she was going to bring her mother with her.

After a week, James returned. He had decided to accept Rebecca's conditions. He had braced himself for marriage and it was too dismal to turn back.

Ruth Hart announced in triumph the news of her daughter's engagement. The family took a cottage at the seashore and James came to stay with them as a boarder. Again, he was slow in coming to the point of saying when the marriage was going to occur. Ruth became fearful again, for she was often afraid that what she desired would not come true, some disaster would intervene. Meanwhile her cooking reached new heights because of her effort to please James. At last Rebecca forced the issue by bringing James's petting further and further until she was able to tell James that they had to get married soon. James felt the pride of the seducer who does the right thing and this was a very important thing for him. The marriage occurred and Ruth Hart enjoyed a mighty relaxation. Now if only Seymour would make something of himself, she would be satisfied, and if Michael would return to his wife and children.

The depression began two months after the marriage and James who had been playing the stock market lost all of his own savings, and much of what Rebecca had given him as dowry was thrown away in an effort to cover the stocks he had bought on margin. Rebecca decided immediately to start a small dress store so that James would not feel that he was supporting her mother and her brother. For the first time Seymour had a job at which he could work at his own hours; he helped Rebecca sell dresses in the store and he worked in the late afternoons and evenings. Rebecca was pregnant and yet sturdy enough to give herself to her new business.

"I always wanted to be in business for myself," she said.

Seymour showed his powers of persuasion as his sister's sale clerk. He was able to kid the customer in the right way by flattering her and telling that she looked like a high school girl. Seymour had always been persuasive but too often he had used this power merely to borrow money for the sake of betting.

Yet the business was not a success because of the depression. And just before Rebecca gave birth to a boy, the whole store front burned down and it was decided to give up the business because now Rebecca had to take care of her child. James had for some time been dissatisfied because Ruth Hart no longer cooked for him the kind of dinners he had been given as a suitor, and he tried again to persuade Rebecca to set up a separate household where they would live alone. Rebecca was clever at putting him off, but his resentment of his mother-in-law became more and more of a compulsion until he said one day that it was his theory that after a certain age, when they were no longer useful, human beings ought to be painlessly executed, as among the Eskimos. James was a man of many theories, but this was unlike most of them. Seymour, hearing this, decided that his mother had been insulted and became furious.

"They ought to put you to death," said Seymour, "you're only ten years younger than Mamma! That's the most awful thing I ever heard anyone say and I've heard a lot in my time."

The quarrel blew over, but the conflict renewed itself, and its true cause was James's disappointment in his marriage which he had expected to be just like his courtship. And now he barely made a living as a dentist, for he was never a very good dentist and he talked too much to his patients. Rebecca decided to go back to work and she went back, but she had lost her touch, her sense of fashion and vogue which had made her a good imitator. Hence, she had to go back to the work-table of the shop, the job she had started with as a young girl many years before. Yet this helped to support the family and to quiet James, for Ruth Hart was useful in taking care of the child, who had been named John and who proved to be a sickly infant. Seymour resumed his old habits, he lost the jobs he was given because of his sister, and now jobs were no longer plentiful and employers were less patient with Seymour than ever before.

Sarah expressed to her friends her extreme admiration for Rebecca, and said that she would not do what Rebecca did for the sake of her mother and brother. But in expressing this admiration Sarah condemned her sister's marriage without being conscious that this was one of her motives in speaking as she did. And she felt perplexed because, in spite of all, it seemed to her that she had made a better marriage than her sister. Michael was the worst kind of husband, but he was not like James who devoted so many of his thoughts to deciding how he might best secure a comfortable life and lessen his own efforts, for as a dentist it was possible for him to choose his own leisure.

Seymour was James's most unfavorable critic. He noted how much James loved a big breakfast, and how slowly he ate, seeming to relish every bite and chew. And he quoted to his mother James's sentence: "To me a good dinner is more important than anything else." But Seymour also liked to eat. He wolfed his food, bending over the newspaper, but there was no doubt in anyone's mind that it was fairly important to Seymour that he be well fed. It was true that Seymour's taste in this as in many other things differed from James and was indeed antithetical, for his liking for pickles, delicatessen, and cake made him dislike the wholesome foods upon which James insisted. So too with James's love of talk. He spoke of very different subjects and he was interested in politics, national affairs, and science, to all of which Seymour was indifferent. He also used the big words, the five-dollar words, as Seymour called them, which had at first impressed the Hart family, for when they were mystified they were impressed, and they suffered from a will to admire James. But again Seymour also loved to talk and he was also a person of theories. He felt that all politicans were crooks and thus dismissed politics from his mind; but his interest in the lives of all human beings resembled the passion of the chess player who reviews or reads about great performances. It was his mother who told Seymour that whether he liked it or not it was true that his condemnation of James was touched off by the fact that they were both infatuated with their own desires.

"You are both selfish in the same way," she said, and in her sixty years of life she had learned to discriminate exactly between different shades of egotism which she called selfishness.

"No matter what is wrong with me," said Seymour, "I am not a fool."

"Everyone is a fool," said his mother, "practically everyone is a fool."

"Maybe," said Seymour, "but I am not a dumb-bell. That's the kind of fool that James is. Every time something happens he makes a speech about how he predicted the whole thing five years ago. He thinks he predicted everything in the last twenty-five years."

These discussions were inspired by the recurring conflict between Seymour and James.

"Just keep out of his way," said Rebecca to her brother. "Remember it is for Mamma's sake."

Again and again James demanded that Rebecca come with him to a different apartment so that he would not have to endure the daily presence of his mother-in-law and brother-in-law. Rebecca postponed matters, she did not argue with her husband, she knew he would forget his desire to be alone for a time, and that when it recurred, he could again be put off. Seymour made a slim contribution to the support of his mother and himself by means of his new job, the job of collecting the balance on magazine subscriptions. He was paid on a commission basis and it was a difficult job, but it permitted him to work in the afternoons and not in the mornings. Rebecca felt that he had improved to some extent because he did not gamble with the money he had collected. They did not know that the reason was not an improvement in character, but the smallness of the sums and the curious change in Seymour's emotions: he no longer believed in his luck.

During the years of the depression each person of the family slowly accepted his own life, the deprivations, the comforts, consolations, and substitutes, and the wasting defenses with which they coped with their own desires and weaknesses. As Seymour accepted his job which made it necessary for him to climb apartment house stairs, so James accepted his wife's family, and Rebecca, who always accepted everything, accepted the violent temper of her husband and the fact that he talked too much, that he made speeches about international politics at the dinner table, boring everyone and appalling visitors with the mannerisms he had learned through a correspondence school course on elocution some twenty years in the past. She knew that James also repelled many of his patients and lost them by orating to them as they sat in the dentist's chair, awaited pain, and with stuffed mouths listened like mutes to his theories and opinions. Sarah too accepted her husband's departure and as Seymour no longer believed in his luck, so she no longer believed that he would return to her and the children. The children were growing up and both were in high school. Jasper was a good student, but he was a difficult boy who read books all the time and did not go out to play like the other boys. Nancy was more difficult in one respect, she liked the boys too much and she went with the fast crowd at high school. Nothing had ever made Sarah as angry as the possibility of Nancy's promiscuity. Nancy denied all under her mother's questioning and she told her mother that she knew very well how to take care of herself. Sarah did not understand the deep-sea necking—the term used by Nancy's friends—in which her daughter indulged, for in Sarah's youth the relations of boys and girls had been less open and less discussed.

"Nowadays the girls of today will do anything," a friend of Sarah's had told her.

Sarah had brooded about this report. She felt, however, that Nancy would not be able to lie to her if she had actually had a serious love affair and permitted some boy to have his way with her.

"Mother, in a technical sense I am absolutely innocent," said Nancy to her mother, smiling about the innocence she meant, which was the preservation of her virginity. "Nowadays if you don't pet, the boys drop you."

Sarah remained perplexed, although appeased. The resentment she felt when Nancy went out with a young man in a car was so great that only by preventing Nancy from going out at all could she have freed herself of this feeling. Since every effort to keep Nancy at home in the evening merely made her disappear during the afternoon, or return late from school, Sarah accepted her own harsh resentment. And she blamed her husband, she said that Nancy was just like her father, and she supposed that the love which existed between Nancy and her father was based on the fact that both were so much interested in the act of making love.

Rebecca tried to explain to her sister that anyone could see that Nancy was the kind of a girl who would not get into trouble, she was adequate to every situation, she just wanted to have a good time like everyone else. But the mere fact that it was Rebecca's explanation sufficed to prevent it from being plausible to Sarah, even if it had not been insufficient for other reasons.

"If you had a daughter," said Sarah, "you would feel like I do."

Rebecca's boy, John, was growing up too and Sarah pointed out to her sister that she was spoiling him in the way that she had tried to spoil Sarah's children when she was an unmarried aunt.

"He is not in good health," said Rebecca who was very sensitive about John, "you have to be careful with an ailing child. You know that he has convulsions."

Meanwhile Seymour's relationship with John was exactly what it had been to Nancy and Jasper when they were still children, and although John did not respond to Seymour's teasing as fully as the sensitive Jasper had, still it was a comfort to Seymour to have a child to tell jokes to, to send on errands, to make fun of, and to teach about major league baseball. As Jasper went forward in high school, he began to read books of which Seymour did not approve. For a time uncle and nephew had had a common interest in O. Henry and Irvin S. Cobb, but when Jasper began at fifteen to read the fiction of Theodore Dreiser and Sinclair Lewis, Seymour was troubled.

"God knows what is going to become of that boy," said Seymour, "if he reads any more, he will turn out to be some kind of freak."

On the other hand, Seymour took pride in Jasper's precocity, and bragged to his friends about his nephew's learning, exaggerating the extent of this learning because of the intensity of his family pride. Jasper heard of his uncle's esteem by accident, when one of his uncle's cronies asked him whether he really was interested in reading dry books. And Jasper was surprised, for he had never had a word of praise from Seymour. But then when Seymour became angry with Jasper because Jasper refused to get him cigars, he attacked his nephew for reading what he did.

"You're going to land in jail one of these days," said Seymour, "reading all these red magazines."

Jasper was astounded and it took some time for him to make out that what Seymour had in mind was the copy of *The New Republic* he had glanced at in his nephew's bedroom. After the quarrel was over, Jasper sought in vain to explain to Seymour that *The New Republic* was liberal and not socialist in politics. But Seymour regarded this as a sophistical distinction.

"All those guys," he said, "are just sore because they are not rich. Give any one of them a million dollars and they would forget all about being reds."

And when Jasper argued in vain that socialism was not a question of personal resentment, but of altering the economic system, Seymour announced as if he had discovered the thought that it was impossible to change human nature. These discussions occurred during the worst years of the depression and Jasper told his mother too that the remedy would be a different social order. Sarah said that if what Jasper said was true, then capitalism would not have lasted so long. It was useless for Jasper to remind his mother of the panics and crashes which had recurred in her lifetime, for she remembered chiefly that they had ended and prosperity had returned.

"Most people have to admit that something is wrong," said Jasper to his mother, repeating an argument he had read. But Sarah was unwilling to believe that the depression was not going to end soon. And she thought her son was obviously wrong when he said that was the result of the competition for profits. Sarah knew that human beings are always fighting with one another and some men are just evil. Her husband was a good example. She had compared her husband to the Kaiser more than once. She was also disturbed because she felt that Jasper was turning out in the way that the lunatic fringe of her youth had turned out, loafers and good-for-nothings who talk parlor socialism and do not earn a living.

Michael was given his divorce by Sarah in the first year of the depression. He had immediately married again and he had died two years after his second marriage, a fact which Sarah regarded as a personal vindication.

"If he had stayed with his wife and children," she often said, "he would be alive today."

Michael's estate was believed to be one of considerable wealth, and Seymour as much as anyone was interested in how much money Nancy and Jasper were going to inherit. He discussed tirelessly with Jasper what might be done with the money which he was going to get when he was twenty-one years of age. The lawyers for the estate tried to suggest to Sarah that the general collapse of values was such that the estate had merely a paper value, apart from some of the stocks and bonds, and even the stocks and bonds might never return to their value in the heyday of the bull market. Seymour told Jasper that this was foolish, and he said that whatever went down must eventually go up, it was like bouncing a ball. Jasper believed that this was true, because he wanted to believe it was true, despite his acquaintance with radical political and economic theory. And the whole family believed that Nancy and Jasper would be rich heirs, for this belief had lived in the family for many years and it was too pleasant to yield to any acquaintance with reality.

In 1937 Seymour made the most revolutionary move of his life, he became a bookmaker. It was soon recognized that he should have done this many years before, instead of being the gambler who threw his money away on betting. Seymour did not prosper as a bookmaker might, but he managed to make a living sufficient to keep his mother and himself in modest circumstances, so that at last, twelve years after James first had demanded it, Seymour and his mother lived in a household of their own and James lived alone with his wife and his son. But the two families lived in the same apartment house because Rebecca was unwilling to let her mother go anywhere where she would be unable to take care of her if she became ill. And Ruth Hart was always in Rebecca's apartment, trying to help her, while Seymour used his sister as a kind of banker, giving her his money to put in the bank for him and drawing upon her resources when he was short of funds.

The entire family had now settled in the fixed forms of middle age. James made a modest living, Seymour made a modest living, Nancy and Jasper went to the city universities, the sickly John was now in grammar school, and the generation of the children provided the only unpredictable and unstable processes in the family life. As the new war came nearer, the prosperity of the family became definite and certain, although modest. And Seymour moved forward as a bookmaker by securing a silent partner who gave him sufficient capital to take as many bets as he felt he dared. The silent partner took half of whatever money Seymour made as a bookmaker and he took none of the risks that Seymour did with the police, who were supposed to stop all professional gambling. Seymour's new ambition was to get a sufficient amount of capital to be free of his silent partner, and then to enjoy the entire amount of the proceeds. But this ambition often seemed out of his reach, because just as his savings accumulated to the five thousand dollars he thought necessary, the bettors made a killing which none could have foreseen and Seymour was back where he started. With the rise in prosperity as the war began in Europe, there was a rise in the amount of money which was available for gambling and all looked well for Seymour until he was taken by the draft. He was just one year too young to be too old for the army, just as the last year of the first World War he had been the right age, and he had not been taken only because the war had ended in November.

Seymour regarded being drafted as a plain catastrophe. He had thought that he would be rejected for physical reasons, but as he said when he returned from his physical examination:

"If you can breathe, you're in."

He went away to Camp Dix, feeling that the nemesis which had hunted him down all his life had now become the whole of society. After his first six weeks of training, during which he visited his mother on every available occasion, he was sent to Texas for further training. He had not been away from his mother an entire night for years before this time and he was afraid that she might die during his absence, a fear equal only to his fear that he himself was going to be killed during the war. In the army, he was popular as a Broadway gambler, his version of his civilian status, and for the first time in his life he had to get up early in the morning whether he liked it or not. But an old injury to his knee provided him with the excuse for sick leave often enough.

His mother, questioned as to whether she missed him, said that she was glad to get rid of him, and although she did feel his absence as a breach of her daily life, nonetheless she accepted his departure with the equanimity with which she had accepted all the chances and changes she had known all her life.

In six months Seymour was discharged because of his poor knee. He returned to the heart of the family in better health than he had ever been before and full of loud praise of the army and of military training for boys between eighteen and twenty-one. This praise of discipline was a new version of his affirmation of conventional morality. Yet it was also a sign of his enjoyment of good health.

"My whole life would have been different," he said, "if I had only been drafted in the last war! I would have learned to take care of myself!"

Yet his return was marked by a complete surrender to his old way of life, his late mornings, long breakfasts, and the attention of his mother.

"Mamma, let the water in the tub," he said again as soon as he returned and again she waited on him hand and foot. The one habit he retained from the army was that of sitting on his bed and putting on his socks by throwing his legs up. His mother did not like this method and his resistance to her criticism of it was perhaps the only proof that his mother's attention, though initiated by her, required his acceptance.

Seymour returned to being a bookmaker and he prospered with the wartime prosperity. His mother was satisfied. She felt that at last he had become a real man, equal to a man's responsibilities. His shortcomings now were part of a system which provided him and her with a decent living. She had hated gambling until Seymour became a bookmaker, but now she was distressed by the effort made by the city officials to stop gambling, an effort which Seymour evaded by going to one of the suburbs and receiving the calls of the bettors in the house of a friend, who was paid for this privilege and who took Seymour home in the evening in his car.

Ruth Hart felt now that the city administration was wrong to try to stop gambling because it was a part of human nature to gamble and when a human being had extra money, he had the right to risk it and enjoy the heady excitement of a bet. There had always been gambling and there would always be gambling, so that it was foolish and irritating that the police made Seymour go out of town.

As he prospered, Seymour's spendthrift habits increased. He liked to eat expensive meals in restaurants and he was not at home for dinner very often. He let his mother give him breakfast, but he preferred to have lunch elsewhere, and when Jasper visited his grandmother one afternoon, his grandmother remarked to him with both pride and irony:

"You see: he is doing me a favor, he is eating the lunch I made for him."

Ruth Hart's health became weaker and she had heart attacks which were serious indeed. Through the years she had had many illnesses and many griefs, until it seemed as if everything had happened to her. She had been bitten by a dog, she had broken her leg on an icy sidewalk, her appendix had been removed and she had suffered the heartbreak of the death of her son. Yet she was cheerful once more as soon as the trial was passed and she rejoiced in her children, her grandchildren, her friends, and the love all felt for her. Bearing in mind how much she had suffered, her daughters said of her that she had more lives than a cat and Seymour said that nothing could kill her.

"How do you manage to live so long?' asked her grandson Jasper who loved her very much and feared the day when she would die.

She explained to him that she knew how to rest. She did not sleep much and she never went to sleep for good until Seymour had returned, but she dozed in the dark, waiting for him.

And then a year after Seymour's return from the army she had the most severe of all her heart attacks. Seymour's behavior became extraordinary. Although he expressed a mocking amusement at all of her behavior when she was well, as soon as she became sick he was sure that she was going to die, this was the long-feared moment, and Seymour, overcome by the emotions he knew when he went to a ball game on which much of his money was staked, became panicky. He walked up and down in the bedroom and then he sat at her bedside, and when the attack was at its worst, he became so sure that she was going to die that he began to moan and refused to stop moaning and would not leave his mother's bedside.

When she was well again, she told her grandson Jasper about Seymour's behavior, speaking with some disdain.

"You should have heard that moaning, Jasper," she said, "he was not like a human being, he was like some animal. I had to tell him to go away, he was making himself such a nuisance."

The truth was that Ruth Hart was touched by her son's terror of her death. But she was ashamed of what to her was unmanly behavior. It was all right for a woman to scream at such times and she herself had screamed more than once at the news of death or disaster. But a man ought not to be like that.

"What will he do when I am dead?" she asked Rebecca. "I think he will go to pieces."

"You are better than a wife," said Rebecca, "that's why Seymour never married. What wife would take care of him like that? What wife would fix her husband's socks half inside out in the morning so that they would be easy for him to put on?"

The reason that Seymour did not get married was doubtful and complex. It was true that he had never had enough money to get married properly, but for a time it was suggested by family friends that he ought to marry some rich widow, and this seemed to show that it was not merely a question of not making a living, since a marriage for money might have been arranged. And when Sarah asked him once whether he had thought of getting married, he said:

"I never saw anyone I liked well enough who would want to marry me." This un-understood answer had to do with a plump and handsome girl who had lived in the same apartment house and whom Seymour had admired very much from a distance, asking Jasper once if Jasper thought that Thelma did much necking, and became pale, as he spoke, so that his nephew saw that he had a crush on Thelma, and observed thenceforward how Seymour avoided Thelma or made believe that he did not know who she was when he passed her on the apartment house stairs.

When Ruth Hart was near her seventy-fifth birthday, Rebecca decided to give her a surprise party. All the friends who had known her and loved her so many years were excited by the idea of the party, though some said that it might not be wise to make it a surprise, for she was such a nervous person. But Rebecca wanted to make it a surprise party because she liked surprises.

It was the first celebration of a birthday which had occurred for Ruth Hart since she was nineteen years of age, the year that she was married. Even Rebecca, who knew her mother was loved, was surprised by the spontaneous delight the idea of the party evoked in all who were invited, and she was astonished outside of her own view of the limitations of human goodness by the queries about what kind of gift her mother would like and the desire to give her a gift which was not inexpensive, so that the cost of the present would demonstrate the feeling about her. As the preparations for the party went forward there was a competition among the prosperous friends to be the one who gave the most handsome gift. And the poor and the old, being without sufficient funds, wanted to bake the cakes they baked best for the party.

Seymour consented to be present at the party, even though for years he had hidden in the bedroom to avoid the friends of the family, and this too astonished Rebecca. Sarah too was touched by the extraordinary affection which everyone showed toward her mother. But she was also critical.

"It's just because she never knocks anyone," said Sarah, "she has a good word for everyone. She does not admit to herself what she thinks about them most of the time."

The morning that the party was to occur Rebecca arose early, as her mother might have, to prepare the party food. When Ruth came from the first floor of the apartment house, where she lived, to the fourth-floor apartment where her daughter lived, to make her habitual morning visit and see that all was well with her daughter's family, Rebecca came to the door and would not let her mother come in. She said she was taking a bath. Ruth went downstairs and by the time the elevator had reached the first floor, she knew that her daughter's refusal to admit her was very strange, since the reason given was unheard-of, her daughter had taken many baths in her presence, this was the first time in her life that Rebecca had been squeamish about her mother's presence or refused her admission to her house.

It took an hour for Ruth to decide that Rebecca was trying to conceal something from her and she felt that all concealment was concealment of evil, she had never known anyone to have a reason for concealing goodness.

Seymour had been told to keep his mother from visiting her daughter's apartment, but he had not come home that night, a habit which was becoming more and more frequent. He had been told by Rebecca to use any possible subterfuge to keep his mother from coming upstairs to Rebecca and if he had been at home there were countless resources which he had spontaneously made use of through the years to keep his mother near him.

Ruth, having decided that Rebecca was concealing a disaster from her, returned in the elevator to Rebecca's apartment to make sure. When Rebecca sent Sarah to the door, Sarah told her, smiling, that she must not come in, supposing that the smile would be sufficient to reassure her mother. Ruth again went to her own apartment, thought more about her banishment and decided that Seymour had been injured or killed in the accident she long had feared. She returned in the elevator again, was greeted at the door by both Rebecca and Sarah who told her that she could not enter now, but that at three o'clock in the afternoon, she would be welcome.

Ruth demanded to be admitted with passion and anger.

"I have the worst children in the world," she said, and since the mention of three o'clock had convinced her that Seymour's dead body was being prepared for the coffin by an undertaker, she cried out:

"Just give me his body and I will never ask you for anything again."

Sarah and Rebecca laughed and said that there was nothing wrong with Seymour, and she was behaving like a child.

"Where is he then?" said Ruth. "He has not come home all night."

Rebecca reminded her of how often Seymour had stayed out all night during the past year and begged her to depart. The laughter of her daughters did not reassure Ruth so much as perplex her.

"Never in my life has anything like this happened: what children! not to let their own mother in the house." And she departed, disgruntled. It still seemed possible to her that Seymour had been injured elsewhere.

By two some of the guests began to arrive and one of them was sent downstairs to entertain Ruth until it was time to bring her to the party. The guest was greeted by Ruth's condemnation of Sarah and Rebecca as the worst children any mother had ever had. During this time Seymour returned for a clean shirt, glanced furtively at the guest, and told his mother not to annoy him when she questioned him about where he had been. Then she told him about being barred from Rebecca's apartment and Seymour remembered that there was to be a surprise party. But he had an appointment elsewhere. He decided to return as soon as possible, and without greeting his mother's guest, who had known him for twenty-five years, he departed once more.

"Let us go and try Rebecca again," said the friend of the family when it was time to go to the party.

"I don't want to see her," said the angered mother. But she went, after she had been urged to make herself pretty, to fix herself up.

When she entered the living room of her daughter's apartment she was confronted by the friends of many years who sang out:

"Happy birthday, dear Ruth, happy birthday, happy birthday!"

At first she was stupefied. Then she understood and greeted them with a child's smile. She was very pleased. But the guests were moved and some began to cry from the strength of the emotion and some started to clap hands—they had not really known how much they admired Ruth—and one of them, moved by the desire to think not only of Ruth, but of such another party, cried out:

"May you live to be a hundred!"

Ruth remarked that she had no doubt the well-wisher had the best intentions in the world, but perhaps it would not be the most pleasant thing to live to be one hundred years of age. However she spoke of her joy in the party and her pleasure that all of them were here. Then all began to present the gifts they had brought for Ruth, and their handsomeness and their expensive-ness were such as to make Ruth say, charming, flustered, and astonished: "O, for me? for me?" as if the gifts were too good for her.

Rebecca and Sarah were the last to give their gifts to Ruth. When they did, Sarah asked:

"Who has the worst children in the world?"

"I have the best children in the world," said Ruth graciously.

And then a friend of the family who had known Ruth when her first child was born made a short speech in which she said that of all the human beings she had known, and she had known many, Ruth was the kindest, the most generous, the most devoted, the least selfish.

Hearing this, Sarah remarked to the lady next to her:

"She can live for six months on a compliment! She thinks about it all day long for six months and forgets to eat."

"That has never stopped her from doing what she thought she ought to do," the friend replied.

Sarah, so long critical of her mother, blaming her for her marriage and for Seymour's character, was nonetheless pleased as well as perplexed by the occasion. She knew that there were not many human beings who would be honored with so much sincerity and conviction.

As the party foods were eaten, there were many stories of what had occurred through the years and much laughter, although, in fact, there was little reason for laughter about the events which were recounted.

When the party was almost over and some had departed and most still sat at the dinner table, but no longer ate, partaking of a last cup of tea, Seymour entered hurriedly. He was very embarrassed to see all these people whom he always avoided, and embarrassed most of all by the bouquet of American Beauty roses he had brought for his mother. He gave her the bouquet, kissed her cheek self-consciously, and then departed.

"I have to meet someone at nine o'clock," he said.

"There is a good side to his character," said Ruth, when he had left. "He is not everything that he should be, but he takes care of his mother, and since he became a bookmaker, he has improved in every way."

And the party ended amid kisses and sincere best wishes, gratitude and a sense that after all there was some goodness in life, after all.

Seymour was forty, his sisters were middle-aged, Nancy was married, and Jasper had begun a legal career. James at sixty-five was what he had always been, and John, Ruth's last grandchild, was in high school, where he made his way painfully because he was a poor student. Nancy had married and moved to San Francisco and had had three children immediately.

"Par for the course," said Seymour to Jasper. "Maybe we ought to send her a booklet about birth control?"

Jasper, returning from Washington where he was a lawyer for one of the New Deal agencies, came to see his grandmother just after the defeat of Germany. Arriving at his grandmother's house at noon, he found Seymour seated at the table in the kitchen in his underwear, being given his breakfast by his mother as he read the newspapers and spotted the page with the yellow drops of his soft-boiled egg.

Jasper greeted the two and went with his grandmother to converse in the living room which now served also as Seymour's bedroom: he had used the studio couch as his bed since his mother was ill, although for a long time it had been Ruth who had slept on the studio couch while Seymour used the bedroom.

Ruth explained this shift to her grandson with some pride.

"You see," she said, "he is really a good son, after all."

"You always look for whatever is good in everyone," said Jasper.

"It is better to be like that," said Ruth, who knew that her grandson suspected the worst of most human beings and felt that he suffered because of this suspiciousness.

Seymour, having concluded his breakfast, entered in his bare feet and underwear and began to dress, as he conversed with Jasper.

"What are the big shots in Washington figuring out now?" he inquired of his nephew of whose presence in Washington he was extremely proud.

"They are figuring out how to keep their jobs and how to get the jobs they have been thinking about," said Jasper.

"I bet they are," said Seymour who approved of such a view of human beings and who liked such observations because they gave him the feeling of being in the know. Meanwhile as he conversed with his nephew, Seymour threw his leg high in the air, leaning back on the studio couch and drawing on his socks in the way he had learned while a member of the armed forces. His mother went to the closet, took his newly pressed pants from a hanger, and brought them to him. Seymour drew on his pants with care and examined the shirts in the dresser. He complained in an off-hand way to his mother because the collars were not starched well by the laundry. Jasper regarded his grandmother. She was watching every move made by Seymour. Seeing his glance, she returned to him and asked him if he wanted a new and handsome necktie which Seymour had purchased, decided he did not like, and then refused to bring back to the haberdashery. Jasper refused the necktie.

"I have enough," he said to his grandmother, although the truth was that Seymour's taste in clothes and men's wear was loud, practically spectacular, so that nothing of his could conceivably be of any use to Jasper.

Jasper regarded his grandmother's scrutiny of his own attire. She took pride in Jasper's success, the only success of the family, and she took much pleasure in his love for her. Yet she felt that he did not look the success that he was and the reason was that he did not dress as he should. She thought that Seymour went too far, perhaps, but Jasper, on the other hand, wore old and unpressed suits.

"He does not look like what he is," she explained once to a neighbor as she introduced him, and thenceforward Jasper made a special effort each time he went to see his grandmother, and when on one such occasion he returned to the apartment of a lady friend she remarked on the fact that his shoes were shined for once.

"What a character you are," she said, "the only time you get your shoes shined is when you go to see your grandmother!"

Jasper had taken the same extraordinary pains on this occasion and he was amused to see that his grandmother looked at him with some disappointment, as before.

She recognized his amused look as having to do with her scrutiny and changed to the subject of Jasper's work.

"You must not work so hard," she said, just as ten years before when he had stayed with her and asked her to wake him in time for school, she had not done so, explaining that she thought that if he was sleepy, he ought to sleep.

Jasper explained as he had many times before that he liked his work.

"Have a good time," she said to him, "there is plenty of time for work." And she wanted to know when Jasper was going to get married, urging him again to marry a rich girl.

"Don't forget," she said, "it is no crime for a girl to be rich."

"I want to find a girl I like twenty-four hours a day," Jasper said to his grandmother.

"That's right," said Seymour from the bedroom, "women are a tough proposition. You better watch your step, Jasper!"

Seymour returned to the living room, tying his necktie with much effort at the precise effect.

"Love 'em and leave 'em," he said to his nephew, who he supposed was a philanderer just like his father.

Jasper smiled and said, "I don't have much time right now to get very much involved."

"That's right," said Ruth Hart, who had not really understood her son's remark or her grandson's reply, "but remember, you promised me that you were going to give me a great-grandchild. After all, Nancy is in California, what good does it do me that she has three children, even if she sends me pictures?"

"Don't forget your promise," said Jasper who was pleased more than he knew that his grandmother desired him to have a child.

"What promise?" said his grandmother.

"The promise that you are not going to die until I have the little girl I am going to name after you."

"How long do you think I can wait?" his grandmother said. "I am getting impatient."

"There's always time enough to die," said Jasper, and rose to depart, full of the pleasure, animal and spiritual, which this kind of conversation, often renewed, had given him.

Two weeks after this occasion, Jasper was summoned from Washington. John had written him a special delivery letter in his schoolboy scrawl, John, and not any one else, because Rebecca felt it wise that John should cultivate his successful cousin. The news was of the serious illness of Ruth Hart. "I am sorry to have to upset you," wrote John in words that Rebecca had told him to choose, "but Grandmother is in a serious condition and has gone to the hospital."

Jasper returned to New York and went immediately to the hospital. He arrived at the visiting hours mentioned in the letter, just after two o'clock, and in the waiting room he found Seymour very excited while Rebecca tried to appease him.

"Where is the money going to come from?" said Rebecca to Seymour.

"I'll steal the money if I have to," said Seymour, his eyes bulging with anger.

It turned out that instead of placing Ruth in a private room, she had been put in a room with two other patients. The hospital, endowed by charity, had different visiting hours for patients and only the ones in private rooms were able to have visitors at any time during the afternoon. Jasper had been wrongly instructed about the visiting hours and he was unable to visit his grandmother.

"But she is all right now," said Rebecca, "it was just another of those attacks."

Seymour paced up and down, as if he were at a ball game, betting. The other visitors regarded the scene with curiosity, for Seymour had shouted and Rebecca had shouted back at him. She explained to Jasper that there was just no money to pay for a private room.

"I will pay my share," she explained, "but Seymour has no money now."

"I told you," said Seymour, "I will borrow it."

"Anyway," said Rebecca to Jasper, "she is feeling much better and she would be all right at home where I could take care of her. But Jasper, that night when I sat up with her because we could not find any hospital that would take us, that night I wished she would die, she was suffering so much."

Seymour departed to borrow money so that his mother might have a private room, and Jasper conversed with his aunt about his grandmother, hearing how afraid she had become because she had supposed, such was the severity of the attack, that she was about to die.

"She gets scared," said Rebecca, "and that is worse for her than anything else, she gets so panicky."

It was too late to change Ruth's room now, a nurse explained to aunt and nephew, who decided to go back to Rebecca's apartment and wait until the evening when patients in semiprivate wards were permitted visitors. They returned in a streetcar, although Jasper wanted to take a taxi, and when they were at the apartment, Jasper was given lunch. He had not wanted to eat at noon because of fear that his grandmother was going to die. And as Jasper ate and as his aunt conversed with him and as the afternoon waned, Jasper heard again from his aunt the long story of the family. Each such recital brought back incidents Jasper had not known about and he felt the glare of discovery, the understanding of events and relationships he had long misunderstood or been ignorant about. Fresh light, new light, light breaking through the massy cumulus clouds—so Jasper felt as he listened, questioning Rebecca. Before this, he had known Sarah's version, most of all, and now, hearing Rebecca's version of Sarah, Jasper knew for the first time what the two sisters had been to each other.

"What a strong human being Mamma is," said Rebecca, "even the doctor was surprised. He said that most human beings would have died from an attack like that."

"I bet that it is because she really does not want to die that she has lived through so much suffering," said Jasper. "Look at my mother. She has been sick for years in a way that Grandmother was never sick. And yet she has taken better care of herself than Grandmother ever did and she is twenty-five years younger."

"Your mother," said Rebecca, "did not have a good husband and your grandmother did."

The conversation turned to the marriage of Jasper's parents, which he had often discussed with his grandmother as well as his aunt. Jasper explained to his aunt that he had been told by a physician that he had probably had a very unpleasant infancy. He knew well enough that his childhood had been made unpleasant by his sorrow for his mother.

"This doctor thinks that I was sick," said Jasper, who had re-marked to friends of his own generation that he had been born with a hangover, the colic.

"You were a fat healthy infant," said Rebecca, "you just had the usual ailments."

"I thought I cried all the time and that that was why we moved from one apartment to another so many times," said Jasper.

"You cried like any child in the cradle," said Rebecca. "The only thing was that your father was crazy about you and when you cried at night, he insisted on turning on all the lights. When a child cries, most people let it cry until it falls asleep. But you found out that you could get a lot of attention by crying and that spoiled you."

This was a new thing to Jasper. He had not known that it was his father and not his mother who made much of him in his infancy.

"I thought my mother spoiled me too," said Jasper.

"It was your father," said Rebecca, "your mother was so miserable about her marriage that she did not pay much attention to you."

This was like a sudden great light in the midst of darkness to Jasper. He had always supposed that his mother, rejected by his unfaithful father, had been devoted to him until he had grown to be an adolescent critical of her. And he had thought that his sorrow and pity for his mother's unhappiness began with the love his mother had fixed upon him as an infant. Now that he saw that this was not true, he saw his own being and character in an utterly reversed form. He had really loved his mother very much and that was the reason he had felt so much sorrow for her unhappiness. His mother had never loved him and that was why he had sought vainly to be in love. The girls who had been in love with him and whom he had thought of marrying were too easy, they did not reject him, they did not turn away from him, as his mother had. And it had been his father who had really loved him! Who had turned on all the lights when he cried and satisfied every wish of the child! More and more memories of early childhood returned and Jasper saw how his father's departure from his mother must have been a great loss to the small boy who was used to being a little king. His father had loved him as Seymour had been loved by his mother.

"Your father thought there was nothing like you in the whole world!" said Rebecca. "I have never seen a man make so much of a child! That's why your mother always thought he would come back to her, no matter how often he went off with other women."

"And that was why she never cared very much for me," said Jasper, repeating what his aunt had said as he understood it more and more, "I was the hope that disappointed her most of all."

"That's what has been wrong with all of us," said Rebecca, "we expect too much from our children. Everyone knows that we expect everything from them which we never had anywhere else. It is time to go to the hospital. Your grandmother will be waiting for you."

As Jasper returned to the hospital, the history of his family arose, illuminated, in his mind, as if he had entered a house at night and turned on the light in each room, and looked at the things which had long been there, but which he saw as if for the first time. Seymour was what he was because of his mother, because he was his mother's child. Yet Rebecca also was what she was because she had the same mother. At the same time, Sarah was the kind of woman and wife and mother she had turned out to be because her mother and her father had liked their other chidren more; that was the reason for her being a grasping being, turned in on herself and incapable of love. And Nancy, turning from such a mother, had hurried to marriage, just as Rebecca, having a different mother, had waited long for marriage. As for John, it was too soon to see what kind of a human being he was, but one could be sure that his being as a child would be the beginning and perhaps the end of whatever he was. And Jasper himself knew now in himself that he looked at the adult world as he had had to look at his mother, suspicious, rejected, ambitious to win more than most human beings desired. What was the freedom to which the adult human being rose in the morning, if each act was held back or inspired by the overpowering ghost of a little child? This freedom seemed to Jasper like the freedom, dangerous, dark, and far-off, to become the father of new children without knowing at all what would become of them, what kind of human beings they would be.

As he entered the hospital room, Jasper saw that his grandmother was exchanging witticisms with the old ladies who were patients. She was overwhelmed to see him and she began to cry while Jasper felt a paralysis of face, so strong was the shock at how shrunken and yellow his grandmother looked.

Ruth Hart introduced the grandson in whom she took so much pride to the other old ladies, who seemed skeptical, for Jasper looked youthful and he did not have the appearance of a successful lawyer.

"I am all right now," said Ruth to her grandson, when she had recognized the fear on his face. "I am going to live for a long time."

Jasper sat by the bedside and held his grandmother's shrunken hand, which had the look and the feel of a chicken's neck. He held her hand as if this were a way of keeping her from departing from this life.

"Don't forget," said Jasper, "you are not supposed to die until I make you a great-grandmother again."

"When will that be?" asked his grandmother, thinking that perhaps Jasper had at last chosen a bride. "Make it soon."

"I will bring some of the girls I know to see you," said Jasper, "and you can tell me which one you like best."

"I must make myself pretty for them," said Ruth Hart, "you must wait until I feel better."

"You are pretty enough as you are," said Jasper.

"I must show them what a fine grandmother you have," said Ruth Hart.

"They don't have to like you," said Jasper, "you have to like them. That's what I will tell them. You tell me which one is most like you and I will marry her."

"She does not have to be like me," said Ruth, although she was flattered, "she just has to be a good girl with some money, a good rich girl and then you will be able to have children soon."

The nurse entered, bearing a tray and announcing that visiting hours were over. Jasper kissed his grandmother, promising to come tomorrow.

As he left the hospital and looked at the clear sky, sparkling with stars, he said to himself:

"The child is the mystery of this life. And the child is the meaning of this life. But the child may be Sarah, Rebecca, Seymour, Nancy, John, or myself. Or he may be my grandmother again, but it is not very likely."

"Do you have a light?" asked a middle-aged man who was also waiting for a taxi and holding a brand-new cigar in his mouth.

"No, I have no light," said Jasper.

SCREENO

For three hours, Cornelius Schmidt attempted to raise himself from the willlessness and despondency which had overcome him. He tried to read the *New York Times*, which today contained the long obituary of a great man, the only kind of story that could awaken any interest in him. He played records on his portable victrola, first a string quartet by Haydn, and then, tiring of this with the third record, playing certain singing records of a celebrated movie actress. But to no avail: the music was lifeless as his own spirit. He then resorted, as often before in such a mood, to the icebox, making for himself a fat sandwich out of materials which would have otherwise not appealed to him. Having eaten the sandwich, he seated himself by the window and watched the quiet October evening rain soundlessly falling through the bright arc of the street light downstairs, four floors below, and pocking and wrinkling the glittering puddles. Automobiles passed with the frying sound which tires make on wet streets. Cornelius took down a volume of poetry of which he was very fond and tried to read it. A poem of his own slipped from the book. He read the first few verses and shuddered, thoroughly disheartened. Drenched by such a tasteless, colorless mood, there was only one refuge, one sanctuary: the movies.

He left a note for his mother on the kitchen table, donned his trench coat, and departed. Anticipation of the movie to be seen already began to rise in his breast. People in the huddled posture which rain enforces passed him as he walked to the business avenue where stores shone wetly and brightly in the rainy night. Two boys were standing outside a candy store and trying to get chewing gum from the box beside the newsstand. Cornelius, in his rising spirits, was tempted to stop and afford them the benefit of his childhood talent for such efforts, his ability to make the machine give freely by a certain trick. But he knew that the boys would merely be shy, or afraid of him, and perhaps even antagonistic. At the age of twenty-five, he said to himself, I am neither here nor there, and can no longer expect to return with ease to the world of the young, that cruel zoo inhabited by a special kind of animal.

He came to the arcade of the movie house, reading the titles printed in electric bulbs framed by other lights which raced backward and forward along the arcade.

JOHN BOLES AND EVELYN LAYE

IN ONE HEAVENLY NIGHT ALSO

SPENCER TRACY IN FREEDOM

SCREENO TONIGHT $475 CASH

The presence of the new lottery annoyed him, for it meant an interruption in the flow of movies while the stage was lit and everyone looked about dazedly. At such times, Cornelius slouched far down in his seat, ashamed for some reason to be at the theatre alone, as if it were a confession of a lack of friends and engaging activities. But Spencer Tracy was an actor who had often pleased him by an absolute unself-consciousness, and Cornelius wished also to permit himself to be moved by the operetta music. Decided, he walked toward the box office, as a stream of people came out of the darkness of the theatre, looking like sleepwalkers.

At the door the uniformed ticket taker gave him a card on

which was printed a kind of checkerboard, having in each box a number. It was obviously the old game of Lotto, the object being to get five numbers which were successive either horizontally or vertically or in a diagonal. In the center, amid numbered boxes, was a box entitled GRATIS; the management gave this box to the audience.

Cornelius completed his examination of this card while walking on the eerie soundless plush carpet of the stupendous lobby, from whose lofty top great chandeliers hung. In a moment, he was in the midst of the ghostly evening of the theatre; two thousand entranced persons stared toward the white and black screen, ignorant of all else. A harried usher led him to an aisle in the middle of the theatre and hastily departed. Once free of the usher, Cornelius walked further down, blind in the soft darkness after the recent blaze of chandeliers, and after some trouble found himself the kind of seat he wanted, one in the middle of the aisle, where he would not be disturbed by those who wished to depart.

Located in his seat, and comfortable at last, Cornelius directed his gaze toward the screen. The newsreel was on, and cavalrymen were leaping high barriers, flying upward from the saddle at the apex of the jump and then settling back again, all of this performed with no little grace. The unseen voice, the commentator who always made Cornelius remember the Oracle at Delphi, was saying: "Uncle Sam does not intend to be unprepared." The scene shifted suddenly, to the accompaniment of sad and heavy music. Flood pictures were shown; a family departed from its almost submerged frame house in a rowboat, the young son of the family clutching his dog in his arms. The face of the dog and of the boy was shown in a close-up. The bleak and baffled look of the dog charmed the audience. Everything moved slowly in the slowly moving water. The commentator stated his sentiments in a histrionic baritone: "Nature shows its might on the Ohio. Thousands are left homeless by the cruel and raging waters." And then with a montage of archetypal newsreel scenes (West Point; a batter swinging; Roosevelt at the microphone; an actress descending from a train) and a martial music which came to a ringing close, the newsreel was ended. The threatre lightened and a well dressed young man came upon the stage before the screen, carrying a microphone with him. The uniformed ushers followed him. In the corner stood a round red poster to which golden discs were attached. When you turned the disc over, the amount of money you had won was revealed by the dollar sign upon the disc.

"Good evening, ladies and gentlemen," said the young man, speaking into the microphone with a knowing and efficient tone. "The management is again glad to offer prizes for the winners in SCREENO. Again we are offering $425 for anyone who gets SCREENO with the first seven numbers called. If no one is so fortunate, then we will add $25 to the amount and next week the sum will be $450. Besides this, $50 in prizes will be distributed tonight to the first ten people who get SCREENO. Now as soon as you have five consecutive numbers, either horizontally or vertically or in a diagonal, please call out loudly and clearly and come down to the stage. Then you will place your disc on the board and you will win some part of fifty dollars. Remember now! five numbers in a row! horizontal, vertical, diagonal. Good luck to all of you! And remember that everyone can't win."

True enough, said Cornelius to himself.

The theatre fell into a semi-darkness, not the movie darkness, but one in which discreet lights shone on both sides of the theatre and both sides of the stage. A white and pink clockface flashed on the screen. It was, in fact, like a roulette wheel, and had numbers running from 1 to 100. In the center was a pointer, which suddenly began to whirl furiously about the clockface, and then slowed down, and then stopped.

"Ninety-nine!" said the businesslike yet airy young man in an authoritative voice. An usher wrote down the number upon a blackboard to the right of the screen. The pointer spun again, at a tremendous pace, so that it was almost a moving blur for a moment, and then clarified into its arrow-like straightness. The actual wheel was, of course, in the projection room.

"Fifty-four!" said the young master of ceremonies, simulating a dramatic tone.

"SCREENO!" cried a voice from the balcony in a mocking voice, while everyone laughed, for obviously no one could have SCREENO as yet.

"I am sorry, ladies and gentlemen," said the young man in an affable voice, "but we will have to ask you not to be humorous about this. After all, money is involved, and there has been much confusion in the past because various people insisted upon trying to be funny."

"All right, Senator," cried the same balcony voice, and the audience laughed again. Meanwhile Cornelius had become very interested. He had both of the first two numbers and had marked them by pushing his finger through the soft cardboard of each box. It would be curious indeed, he said to himself, if I won. Probably no one here could make better use of the $425. But I have never been lucky and I am certainly not a prize-winner.

The pointer was revolving again. "Thirty-nine!" announced the young man. The audience was not yet warmed up, because too few numbers had been called for anyone to be on the verge of winning. Cornelius, however, also had this third number and was pleased no little by the course of events.

"Forty-nine!" announced the young man.

"Raspberries!" cried the same voice from the balcony.

"Please!" said the young man in a tone of unctuous and good-natured irony, "I must ask you to restrain yourself, my dear friend in the balcony. Otherwise we will be forced to suppose that you are intoxicated, and since there are more suitable places than this for those in that state, we will have to ask you to leave. Your money will be refunded."

"I won't go. I've been kicked out of better places than this," said the balcony voice. The young master of ceremonies signalled to one of the ushers, indicating the necessity of action. Cornelius had paid little attention to the disturbance, for the number forty-nine was on his card also. He needed only one more number in order to win, and was enormously excited. He felt that something was about to go wrong; good fortune was always too precarious, too contingent, too arbitrary an event to be, in truth, good fortune. *Non forat ullum illaesa felicitas,* (unbroken prosperity is unable to bear any evil—if I have translated Seneca correctly). The disturbance from the balcony impressed him immediately as a possible source of reversal and he turned a resentful face toward the balcony, faced forward again, and waited for the pointer to turn again. It did.

"Eight!" cried the young master of ceremonies. A hasty glance convinced Cornelius that he did not have the number. Two more chances to win the big prize, and buy fifty volumes in the Loeb Classical Library. The pointer turned weakly this time.

"Fourteen!" cried the young man into the microphone which made his voice even more official than otherwise. Cornelius did not have the number. He assured himself that the game was a fraud, that the management was obviously not going to permit anyone to win so much money and that the whole business would obviously be controlled in the projection room or by arranging the numbers on the cards. There was only one more chance, a drop in the ocean. He slouched back in his seat, chiding himself for his great excitement.

Meanwhile the pointer was turning quickly, and then weakly.

"Twenty-five!" the master of ceremonies called out.

"Twenty-five! Twenty-five!" said Cornelius to himself, and then, finding the number on his card as the fifth consecutive horizontal number, he rose in his seat and shouted:

"SCREENO!" in a too loud voice which broke, and began to issue from his aisle, tripping over the feet of the people seated near him, some of whom were solicitous of his walk, and eager to provide good advice as he passed. The attractiveness of the winner shone in him.

"Twenty-five! Twenty-five!" said Cornelius to himself. "My age! My gold mine!" He felt the eyes of the whole immense audience upon him as he walked to the stage and the self-consciousness which had always tortured him made him walk with too careful steps.

An usher took his card, and checked it with the numbers on the blackboard. The young man came over to oversee the usher. It seemed as if something was wrong, someone had miscalculated, to look at the young man. The checking was done several times. Very bureaucratic, said Cornelius to himself. Recovering, as the checkup proved that Cornelius had indeed won, he shook Cornelius's hand and the whole theatre lighted up.

"Lucky fellow," cried the balcony voice, amusing the audience again, by the envious tone in his voice.

"Congratulations," the young man said, "the sum of $425 is yours." He led Cornelius before the microphone. "Now before I pay you, will you tell us your name and address."

"Cornelius Schmidt," whispered Cornelius (the whisper, but not the words resounded in the microphone). "845 West 163rd Street."

The young man repeated this information into the microphone as if it were a matter of great importance.

"Cornelius Vanderbilt," shouted the balcony wit, "Park Avenue."

"And what do you do?" the young man asked both Cornelius and the microphone, as if no one could do anything which would not come under his authority.

"Oh," said Cornelius, "I do many things," into the microphone.

The audience laughed, and Cornelius, pleased, grinned in spite of himself. But he was uneasy. He did not wish to tell the truth, that he was a writer, for he was an unknown writer, and besides the profession always appeared to him as seeming peculiar and anomalous to others. On the other hand, he did not want to say he was unemployed, his usual subterfuge, because that also seemed a shameful admission. And then he was ashamed of himself, angered at himself for not wishing to tell the truth, for being ashamed of a noble calling, so that he forced himself to the other

extreme, and specified his kind of writing and told the function-
ary that he was a poet. He knew this would be equivalent to sissy
or bohemian for some of the audience.

"Mr. Schmidt is a poet," announced the young man unctu-
ously, patronizingly, and then, desiring to be humorous himself,
he spoke cutely into the microphone:

> He's a poet,
> His feet show it,
> They're Longfellow's!

The audience roared as the young man drew out the last word
with a triumphant tone, and Cornelius blushed and wished he
were elsewhere, and became extremely angered at the young
man, who had previously merely annoyed him. As a matter of
fact, Cornelius's feet were by no means small, and, becoming still
more self-conscious, he tried to withdraw his shoes somehow
from public view.

"I am sure we would like to hear one of the poems of so fortunate a young man," said the official young man. He was trying to
delay matters until one of the ushers could bring enough money
from the box office to pay Cornelius. "Please," he said, "recite
some verses for us."

"Oh, no!" said Cornelius firmly, backing away. The young man
gestured to the intrigued audience which then began to applaud
in unison to express its desire to hear Cornelius recite his verses.

Angered again, and in his anger going again to the other extreme, Cornelius decided to recite for them. All of his happiness
in winning had disappeared, and a mood of stubborn resentment
had come upon him.

"Very well," he said harshly into the microphone. "I will recite
some appropriate verses for you." Changing his tone to one of serious and dramatic import, and permitting a certain implication
of tiredness, illness, and despair to creep into his voice, he began:

> Think now
> History has many cunning passages, contrived corridors
> And issues, deceives with whispering ambitions,
> Guides us by vanities. Think now
> She gives when our attention is distracted
> And what she gives, gives with such supple confusions
> That the giving famishes the craving. Gives too late
> What's not believed in, or if still believed,
> In memory only, reconsidered passion. Gives too soon
> Into weak hands, what's thought can be dispensed with
> Till the refusal propagates a fear.

He ended appalled at himself, as if he had made a shocking confession. But he saw that his effort was a failure for his tone had been false, too serious. The audience had been silenced and puzzled by the verses, but the young man, curiously enough, had been impressed.

"Are those your own verses?" he asked.

"No. I wish they were," said Cornelius. The audience wakened at this and laughed.

"Those verses were written by the best of modern poets," said Cornelius, "a man named T. S. Eliot, whom all of you ought to read." Even in saying this, Cornelius knew that this advertisement was a foolish thing.

The usher arrived with the money just as the persistent balcony voice called out, "Let's go on with the show," and the audience began to clap again, wishing to have its chance at the other prizes.

But then, as the money was delivered to the young assistant manager, and he began officiously to count it out, shuffle it, and arrange it, before paying Cornelius, a hoarse and disused voice cried from the balcony:

"SCREENO! SCREENO!"

A silence fell upon all, and all turned backward to look for the author of the impassioned outcry.

"SCREENO!" came the voice again, this time nearer, as the new winner approached the stairs from the balcony to the orchestra. The young assistant manager and the ushers looked at each other in dismay. Something had obviously gone wrong, for usually no one won the jackpot; two winners was inconceivable and would lead to bankruptcy. Someone was going to lose his job because of this.

In a moment, the new winner was on the stage. He was a small and slight old man, carrying a violin case and wearing glasses. In his unpressed black suit, he looked very much like a waiter in a cheap restaurant. He was completely out of breath, completely beside himself. An usher took his card from his quavering hand and began to check it with the numbers on the blackboard. The young assistant manager came over to superintend the checking, obviously hoping for some mistake. Meanwhile, Cornelius stood by suddenly ignored, having nothing to do. He had not yet been given his money, but was blissful with ideas of its expenditure.

"If the manager loses all this money," said one usher to another, "it will be the biggest collapse since the Fall of the Hapsburgs."

"My name is Casper Weingarten," said the old man, unasked, intruding himself upon the huddle of the assistant manager and the ushers. He was very nervous, very excited. "I am a musician," he said, but no one paid any attention to him, except Cornelius.

And then the young assistant manager came over to the old man and, holding the card up, showed him that he had not won, that he had mistaken a 7 for a 1 because the print had been on the left-hand side. "Perhaps you'll win one of the other prizes," he said, courteously, "since you already have four numbers in a row."

"You mean I don't win?" said the old man. "Why not?" he said, having understood nothing of the explanation. His mistake was explained again, while he stared at his card.

"No!" he said loudly. "This is a 1, not a 7. I win. Give me my money." His voice was weak and now that he raised it, it was curiously pathetic, and like the voice of an angry child. And to make matters worse, he began to cough.

"My dear man," said the assistant manager, resuming his official tone, "I am sorry but you are mistaken. You have not won. You have mistaken a 7 for a 1 because the print was faint. After this, all of the cards will be clearly printed, so that such mistakes cannot occur."

Cornelius came over to look into the matter for himself. He took the card in his hand and looked at the number in question. The old man looked at him, and then turned to the assistant manager, saying:

"Give me my money! I have won!"

"You are being very unreasonable," said the assistant manager, beginning to look harassed. The audience now began to clap to indicate its desire for proceeding with the rest of the game. The assistant manager explained what had happened to the audience with great care and tact.

"Give me my money!" shouted the old man, as the young man was speaking to the audience.

"Please return to your seat," he said to the old man, "so that the game can go on."

Meanwhile Cornelius had looked carefully at the number in question and decided that the assistant manager had no ground for deciding that the 1 was a 7. There was a blur beside the upright bar of 1 which might conceivably have been meant to be the horizontal bar which completed the 7, but the faintness of the blur was not sufficient to justify the assistant manager.

"Look here," said Cornelius tactfully to the assistant manager, "it seems to me that you can only assume that this is a 1. The blur is too faint to make it a seven."

"I know it is a 7," said the assistant manager angrily, and when he said that, Cornelius recognized immediately that he was so sure because the cards had been prepared in advance to obviate the possibility of two winners of the jackpot, or even one. Seeing this, Cornelius began to feel sick and angry, as he always did when confronted with fraud or cheating.

"All my life I've been cheated," said the old man, wringing his hands. "Give me my money." An usher took his arm, as if to lead him from the stage, but the assistant manager deterred him, unwilling as yet to resort to force.

"Look here," said Cornelius firmly, "either you pay him or I am going to speak to the audience about this." In reply, the assistant manager began to pay Cornelius, counting the money with clipped tones as he placed it in Cornelius's hand. The old man grabbed the assistant manager's arm when he finished, saying:

"Where is my money? Don't cheat me, I've had hard luck all my life."

"My good man," said the assistant manager, "Your hard luck is not my fault, nor this theatre's responsibility. Please do not cause a disturbance. Now if both of you will leave the stage, we can go on with the other prizes and with the show."

In answer, the old man sat down upon the stage, looking grotesque there, with his head turned up. "I will sit here until I am paid," he said tearfully.

The scene was becoming unbearable for Cornelius. The old man seemed to have decided that this money was as important as his life. As far as Cornelius was concerned, he had been cheated. This was too much for Cornelius.

"I am going to tell the audience about this," said Cornelius.

"No, you're not," said the assistant manager, but Cornelius reached the microphone before the assistant manager could get there.

"Listen!" said the assistant manager, in a wearied breathless panicky voice, "I'm going to lose my job for this. Have a heart."

This new object of sympathy made matters even more complex for Cornelius. But then he looked toward the old man seated on the floor. He had begun sobbing, and he had taken off his glasses, wet by his tears, and was drying them with a rumpled handkerchief.

This sight decided Cornelius. He grasped the microphone and addressed the audience.

"Ladies and gentlemen, the management refuses to pay this

man the sum which he has won, claiming that his card was badly printed. This is only a pretext. I have examined the card and there is no justification for the management's claim. The management is trying to welch on its obligation."

The assistant manager stepped forward immediately to reply. Cornelius's speech had obviously had a genuine effect.

"Ladies and gentlemen, this young man may be adept at poetry, but he cannot see what is directly in front of him. He is attempting to take advantage of the management's generosity. Not satisfied with having won the sum of $425, he is trying to get a similar sum for someone he has just encountered. Meanwhile it is becoming late, and if this stage is not cleared immediately, it will be necessary to postpone the plans for the remaining prizes. The operator in the projection room is a union man and cannot be persuaded to remain a moment overtime; and since we cannot postpone pictures, we will have to postpone the remaining prizes unless these gentlemen leave immediately."

"You're a fine manager," cried the balcony wit.

But the audience was won over, for no one wished to lose his chance at the remaining $50. There was a murmuring of voices and someone cried out:

"Go home and give us a chance."

"Ladies and gentlemen," said the old man in a broken voice. He had arisen upon seeing the effect of the manager's speech. "These people are trying to cheat me. I have won. I am a musician. I would not do anything dishonest even if I am only a musician in a restaurant," sobbing, "this has always happened to me when something good should have happened. There was a quarrel at my daughter's wedding, the happiest day of my life. Now I have to live with my daughter-in-law," and still sobbing, "I could have my teeth fixed with the money. They have been bad for years. Don't let them cheat me."

A counter-reaction spread, although the vulgar reference to teeth had been unfortunate. Cornelius was prepared to commit any act in order to bring a halt to the old man's sobbing: scenes, rows, disturbances in public places had always had a direct solar plexus effect upon him.

"This is a bottomless pit," said one usher to another.

"Ladies and gentlemen," said the assistant manager, "although we are convinced that we are right, we are ready to put this whole matter into the hands of a committee of three objective members of the audience."

"Oh," said Cornelius to himself, "they are going to start the whole objective and subjective business again."

There was a pause while three members of the audience were solicited to act as judges. The assistant manager, still attempting to maintain his benevolence, offered free theatre tickets for the following week as reward for jury service. A dentist, a lawyer, and the owner of a haberdashery store came forward. The dentist, a sympathetic man, immediately offered to fix Weingarten's teeth cheap, for a nominal sum. The old man ignored the offer, offending the dentist.

"Give me my money," he said weakly, almost an echo of his former voice.

The committee was given the disputed card and went into a conference in a corner. But before they had been there long, an enterprising usher found another card on which the 1 had been printed with a blur next to it. The card was brought up to the stage and in a moment everything was settled once and for all.

The assistant manager announced the discovery. The lawyer announced the committee's decision. The audience applauded, satisfied that justice had been done. Casper Weingarten sat down on the stage again. Cornelius looked helplessly about him, and the audience began to clap and hoot.

"Why don't you go home," said one.

"Call a cop," said another.

Cornelius stepped forth and said, painstakingly, "Can't you see that the fact that two cards have the same blur on them proves nothing. It may be a 1 in both cases. You are permitting yourselves to be deceived."

But the audience had decided once and for all. It was now

intent upon going on with the game and then on with the show, and answered Cornelius by hoots and whistles. The ushers came forward.

And then, threatened by the ushers, Cornelius made the worst mistake.

"Be logical," he said angrily, "don't be hopelessly middle class about this. The management is trying to cheat an old man."

"This poet is a radical," said the assistant manager, seeing his opportunity to win a complete victory. "You heard what he just said: middle class. He is a radical."

"C.I.O." called the balcony wit, with a rising inflection on the O, as one would say "I'll be seeing *you*." The audience giggled, enchanted by this, and the cry was taken up immediately.

"C.I.O. C.I.O. C.I.O.," came various voices throughout the house.

Cornelius recognized that nothing more could be done with the audience. He went over to the old musician, still seated upon the floor and drying his glasses again, for he was still weeping.

"Look, old man," said Cornelius, "there's nothing to be done about this. You'd better come with me."

"No," said Weingarten, categorically.

Cornelius meditated with himself for a moment and then said: "Listen, I will give you half of the jackpot. Come on before you're arrested."

"Call a cop," cried the same voice that had previously made this suggestion.

"No," said Weingarten, "I don't want your money. I want mine. Give me my money," he said towards the assistant manager.

Cornelius considered matters with himself again and came to a decision. Easy come, easy go, he said to himself, and then he told the old musician that he could have the whole jackpot. The manager protested immediately, but Cornelius took the bills from his pocket and began to count them out and give them to the musician, who accepted them with a guilty look and trembling hands.

The audience saw what was happening and applauded vigorously, not because it was genuinely moved, but because it felt that it ought to applaud. Such applause is heard at public gatherings when an abstraction too vacuous is mentioned or tribute is paid to a man long dead. The assistant manager, trying to move in on Cornelius's credit, came over to shake hands with Cornelius. Cornelius, tempted to reject the proffered hand, accepted it because he wished to cause no further disturbance.

The old man had risen and come over to Cornelius.

"Thank you very much for your kindness," he said in the estranged voice of those who have been weeping or overexcited.

"Not at all," said Cornelius formally. Both descended from the stage together.

"We will have to forego the remaining prizes until next week," said the assistant manager, "but the fifty dollars will be added to next week's total, and there will be a hundred dollars in prizes besides the usual jackpot. In addition, two four-star pictures will be playing."

The theatre darkened as Cornelius and Weingarten walked to the exits, the film went on with all its soft floating figures and pleasing movement. How much actuality, after all, can an audience stand in the course of one evening?

"Are you going my way?" said Cornelius to Weingarten.

"No, I think I'll see the rest of the show. Thank you very much, much obliged," he said, still weighed by guilt.

The problem now, said Cornelius to himself as he walked through the soft carpeted lobby, is to keep this from my mother, who will consider me quixotic, as indeed I am. But how small a price for the sense of generosity and dignity which I now have, even though the act was forced upon me by my maudlin sympathy for the old man. Probably I have been foolish, and yet how reasonable I feel at present, and how joyous.

Saying this, in his joy, he issued into the chill and disorder of the street, the fresh air and different light striking him. The rain had ceased, but a thick fog had come upon the city. And as he walked home through this fog, in a pure enjoyment of his feeling, Cornelius recited to himself this poem by a fourteenth-century

Scottish poet, halting sometimes in the middle of a line because he did not remember it too well, or halting in order to correct his imperfect accent:

> Be merry, man! and tak not sair in mind
>   The wavering of this wretched world of sorrow!
> To God be humble and to thy friend be kind,
>   And with thy neighbors gladly lend and borrow:
> His chance to-nicht, it may be thine tomorrow;
>   Be blithe in heart for ony adventure;
> For oft with wise men, 't has been said aforrow,
> Without gladness availis no treasure.
>
> Mak thee gude cheer of it that God thee sends,
>   For wand's wrack but welfare nocht avails.
> No gude is thine, save only that thou spends;
>   Remanent all thou brookis but with bales.
> Seek to solace when sadness thee assails;
>   In dolour long thy life may not endure,
> Wherefore of comfort set up all thy sails;
> Without gladness availis no treasure.
>
> Follow on pity, flee trouble and debate,
>   With famous folk aye hold thy company;
> Be charitable and humble in thy estate,
>   For wardly honour lastes but a cry;
> For trouble in earth take no melancholy;
>   Be rich in patience, if thou in goods be poor;
> Who lives merry he lives michtily;
> Without gladness availis no treasure.

So saying, joyous, with a sense of having done proudly what he wanted to do, and with the fog hiding from him most of the street and surrounding his head, he came back to his house and the room where he would be once more alone.

AFTERWORD

However we may regard the story of Delmore Schwartz's life—as pathos, melodrama, or an experience both terrible and resisting easy explanation—there is a real danger that his work will be brushed aside as he himself becomes the subject of a lurid cultural legend. I don't want to be righteous about this, since I find Schwartz's life as fascinating (though also frightening) as anyone else does. The image of the artist who follows a brilliant leap to success with a fall into misery and squalor, is deeply credited, even cherished in our culture; it is an image that, despite sentimental exploitation, has a costly share of reality behind it. Nevertheless, we ought to insist that what finally matters is the work that remains, far more so than the life that is gone. What matters is the stories, poems, essays Schwartz wrote, perhaps most of all his stories, five or six of which are lasting contributions to American literature. The rest is pain, gossip, regret, waste.

Schwartz's most famous story, "In Dreams Begin Responsibilities," came out in 1937, as the leading piece of fiction in the first issue of the new *Partisan Review*. Those of us who read it at the time really did experience a shock of recognition. The intellectual heavyweights of the *PR* group had been mobilized for this opening issue, and they performed in high style. Young readers like myself who looked forward to the magazine as a spokesman for "our" views on culture and politics—that is, the views of the anti-Stalinist left—were probably more interested in the polemics than the fiction. Still, we did read Schwartz's story, if only because the editors had put it at the top of their table of contents; and we were stunned. Many people I know have remembered the story long after forgetting everything else in the first issue.

We were charmed by the story's invention, though this could hardly explain the intensity of our response, since you didn't have to be a New Yorker, you could as well live in London or Singapore, in order to admire Schwartz's technical bravura. Still, it was the invention—the sheer cleverness of it—that one noticed first. A movie theatre becomes the site of dreams; the screen, a reflector of old events we know will soon be turning sour. The narrator watches father propose to mother at a Coney Island restaurant. Already, during the delights of courtship, they become entangled in the vanities and deceptions that will embitter their later years. But what can the audience do about it? The past revived must obey its own unfolding, true to the law of mistakes. The reel must run its course: it cannot be cut; it cannot be edited.

When I first read the story, at the age of seventeen or eighteen, I felt my blood rise at the point where the narrator cries out to his parents on the screen: "Don't do it. It's not too late to change your minds, both of you. Nothing good will come of it, only remorse, hatred, scandal, and two children whose characters are monstrous." The hopelessness, and as it seemed then, the rightness of the son's lament appealed to my deepest feelings as another son slipping into estrangement. Naturally, this struck me as the high point of the story, the cry against the mistakes of the past.

Only later, when I would now and again reread the story, did I come to see what I could not yet see in 1937: that its tragic force depends not so much on the impassioned protest of the young narrator as on the moment in the last paragraph when an usher hurries down the aisle of the theatre and says to him: "What are *you* doing? Don't you know that you can't do whatever you want to do?" This voice of remonstrance, as it speaks in Kafka-like accents for inexorability, fulfills the story both on the plane of invention (the business in the movie house) and the plane of implication (how presumptuous yet inevitable that we should want to unwind the reel of our lives!). Once you see that the usher's statement has to be given a central place in the story, then you also realize that the narrator's outcry, whatever our sympathy for it, is not so much a protest against mistakes as a protest against life itself, inconceivable without mistakes.

There is still one thing more, and it comes in the last line of the story, a phrase that would serve almost as Schwartz's literary signature: the young narrator wakes up on a bleak winter morning from his dream of a movie depicting the past of his parents, and outside, on the window sill, he sees "a lip of snow." It is a lovely, haunting phrase—the plenitude and renewal of nature become through metaphor a human shape, soon to melt, but still, the shape of that part of our body with which we speak and love. Through all the wretchedness of Schwartz's later years as man and writer, he would now and again invoke such images of snow as an enchanting presence, the downpour, as if through God's or nature's generosity, of purity, beauty, evanescence.

The tone of "In Dreams Begin Responsibilities"—flat, gray, a little sluggish, but with sudden spinnings of eloquence and literary self-consciousness—is distinctively urban. It speaks of Brooklyn, Coney Island, and Jewish immigrants fumbling their way into the new world, but also of their son, proudly moving toward the culture of America and finding there a language for his parents' grief. This sense that Schwartz had found both voice and metaphor for our own claustral but intense experience—this, more than any objective judgment of his technical skill—must have been the source of our strong response. We heard a voice that seemed our own, though it had never really existed until Schwartz invented it: a voice at home with the speech of people not quite at home with English speech.

For a decade there followed story after story in which Schwartz wrote about his characteristic themes: the pathos and comic hopelessness of the conflict between immigrant Jewish families and their intellectual children, the occasional recognition by those children that they had left behind not only a ghetto parochialism but also a culture of value, and the quasi-bohemian life of New York intellectuals in the 1930s and 1940s, with its frantic mixture of idealism and ambition, high seriousness and mere sententiousness. These wry, depressed, and insidiously clever stories—"America! America!," "The World Is a Wedding," "The Child Is the Meaning of This Life"—were put together in a form that Schwartz was making his own: longer than the story but shorter than the novelette, with little visible plot but much entanglement of relationship among characters, stylized dialogue replacing action or drama, and a major dependence on passages of commentary, ironic tags, deflated epigrams, and skittish ventures into moral rhetoric.

The risks of this kind of story were very considerable. To an unsympathetic reader, Schwartz's stories could seem ill-fitted, self-conscious, excessively parochial in reference and scope. Some of the inferior ones are precisely that: manner becoming merely mannered, an adept mimicry of itself. But this hardly counts, since a writer must be judged by his strengths, not the necessary failures along the way.

One charge frequently made against Schwartz's work, however, merits a closer look. The "tougher" literary people of his time—and it was then very much the fashion to be "strict" and "severe" in judgment—often said that Schwartz's work suffered from self-pity. They were sometimes right, but in the main they lacked the patience to see that in stories about the kinds of people Schwartz was describing self-pity is a necessary theme—how else can you write about young intellectuals, at once lost in the coldness of the world and subsisting on dreams of later achievement and glory? Schwartz had the rare honesty to struggle with this out in the open, struggle with it not merely as a literary theme but a personal temptation, so that in his best work he could control or even transcend it. A good many other, less honest writers learn to mask their self-pity as comic heartiness or clipped stoicism. But no one reading "America! America!" or "The Child Is the Meaning of This Life" is likely, I think, to suppose that the self-pity which plagues some of the characters is unresistantly shared by the author.

The stories Schwartz wrote in the years between "In Dreams Begin Responsibilities" and the publication in 1948 of his collection *The World Is a Wedding*, capture the quality of New York life in the 1930s and 1940s with a fine comic intensity—not, of course, the whole of New York life but that interesting point where intellectual children of immigrant Jews are finding their way into the larger world while casting uneasy, rueful glances over their backs. These were stories that helped one reach an emotional truce with the world of our fathers, for the very distance they established from their subject allowed some detachment and thereby, in turn, a little self-criticism and compassion. (Not too much, by the way.) Sliding past the twin dangers of hate and sentimentalism, Schwartz's best work brought one to the very edge of the absurd, I mean to that comic extremity in which the characters of, say, "New Year's Eve" and "The World Is a Wedding" were wrenched almost to caricature even as it remained easy to identify their "originals." It was as if ironic distancing, even ironic disdain were a prerequisite for affection, and thereby one could gain through these stories a certain half-peace in contemplating the time of one's youth. The mockery Schwartz expended upon the New York intellectuals and would-be intellectuals can be caustic, even bitter and, to be honest, sometimes nasty; but it is not dismissive, it does not exclude, it does not relegate anyone to the limbo of the non-human. Finally, Schwartz's voice is sad and almost caressing, as if overcome by the waste of things.

What is more, this comedian of alienation also showed a gift for acceptance, a somewhat ambiguous reconcilement with the demands and depletions of common experience. Schwartz's work gained its fragile air of distinction partly from the fact that he avoided the pieties of both fathers and sons, established communities and floundering intellectuals. I am not speaking here about Schwartz the person. As a writer he came to see, especially in "America! America!" and "The Child Is the Meaning of This Life," with the eyes of both fathers and sons, or perhaps from a distance greater than either could manage, as if he were somehow a detached student of the arts of misunderstanding.

In the early stories (more disturbingly in the later ones) there was also a strong awareness of the sheer foolishness of existence, the radical ineptitude of the human creature, such as reminds one a trifle of Dostoevsky's use of buffoonery in order to discharge aggressiveness against both readers and characters. The *persona* of buffoonery, which goes perfectly well with a sophisticated intelligence, brings with it some notable dangers, but at its occasional best it enabled Schwartz to catch his audience off guard, poking beneath the belt of its dignity, enforcing the shared ridiculousness of … I guess, everything.

By the time Schwartz published *The World Is a Wedding*, he had developed his own style. Some years ago I tried to describe this style, and since I can't now do any better, I beg the reader's pardon for quoting myself: "it seemed to be composed of several speech-layers: the sing-song, slightly pompous intonations of Jewish immigrants educated in night-schools, the self-conscious affectionate mockery of that speech by American-born sons, its abstraction into the jargon of city intellectuals, and finally the whole body of this language flattened into a prose of uneasiness, an anti-rhetoric."

An anti-rhetoric is of course a rhetoric. But more important: in his stories dealing with immigrant Jewish families Schwartz may have begun with an affectionate and deliberate mimicry of immigrant speech, but very soon, I think, he yields himself to it almost entirely. Yielding himself, *he simply writes that way*. It becomes his language. The world is a wedding? Then turn back shyly, ambivalently to the past—though not quite yet with ceremonies of marriage.

It is in "America! America!" as the "young writer of promise" listens to his mother, Mrs. Fish, tell the story about their neigh-

bors, the Baumanns, that all of Schwartz's themes come to fulfillment and his literary voice strikes its characteristic note. Hearing
his mother, recognizing the intuitive wisdom and depths of experience out of which she speaks, Shenandoah Fish experiences
a revelation of how smug he has been in his judgment of the Baumanns and all the people like them, how unearned and unwor-
thy has been "the irony and contempt" he has shown them. It is
this humane readiness to see both links and breaks between the
generations that helps to make this story so rich a portrait of immigrant life.

> ... He reflected upon his separation from these people [the
> immigrant Jews], and he felt that in every sense he was re-
> moved from them by thousands of miles, or by a generation
> ... whatever he wrote as an author did not enter into the lives
> of these people, who should have been his genuine relatives
> and friends, for he had been surrounded by their lives since
> the day of his birth, and in an important sense, even be-
> fore then.... The lower middle-class of Shenandoah's par-
> ents had engendered perversions of its own nature, children
> full of contempt for everything important to their parents.
> Shenandoah had thought of this gulf and perversion before,
> and he had shrugged away his unease by assuring himself
> that this separation had nothing to do with the important
> thing, which was [his] work itself. But now ... he began to
> feel that he was wrong to suppose that the separation, the
> contempt, and the gulf had nothing to do with his work;
> perhaps, on the contrary, it was the center; or perhaps it
> was the starting-point and compelled the innermost motion
> of the work to be flight, or criticism, or denial, or rejection.

Of dismay and disintegration, chaos and ugliness, waste and
malaise there was more than enough in the life, sometimes also
the work, of Delmore Schwartz. Yet there is something else in his
poems and stories, so rare in our time and so vulnerable to misuse

and ridicule I hesitate to name it. What complicates and enriches Schwartz's comedy is, I think, a reaching out toward nobility, a shy aspiring spirituality, a moment or two of achieved purity of feeling. Surely this is what his friend, the art critic Meyer Schapiro, must have had in mind when he wrote the last few lines of a poem about Schwartz's death, remarking of his work:

> It has the beauty of his honest thought,
> Of gravest musings on the human state,
> On thwarted dreams and forced deformities
> And ever-resurgent hopes of light.

—IRVING HOWE